A Sister's Dream

Elizabeth Gill was born in Newcastle upon Tyne and as a child lived in Tow Law in County Durham where her family owned a steelworks. She has spent all her life in Durham but recently moved to North West Wales to be near her family. She can see the sea from her windows and spends a lot of time eating seafood, drinking orange wine and walking the family Labrador, Izzie, on the beautiful beaches.

Also by Elizabeth Gill

A Sister's Dream

Elizabeth Gill

QUERCUS

First published in Great Britain in 2025
This paperback edition first published in Great Britain in 2025 by

QUERCUS

Quercus Editions Ltd
Carmelite House
50 Victoria Embankment
London EC4Y 0DZ

An Hachette UK company

The authorised representative in the EEA is Hachette Ireland,
8 Castlecourt Centre, Dublin 15, D15 XTP3, Ireland (email: info@hbgi.ie)

Copyright © 2025 Elizabeth Gill

The moral right of Elizabeth Gill to be
identified as the author of this work has been
asserted in accordance with the Copyright,
Designs and Patents Act, 1988.

All rights reserved. No part of this publication
may be reproduced or transmitted in any form
or by any means, electronic or mechanical,
including photocopy, recording, or any
information storage and retrieval system,
without permission in writing from the publisher.

A CIP catalogue record for this book is available
from the British Library

PB ISBN 978-1-52942-114-9
EBOOK ISBN 978-1-52942-113-2

1

This book is a work of fiction. Names, characters,
businesses, organizations, places and events are
either the product of the author's imagination
or used fictitiously. Any resemblance to
actual persons, living or dead, events or
locales is entirely coincidental.

Typeset by CC Book Production
Printed and bound in Great Britain by Clays Ltd, Elcograf S.p.A.

Papers used by Quercus are from well-managed forests and other responsible sources.

For the people of Porthmadog u3a.
Thanks for making me feel so welcome.
You are a kind and generous crowd.

One

It was mid-winter and the days were short and dark. Sometimes the light disappeared after one o'clock. Sometimes it didn't appear at all. Catrin Morgan knew that because here in this bitterly cold place she was only allowed to gaze at it from the windows. She was closely watched.

She had ticked off the days at first but now she had lost count of them. The leaves had been turning colour when she first arrived and it had been September. Now it was well past Christmas. She knew this because she and the other girls had been huddled into the icy chapel as they were on most days but there had been carols and the readings were about the birth of Christ.

Not that Christmases at home in Dolgellau in North Wales were anything to get excited about, but Mrs Brandon, the cook, made mince pies and Christmas cake and puddings well before, sometimes as early as October, at least for the puddings. She would feed the

1

Christmas cake with rum. Nobody had the day off – even though Mr Morgan did not invite people to stay or to call in, they did anyway and Mrs Brandon would not have let them have tea or coffee without something to eat. So even though the master did not speak of it, Christmas was celebrated and early in the evening they would have a big party in the servants' quarters. In the old days before her mother had died there had been a proper dance for the servants in the ballroom and her mother had danced with all the menservants and her father with all the maids. She had vague recollections of the maids looking forward to Christmas when they were summoned into the big drawing room. Her mother would have bought gifts for everyone and each maid was so excited by the pretty ribbons, the lengths of coloured cloth, the dainty handkerchiefs and little bottles of scent and each one was different, especially chosen by their beloved mistress. The male servants were given scarves and caps and gloves and bottles of rum and everyone got a small bag of money. All the houses in the area were given special baskets of game and pies and pâtés, sweets for the children, chocolates for the woman of the house and ale for the men. She remembered those happy times but they were long since gone. After her mother died it was like the light went from the house and had not been there again.

She vaguely remembered her brother going away and

not coming back but she could recall little of what her life had been like after that. Her father had not wanted to see her, she didn't understand why, just that she did not belong there, had no place at the dining room table or in the drawing room by the fire and no bedroom of her own. She spent her days in the kitchen and her nights sleeping with the maids in a big attic at the top of the house.

As she got a little older, she had spent some nights with the blacksmith's family. She could not think when that had started either, just that the blacksmith and his wife gave her meals and were kind to her, treating her like one of the family and increasingly often she stayed with them and slept with the other children. They had half a dozen. Joe was the eldest and the same age as she was. They were sixteen, and amongst his family, she had learned to love Joe and to think that he loved her.

She and Joe would creep into the big bed at night while the younger children slept and, with their eyes closed, talk about all the good things that they would do, how they would get away and travel the world and see all the countries that were so different from their own. Best of all she liked to cuddle in against him and that was when she slept the best sleep, she felt so warm and safe and loved and they ate well so her stomach was full. Their house must be one of the most wonderful places in the world, she thought.

She and Joe were in love and after she realized that it was so, she gave him her mouth and her body and all the hopes in her young life and he accepted them. She could hardly bear to think of it because Joe had taken all that she had to offer, and when their love had made such changes as she had not thought of Joe had dismissed the idea, scoffed at it, it could not be so he said, and then it was that his father got a better job somewhere else and Joe was gone and there was nobody to bear the burden but Catrin. In her bitterness now, she hated Joe for his betrayal of her. His father had taken action, had got his family out of there, caring nothing for what might happen to Catrin, and then her father had got wind of it and so she was banished to this freezing place.

Now in the middle of nowhere, hundreds of miles from home, she missed them all – Mrs Brandon, the maids, but most of all the easy life she had had before this happened. Was it lost? Would she be here for the rest of her days? She was starting to think so and it was a dismal thought.

Nobody talked much. What was there to say? Some of them had strange accents which she did not understand. It was not that she was shunned, it was just that English was her second language. She had known English when she was younger and her mother was still alive. She remembered her mother speaking in that language and how sweet her voice had sounded, but the memories were fading fast and in her life now Welsh was spoken every day so she had to think hard to accustom herself not only to English but also to English as it was said here in what apparently was the north-east of England and many of the words were unfamiliar to her.

She had been brought here from her home without notice and she had been so afraid that she had made no sound. It was as if she had died or been spirited away. In the old carriage sat a woman dressed all in black. She did not speak to Catrin and they were moving quickly. Then it had been railways. She had never been on a train before and there seemed to be a great many of them.

She had tried to break free, had attempted to find out what was happening to her, she was so scared but the woman just ignored her and she was much bigger and stronger than Catrin. Catrin was tall but slender and no match for an adult. Nobody cared that she had been taken against her will. When she cried and protested nobody took any notice. She was just another badly behaved girl to them and even if they did look, they looked away again without concern.

After she gave up struggling and protesting and she was soon so scared and tired that she could do no more, the woman was not unkind. She gave Catrin food and water, and in stations went with her so that she could relieve herself, but that was all. The journey seemed to her sixteen-year-old self to go on and on, further and further away from the life she had lived.

Was she being abducted? If she was then why was the woman civil to her? Was she being taken away to be killed? Why would anyone want to do such a thing and why take her away? Surely she could have been killed in Dolgellau more easily and at no expense so that was not a solution of any kind.

Eventually they left the stations behind and were put into the back of an enormous car and after that they arrived at their destination which was a strange-looking building in the middle of nowhere from what she could discern. The wind and hail stung her face when she got out of the car and was ushered by the woman in black into the building.

She heard the car leave and that had been early autumn. It felt like a very long time ago. At first she had been desperate to go home but since she was not allowed beyond locked doors there was little chance of that. The other girls were heavier than she was and some of them who were very heavy indeed disappeared and did not come back.

She was given needlework to do and since she was very bad at it the garments she was stitching were spotted with blood. There were complaints about this because these were apparently sheets and so she was sent to the kitchen and there she found herself happier because she understood how kitchens worked.

The women who ran the kitchens were not unkind either. They were brisk to begin with but as she was so dexterous at peeling potatoes and apples, turnips and carrots with such a thin skin taken off, they could not complain. In time, as they saw she had been in such places before, they asked her to make pastry, and bake cakes.

She was thankful then for Mrs Brandon who had always been sympathetic to her that she was almost like a mother to Catrin. She missed Mrs Brandon most of all and wondered if Mrs Brandon missed her, and then she remembered that it was the cook who had discovered her being sick in the mornings every day for two weeks and how Mrs Brandon had looked pained though Catrin had no idea why. So perhaps Mrs Brandon had caused her to be sent away and she ceased to think of the kindness and worried about the vindictiveness of such an act and wished she understood why. Would she ever go back there? Would she stay here for as long as she lived, locked away in this dark place?

She remembered the first snowfall for an obvious reason. It was dark and she was looking out of the window from her little bed in that great big room where a lot of other girls slept and it began to snow. It came down in the silence where there was no wind, it fell like a thief in the night so softly, almost stealthily as though it did not care to be noticed.

An hour later she found herself in such pain that she doubled over. It got worse and worse. One of the women who worked in the kitchen came to her and took her from the big room and put her into another room where several other girls were in pain, though it seemed to Catrin that their pain could not be worse than hers.

After that there was nothing beyond the pain, she thought that she must surely die, her body could not endure the agony, which went on and on. She didn't know how many hours, how many days her body endured until quite suddenly it went away and she heard a crying and there was a child.

She was astonished at first and then not so. She had pretended that she was not growing to this enormous size and shape and she had heard the cries of other girls. She understood very well what was happening to her now. She was to be punished, sent away probably for good and it was so shameful and she was so guilty of misconduct that she would have to stay here for ever.

The baby was taken from her, literally snatched from her the moment she realized she had given birth. Catrin didn't even see it. She didn't know whether it was a boy or a girl or what it had to do with her. At first she was glad that they took it away because it had caused her so much pain. After that her breasts had become swollen and almost as painful as the birth had been, they were engorged and she was left alone to deal with it. Nobody helped her, nobody came to her and milk ran down between her breasts and down her stomach to her legs. The pain eased in time and her breasts went back to being as they had not been before but misshapen, lumpy, odd but at least the pain of every kind had gone. Then she felt bereft. It was as big a feeling as losing her home and being taken away. There was suddenly this enormous space, a huge hole which the child was not filling. First inside her and then outside. How could it have done such a thing? Now the pain in her body was nothing when compared to the aching that went on in her mind and heart. She felt as though pieces had been torn off her and they had left great gaping wounds which could not be staunched. Nothing could mend it, nothing could bring it back.

There was no point in saying anything. She did not even know anyone's name. She was now put into a different part of the building and there were a lot of other girls in a similar way, no longer with big bumps in front of them. They were silent and she knew that like her they were grieving and they were bereft. She felt that she would never speak again. There would be no point. She could die now and it would be no loss.

Two

Dolgellau, North Wales

A few days later she left the place and went once again into the back of the car, into trains and finally into the old carriage which took her home. She was grateful to be there. It was the only thing she felt. She went to her own bed in the attic and tried not to think about what had happened to her, that she had had a child.

Nobody spoke to her, they just looked. In the kitchen Mrs Brandon had nothing to say and did not even acknowledge her presence but barked out orders as she never had done. Catrin could only accept what she was told. It would get better.

It did in some ways. She worked in the kitchen and gradually people spoke to her as the old maids went and new ones who knew nothing of her came but it was never the same again. She had changed and they had changed towards her and she did not understand. She was almost invisible, she was just a thing that might be around and was of no importance.

Sometimes she went and took a horse from the stables and rode miles and miles. She had ridden since she was a small child, perhaps some kind soul had put her on horseback as a toddler, and held her there and given her confidence. She didn't remember but it was a good thought and it made horses and the freedom she felt while riding the most important part of her life. There again nobody spoke but she was not stopped. The stable lads crept looks at her at first but from somewhere she had found how to repel everybody. She knew what they were thinking, that she had laid with one lad and would therefore lie with another but it did not take much for her to glare at them or set herself so that she could kill them if she had to. She carried a knife on her just in case some idiot should try to force her against her will but nobody did and after that she was alone as she had never been before.

If the weather was clement she would sleep there with the horses and cats and sheepdogs. They were easier to deal with than people, they did not judge and were accepting. She began to help in the stables and the yard, sweeping the yard, cleaning the cobbles, brushing and combing the horses.

The stable lads were polite by then, the head man being a Scotsman who said very little but called her Miss Morgan and none of them was intrusive in this world she had begun to devise for herself. It was as though she was wrapping a warm blanket around her in all that she did.

Often she shared the stable lads' fare or called in at the odd shop where she was known and they would always give her a little of whatever they had since she had no money. She presumed her father paid the bills or somebody would have said something.

However, other people in the village stared and some avoided her so she stopped going anywhere but the stables. She had no friends, nobody cared.

Sometimes she would stay in different places if the weather was fine. She wanted to get away. She often stayed from there for four or five days but in the end there was nowhere else to go. She began to wonder if the rest of her life would be spent like that and she would never see her baby again.

That summer things changed, there was a bustle about the place such as never before and when she asked one of the youngest maids — a girl who had only been there for a few months — what was going on the girl looked at her as though she was stupid and said,

'Why, the young master's coming home. Any day now. Mr Morgan is said to be pleased.'

Old man Morgan, as he was known in the town, her father, never spoke to her though she saw him sometimes around the house. It was just from overhearing others talk that she learned anything. This was news indeed. Catrin didn't know what to do. Should she stay away from the house? She was curious but she thought her brother had nothing to do with her. He had gone away when she was four and he was six. Now she was sixteen and he was eighteen. He must have finished his schooling. Was he going to come back here to live? She didn't know how she felt about that. Part of her was interested to see him, part wanted to hide or run away. It would be very strange. Would he ignore her as her father did? Would he not want to know her? Would he think that she was a bad person because of what had happened to her?

On the day that he was due home she stayed away. But she couldn't go far because she wanted to go back and at least see what he looked like. She therefore took to hiding just inside doors to catch a glimpse of him and when she did she was surprised. They looked nothing alike. He was tall and dark and slender whereas she had red-gold hair and blue eyes though she was tall and slender too. She thought that had been her mother's colouring and perhaps something to do with the fact that her father did not want to see her, but he was like their father, as least she thought so, not being quite sure how their father looked. She had never been that close.

June became July and in the kitchen all the talk was of the young master. They didn't take any notice of her, even when she went to the pantry and helped herself to food. She didn't offer to help, that would have been odd to them now, but she was entitled to take whatever she chose from the cold food in the pantry or she could have hot meals with them. The food was always good and just at the moment it was even better, presumably because her brother had come home.

There was cold beef for sandwiches and lettuce, tomatoes and cucumbers from the hothouses and the garden was at its best. Summer pudding, which was Mrs Brandon's speciality, and various jellies and sorbets, cheese and also raspberries and strawberries and lots of thick cream. There were various pastries and pies. There was always more than enough to eat and usually Catrin was grateful for it. Today however she was eager to see the boy who had come home but that he didn't look much like a boy. She'd caught a glimpse of him in the hall. He was almost a man. That surprised her. Perhaps living away from home made you grow up sooner though not sooner than having a child when you were sixteen, surely.

She left the kitchen, having taken enough food to see her through a couple of days and slept outside. When she got back and was grooming one of the horses there was a shadow across the stable where the sunshine fell in at the open doors and she heard a polite English voice say,

'Are you Catrin?'

She turned. She had heard him. Her ears were sharp.

All her senses were keen in case she was made to do things she didn't want to do ever again, but she had deliberately ignored the soft sounds of his feet because she did not recognize them and there was hesitancy that nobody else who came to the stables would feel.

He didn't speak again and in the end she put down the curry comb she had been using prior to plaiting the pony's mane and turned to him. She thought he looked shocked. She knew what she looked like but until now had thought little about it. Her hair was loose and streamed down her back almost to her knees as it had never been cut, her feet were bare and must be dirty and her hands also, she thought, trying not to look at them.

She rarely changed her clothes. Nobody ever thought to give her new ones and it was left to the maids to share what they had, which wasn't much so she was virtually in rags but that did not matter. The rain cleaned her clothes and body when it did rain, and it was warm at this time of the year so she didn't think about it. In cold weather she put on extra layers, like coats and boots, scarves and hats and gloves, all of which were in the servants' cloakroom beside the back door and could be taken by anyone who needed them.

Her brother must be a huge contrast, she thought. He was very well dressed. She knew because she was not used to expensive cloth and his raiment became him as she had never seen clothing do before. It had been tailored just for him even though he was so young. Like another skin somehow. His tone was so English, at least that was what she thought, as though he had never heard a Welsh voice.

'Why don't you live at the house? Why are you dressed like that?'

She didn't answer him.

'I didn't know what had happened to you and my father didn't reply when I asked. What is going on?'

'I don't see him,' she finally said, but in her own language.

He stared. 'I don't understand what you are saying.'

She tried to think of the words in English but struggled. She never used English. She didn't think anybody around her did and although she heard and interpreted what he was talking about, it was more effort to say it and she couldn't be bothered.

He gave up the questions, which she thought wise of him, but he came further in and admired the horse and even stroked its face.

Eventually curiosity got the better of her.

'What are you doing here?' she asked him in English. Once she had said the words the language came back to her as though her brain was transferring her thoughts from one to the next and back as though rusty.

'I'm going to Edinburgh to study medicine and my father invited me.'

'Was it the first time?'

'Yes.'

He had nothing more to say and she was unsurprised. She sometimes caught glimpses of her father – or his father – depending on how you thought of the man. It seemed to her that fathers were very strange people if that was how they went on. The other fathers were people she knew vaguely and had nothing to do with.

She had no friends. The stable lads didn't count. They were just lads and now treated her like one of them. They made little conversation. In the kitchen or in the attic bedroom silence always fell when she entered so she spent very little time there.

'What do you do all day?' Strange that he should say it when she had been thinking the same about him. Was that what brothers and sisters did? When she couldn't think of an answer he said,

'Do you go to school?'

'Nobody here of my age goes to school. Everybody works.' It was true, the lads on the farms, the butcher's son and the grocer's son and the hardware shop's two sons all worked with their fathers. Some lads went away to work in the slate quarries and here there was still gold mining and the lads whose fathers had always done such things followed them into it.

The girls went into service and often had to move away because everybody must earn money. Except that she did not. She didn't really do anything, she admitted to herself now.

'Where do you live?' The questions were underway once again.

She shrugged.

'Why don't you live with our father in the house?'

'He doesn't want me there.'

'Why not?'

She was not going to tell him what had happened to her but then she never had lived in the house as the daughter of it, not at their father's level, just as a maid. She had been nothing but a kitchen maid. Now she wasn't even that.

'I don't think he likes us very much,' her brother said bitterly. 'After she died he didn't want us there. Do you think we reminded him of her? And if so why would he not want us there all the more? Did it hurt him so unbearably to have us near?'

'What's he like close to?' she asked.

'Very quiet. He never goes anywhere or sees anybody. He sits among his books all day. I suppose with a life like that you can't have much to say. He did ask me questions about Edinburgh. I think quietly he's quite proud of my achievements. He seems to enjoy having me here though it obviously didn't dawn on him before I got this far that I might have come back here more often.'

'Where did you go?'

'We had family in the Durham dale and in Northumberland though they weren't up to much, just old people who felt obliged to give me a holiday for a few days and they were like him, very quiet and rather boring. And they are all dead. Sometimes I stayed with other boys and their families and that was better.'

'Didn't you ever want to come home?'

'I did to begin with. I felt totally abandoned, as if I had lost both my parents, and as for you – I remembered so little of you over the years that I tried to stop thinking about you. I just hoped you were having a better time than I was, but I turned out to be good at cricket, rugby, Latin and Greek so I had to be thankful for small mercies and get on with it. Once I realized that I wanted to be a doctor and had some sort of goal in life it all felt a little bit better, but when I went to stay with people I saw that they lived in a different way than I remembered living here.'

This was such a long speech that he was silent after it and she could think of nothing to say. She finished plaiting the horse's mane and she had by now looked after all the horses. She didn't really need to, the lads were good but they knew that it was something she liked doing so they let her. She had to fill her days with something.

'I could ask him if you might come and eat your meals with us?' her brother suggested.

'No,' she said flatly.

He mooched off back to the house and as she watched him go she knew that she and her brother and her father were all lonely. Was it something they had in common or was everybody's loneliness different than everybody else's, but when he had gone she missed his presence somehow and wondered how to get it back?

She waited to see him again, hanging around the yard and by the river and the fields. It was a long hot summer, far too hot for the horses and cattle who were plagued by flies. She spent a lot of time washing down their faces and coats, legs and back ends with a weak solution of vinegar and water which stopped the bluebottles from gathering. She thought all the animals were grateful.

One day, when she was sitting by the river, her brother appeared with a hamper. He proceeded to sit down and open it. She was rather touched and watched in delight as he took from it cooked chicken and newly baked bread, white cheese and various pickles, strawberries and meringue and a bottle of something called champagne. It tasted very strange, the bubbles popping up the slender glass he handed her and aiming at her nose.

'Did Mrs Brandon not mind you taking all this?'

'I didn't ask, I just ordered it,' he said with delicate carelessness. 'I am the young master, everything I do is good.'

He said it as though he were talking about somebody

else. There was a lack of pleasure in it, a want of more and she could hear and feel it. As she watched her brother looking out across the river as though he saw something in the distance which was fascinating, she remembered. He was Rhodri and when he had been small and she had been smaller she could see herself running after him with tottering steps, calling 'Roddy, Roddy, wait for me.'

But he had not waited for her, he had not been allowed to. She had been left here all alone and he had been all alone too and their father sat in the library like a withered plant, his life gone and nothing left but the minutes passing by slowly, interrupted only by visits to the dining room or having food and drink brought to the library or the study or wherever he sat. Did he go outside? She didn't think he did. Other people managed everything.

The strawberries and meringues glistened with sugar and cream in little glass bowls. There were small silver spoons for eating them. She had not had such a thing before and was rather taken with it and by the contrast of the champagne which she had thought sweet before and now was dry on her tongue.

That afternoon was the best she could remember. She tried to hold on to it in fear that there would never be another, but she knew very well that you could never hold anything good. It was only the bad memories that chased you around your bed at night.

They both fell asleep in the warm grass with the sound

of the river running low over summer stones and it was only when Roddy roused himself and said he must go and have dinner with his father that they got up and even then he hesitated.

'What will you do now?' he said.

It had not occurred to her that there would be an afterwards, as though her brother had made time stand still and she could not set off again. She would be pleased to stay there in the pleasure of his company but it was not to be. He put the glasses, the plates, the little dishes, the silverware and the champagne bottle back into the hamper and got up. She didn't know how to answer him. Everything that came to mind seemed so inadequate.

She watched him make his way across the fields towards the house. There was something special about his back and it made her think of a time when she remembered her parents walking away from her and her father's back had been like that. She could not remember the movements of her mother, had never been able to bring the sound of her voice to memory, not even a song.

Whether their father knew what was going on, Catrin was uncertain. Did he even think about what life went forward beyond the doors which led outside? She doubted it. After the picnic she was so happy that she worried. Life had never been like this so why should it change for the better now and then she told herself that it didn't matter, she must enjoy the little she was given.

Roddy would go off to university and she would probably never see him again. She doubted she would see him the next day but she did and the one that followed and the one after that. She dared take nothing for granted but she began to get up with the pleasurable feeling that she would see him.

She had begun sleeping in the attic again. She had the feeling that Roddy would think it a lot more respectable if she slept indoors though in such weather she was not sure it was an advantage. He seemed to grasp the idea because one night when he had stolen out after dinner and knew that she was waiting for him down by the river he brought with him cushions and a couple of light blankets, although that made her laugh, for she had stayed out many a night with neither one and been comfortable.

As usual he brought food with him. What Mrs Brandon would think Catrin could not imagine but then Mrs Brandon was too good a housekeeper, cook and servant to question the young master. What he wanted he got, she felt sure, and so there were puddings and cakes and bread and pâté which she called meat paste. It tasted good anyway and she was so pleased to be in his company that she tried to think of nothing but this.

They fell asleep together. The last person she had slept close to in the evening was Joe and the consequences had been appalling but this of course was nothing like that. She was so proud to have a brother like him, she kept her eyes open as long as she could just to drink in that he was there with her. She understood now why people made paintings and photographs because you had to capture whatever you loved and it was the closest you could get to halting time. She wished she could stop it now and keep him here forever.

The summer weeks went on. The river was low and clear and she would put her feet into the icy water. She showed Roddy how to catch fish by finding them under the bank and sliding your hands around them but he was not very deft and ended up wet and laughing because he had had no experience of such things. Neither could he ride a horse. She was surprised about that and soon they would go out on the horses every day.

Roddy read a lot. He talked to her about this because it was what he did so that his father would not wonder that he was out all the time and possibly object to what he was doing, but there came a day towards the end of August when Roddy was reading poems to her and he stopped and said would she like the book whereupon she blushed and stammered for she could not read very well. She had taken little effort and was out of practice and she did not want to show her ignorance in front of him.

'How stupid of me,' he said in apology, 'I didn't know that you had never been to school.'

'Lots of people don't go,' she said in mitigation.

'Yes but they aren't my sister.'

He said it so proudly that she was pleased and when he offered to teach her to read and write better she could not contain the way that she felt.

It began to rain for the first time in weeks but there were many buildings that belonged to the house and above one of the old coach houses there was a loft for storing hay. It had a window which looked out over the back fields so they spent the rainy afternoons there and slowly she remembered the little she had been taught as a child and was surprised how eagerly the reading and writing came back to her. She was aware of a pleasure which she had never thought attached to such things.

Roddy also played the piano and said he wished he could teach her for it was but another skill as to using your hands for what you wanted, rather than what they wanted. She told him that her hands could tickle fish and peel potatoes and he could do neither of these things.

She became aware that his time here was limited. He would be going to Scotland by the second week in September. It made her very sad. Every time she thought about it, it upset her until he told her that if she wanted he would take her with him.

She knew almost immediately that she couldn't do it. She was not this person that he saw, that she hoped he saw. That he liked her, that he might even want to take her with him would have to be enough.

'What have you got here that you would stay?' he said and she couldn't answer him.

'I'm a country girl, I belong here. I don't even speak English much.'

'You do when you stop thinking about it. You've been speaking English to me for weeks. And you speak it as I do who has been in England for years. You have a very good ear. I think once you learn something like that it stays with you. You would have to change of course.'

'Change what?' She eyed him. It was raining yet again, it didn't usually rain in September but they had been lucky in August and were obviously not going to get an Indian summer.

'The way you dress and you would have to put up your hair. The sisters of the boys that I know are very modest and they look up to their brothers and think how special they are.'

'Why would anybody do that?'

'Because it's the accepted way. Girls are meant to say little, listen a lot and be deferential.'

'Well, it's just as well I'm not going anywhere. I can't see me being like that.'

'You could pretend if it was going to get you places.'

This had not occurred to her. What a strange way to go on, she thought but then she had no society, she knew only the servants here and they did not treat one another in such a way but then her father had no indoor male servants. The men did the outdoor work so it was a different way of going on which she had never considered.

'Why don't you want to come with me, Cat?'

It was the first time he had called her by her childhood name and it made her feel sick and it hurt her.

'I cannot. You will have to accept it. You and I are nothing alike,' and she knew that if he persisted she would get up and run away and he must have known it too because he shut up.

When she was alone Catrin felt bad. Did she really not want a chance of a new life? But she was right. They were so unalike she could barely think of him as her brother. He didn't look like her and their experiences of life were totally different. He didn't know her. He wouldn't like her if he got to know her well, she felt sure. Then what would happen?

As the days counted down towards his leaving she knew that she would never see him again and that was too hard to consider. He had been so kind to her. How could she go back to the loneliness? She had not thought of it as such, it was just as her life could be and she had had to content herself, but now she had an opportunity and yet she was too scared of what might happen if she took it.

He was strange to her, he spoke in another language.

It was not that it was English, it was that he was educated and clever and she knew how much he was looking forward to going to Edinburgh to learn how to be a doctor. She tried to stay away from him but he knew all the places she would be so nowhere was safe. Also it was easy enough to live outside when the sun shone but rain fell every day so that she had to keep close to the house and even to sleep upstairs and take her meals with the servants.

She soon became aware that not only had they taken to not speaking to her but that she did not speak to them. She tried making conversation with the newest kitchen maid but the girl just looked at her as though she saw a snake. That evening she was summoned to Mrs Brandon's sitting room.

The housemaid, Eliza, gave the message as briefly as she could but Catrin could not imagine what the cook and housekeeper wanted with her. Mrs Brandon had not talked directly to her since she had come home after having her baby. She knocked on the door and found the woman looking confused and embarrassed.

She said as though trying to be friendly, 'Do come in, Miss Catrin.'

She had never put the 'miss' in front of Catrin's name before and Catrin felt sure that Mrs Brandon had no liking or respect for her but she did as she was bidden and closed the door.

Mrs Brandon urged her to sit down across the fire and Catrin was grateful for the fire, which was giving out a lot of heat, and for the room, which was so comfortable. The chair she sat down in was the best she could ever recall so she sat and waited for whatever Mrs Brandon had to say.

That lady did her utmost to look straight at Catrin and failed so she said to the fire, 'Master Rhodri has spoken to me about taking you with him when he goes north. I think he felt the need to ask somebody what to do and he didn't wish to approach your father.'

'There wouldn't be much point. I don't suppose the man would recognize me or my name.' Catrin was surprised how bitter and resentful she sounded. She could not remember ever having said anything like this before and Mrs Brandon was obviously upset by it because the look she finally gave Catrin was one of disgust.

'You must not speak about the master like that. He does his best for everybody.'

'Does he? Well, it doesn't include me and never has done.'

'Master Rhodri is in earnest. He thinks he can provide a better life for you than what you have here and yet you are resisting.'

'I can't go. If he ever found out what I had done he would send me back here, you know it and so do I.'

'There's no reason why you shouldn't start a new life.'

'Because I have nothing here? Because nobody talks to me or cares about me? Somebody would be bound to tell him and then what?'

Catrin got up and left the room, shivering in the hall outside the door because the hall was always chilly in bad weather. Wind and rain were beating against the stained-glass windows there, making the colours run one into another. Catrin didn't hesitate. She ran down the hall and stairs and out of the front door and into the bad weather.

She cried. She hadn't cried in a long time but it was as if there was no difference between the rain and her tears. The one would hide the other. It would not however hide the sobs that began to escape and so she ran until she reached a big barn which was often empty and then she sat down on the cold floor and let her crying run its course. She went to sleep even though it was draughty and when she awoke she felt as though she could go back to her life, she would manage it. She did not need to leave here, she could organize some life of her own and once her brother had gone it would be easier. She had managed before and she would manage again. She must not give in. She must not see him any more.

She kept well away from the house for several days until she knew that he had less than a week left. Then he discovered that she was having meals and sleeping at the house because the weather was bad and he even went into the kitchen in search of her, horrifying Mrs Brandon and the maids as they sat down for their tea.

'Here you are, Catrin,' he said frowning at her. 'I want to talk to you.'

'I don't want to talk to you,' she said and ran out of the kitchen and into the backyard but he caught her by the arm.

'You're avoiding me. I want you to come to Edinburgh. I want you to have a new life, a chance. If you give it six months and don't like it I will bring you home.'

Catrin tried to free herself from him but he held on. He wasn't hurting her but she could see that he was in earnest.

'I can't go. I can't ever go anywhere,' she said and she was losing her temper now.

'Why? If you give me reasonable explanation I will accept it,' he said.

'I had a baby. All right?'

He let go of her then as shock and amazement took over his face. She pulled free and he let her but he was as determined as she and followed her across the yard and into the comparative warmth of the stables. The boys were about and he would not talk to her there, she thought, but it was not the case.

'Why didn't you tell me?' He seemed unaware of other people. The boys stopped what they were doing and even left the stable as though they did not want to overhear the conversation and who could blame them, she thought.

'When was this? When was it, Catrin?' He was glaring at her now. 'Was this recent? Did somebody do something awful to you? Tell me about it, tell me what happened.'

'So that you can judge me?'

'You've already judged yourself by the sound of it, it can't be that much harder to tell me.'

'I wanted you to think well of me. Now you will never do that again. You could not take me into polite society such as your rich friends and their families. You couldn't do such a thing.'

He was nonplussed, she could see.

'Tell me what happened?'

'It was one of the stable boys.'

It was the first thing that came to mind and somehow easier than the truth since she had cared for Joe and it had all been for nothing.

'Nonsense,' her brother said immediately. 'You've just made that up.'

'How do you know?' She regarded him with new respect. How discerning he was proving to be.

'Because they treat you like one of them. They seem to be your only friends such as they are able.'

'So maybe one of them got too friendly.'

'You are a very bad liar,' her brother said. 'Did

somebody take advantage of your ignorance? Did some man force you?'

'Would that make any difference?'

'Of course it would.'

'Of course it wouldn't. A girl is supposed to resist, she is meant to stop a man from doing such a thing and so if it happens it is her own fault because she didn't try hard enough to get away.'

'That's ridiculous,' he said. 'I am going to be a doctor and I know exactly how these things happen and how strong a man is. You're just a slip of a girl. How on earth could you stop somebody?'

'Well, I didn't, so there. I loved him. I thought he loved me. He didn't purposely deceive me, he just wanted to – to have me and I wanted him.'

This time she ran and he did not run after her and she assumed that he could now accept what she said. He would leave her alone and he would soon be gone and she would have some peace. Anyhow, Mrs Brandon had spoken to her so things might get easier. She would take charge of her own life, she was old enough. She could change her name and leave and find a position in somebody's house. She could work in anybody's kitchen and make a good job of it.

But then everybody for miles around knew who she was, her looks were so distinctive, with her bright golden hair, her blue eyes, and she was tall and slender for a girl and she was free in her manners. Also, they knew her father and must wonder at how she dressed, how she lived, but not why any more. Everybody knew that she had had a child and they shunned her. How would she ever get out of here with no money and no aid? In the end she resolved to go to her brother and ask him for enough money to get her away and then maybe he would be satisfied and they would never meet again. That was all she wanted, to pretend that nothing was any different, that he had never come here, that nothing more would alter. She didn't think she could bear any more. She was only just growing used to the way that she had let herself down so spectacularly. It seemed that there was no way back.

Introducing the subject of money to her brother was not the easiest thing to do. He had taken to going riding when the weather was bright, which it was almost every evening after the skies cleared. It made for beautiful sunsets, something she loved dearly. So, the next evening when he went to the stables she went with him and suggested they should ride together.

She moved ahead and let her horse go as it wanted to, but he kept up with her. They always stopped in the same places and this one was at the top of a hill where all the countryside spilled out around them, so green and orange and brown. There were the mountains and, well below, the fast-running rivers, which were now dark and muddy because of all the recent rain.

She waited for him to dismount and then looked straight at him and said,

'I could manage some kind of life if I had enough money to move away from here so that people don't know who I am. If I could get away properly to somewhere like Llandudno I could go to work as a kitchen maid or cleaning bedrooms in a hotel. I can cook so I could start at the bottom and maybe become like Mrs Brandon in time.'

'You are nothing like Mrs Brandon,' he said, clearly affronted and frowning. 'It would be beneath you to do such a thing.'

'Nothing is beneath me.'

'Of course it is. Mrs Brandon is a nice enough woman but you are clever and well born and of a good family. You could never do such a thing.'

'It would be better than staying here like this, surely. I would need no more than a few pounds, I'm sure you have enough, your father seems to lavish money on you. It would be like nothing to you and you could forget about me. You would have done your duty and could salve your conscience—'

'See how you speak? You may not have had any education but you pick things up so quickly and you can read and write so well after only a few weeks. You are beautiful and charming and clever.'

'I had a child. They took it from me but I had it. I am

35

somebody's mother. Even if I never see that child again the fact remains. If it lived or if it died things like that cannot be undone. Don't you see?'

'Maybe if you talked about it I would understand.'

'I don't want to talk about it. It happened and this is my life and nothing you say can make any difference. I have to live now as if it had never happened, to cut it from my heart and mind.'

She would have got up on her horse, this she could do just by swinging herself on to it with one foot in the stirrup, but her brother would not be put off. He got hold of her waist and pulled her so that she turned around within his grasp and tried to hit him. He held her off easily.

'I will let you go but you must promise to tell me what happened.'

'I don't see why I should.'

The moment she stopped fighting he let her loose and they both stood back rather in awe of one another.

'If I tell you will you give me some money so that I can leave this place?'

'Yes.'

'Promise?'

'I promise.'

The sun was going down and the sky was blue and fiery and great streaks of pink lit the whole area. Catrin could not help but think that she could never leave here, she loved this place so very much.

Nearby was a wood and in the best position for seeing the view there was a bench under the tree so she led him there. It was quite dry now. They sat down.

She told him about the awful house up on the hill at the start of the descent into Weardale. She told him about the pain and despair. He was not looking at her so she did not look at him and it was easier that way to keep on talking until it was all told, feeling that nobody had cared for her. The tears began to fall and she thought how awful that she had cried twice recently which was possibly more than she had ever done.

She saw through his eyes what her life was like, how truly awful it was and she knew that she must get away from here and try a new life, in another place and never ever come back. She did not belong here. She had been foolish to think she could go on like this forever. She could not, that much had become plain.

In the end they decided not to say anything to their father. What would be the point? Catrin would go with her brother and try the kind of life she might have and if it did not work then he would bring her back to Wales and they would try something else. She had to be content with that.

They went to the dressmaker and there he left her in the capable hands of the old Scotswoman who was delighted to make clothes for anyone. If she knew who they were she was sensible enough to say nothing. She made three dresses for Catrin in the few days which followed. She also took her to the cobbler, bought her underwear and nightgowns and she instructed Catrin how to put up her hair, after snipping off the bottom four inches, the better to contain it, she said. Looking in the mirror finally Catrin barely recognized herself.

She felt like a turncoat and kept in mind his promise, that if she didn't like it he would bring her back home. Edinburgh was a very long way and they would travel by train. Catrin tried not to think that they might be within a few miles of where her child was, if the child lived. She tried to think that the child was safe and loved. It was the only way she could think of it at all.

Three

Therefore as they passed through Durham she ignored the view of the little city below, the streets, the cathedral, the castle. People were walking, shopping, carrying various goods to and from the shops and places of business. It seemed so strange that somewhere down there was the child she had given birth to and nobody knew.

She did not want to linger for fear someone would recognize her. She knew this for folly, why should anyone know it was she, looking so very different and besides from what she knew the station was quite a distance from the place where she had been obliged to give up her child.

They went through Berwick. The view from the coast of Northumberland and into Scotland was beautiful and Roddy insisted that they sat on the right side of the train and that she could have the window seat the better to see the little stone houses and the waves which crashed up the beaches of the seaside towns. In some cases she caught a glimpse of small fishing boats in harbours or pulled up on to the sand.

Edinburgh was vast or so it seemed to her. Everything moved so quickly. The streets were filled with people and traffic of every description. The streets were also narrow, so close together, but the city was almost elegant with its Georgian squares and gardens, and she got to see the majesty of the castle, which stood out proudly.

Roddy had rented a house and with it various servants. Catrin found it embarrassing that they were the servants and she was not. There was also a young woman who seemed not much older than she was, Miss Caller, who was to educate Catrin in every possible way – history, geography, Latin, Greek and mathematics. They were to walk in the park together when the weather was fine and sit over their books when the weather was not.

It was a strange way to live and took several weeks to get used to. She was not the person she had been, not to herself or to these servants. The governess was polite and confined her conversation to the topic in hand, but as the autumn nights grew cold and dark Catrin became comfortable with the other girl though they kept one another at a distance.

She felt strange in some ways. She was constricted as she had not been. Her hair was put up each morning by the little maid who looked after her and whose speech Catrin did not understand, her accent was so thick. At night the little maid gave her hair a hundred strokes and then plaited it so that it should not tangle. In some amusement Catrin remembered how she had done the same to the horses and it was odd.

The little maid brought her tea in the mornings and opened her curtains and placed hot water on the dresser, lit the fire in the bedroom and helped her to dress. It was hardly surprising that Catrin grew used to the luxuries of her life though the clothing she wore was so tight that she found red welts on her body when she was freed of it and into her nightgown.

The house that Roddy had rented was large to her but attached to other houses and it seemed odd that people walked past. It was part of a square with lots of grass in the middle and sufficient room for vehicles to stop right by front doors. There were many rooms, all of which had fires and she came to realize that her brother had plenty of money to use for such purposes and he stinted neither of them in any way.

The beds were big and comfortable and her bedroom was large enough for a writing desk, a chair by the window, and for shelves which she soon filled with books. There was also a dressing table where she could gaze into her own eyes while the little maid brushed her hair.

Edinburgh felt huge and people were in such a hurry. Roddy was always out and about as he called it, he was a busy student and had classes to go to and people to meet so, but for the governess and the servants, Catrin was almost always alone. It was easy to be lonely among so many people but she had the comfort of her home to make up for it.

Miss Caller was determined to change the way that Catrin spoke English. Miss Caller had an Edinburgh accent but that apparently was acceptable while her Welsh accent was not. What the difference was she could not discern. Miss Caller knew nothing of Wales and suppressed a shudder the once they spoke of it as though heathens lived there but Edinburgh was the height of sophistication. This seemed odd to Catrin. Surely people were the same everywhere.

Miss Caller was teaching her embroidery. It reminded her so much of the dark days when she was pregnant and stitching the edges of sheets that she hated doing it. She was meant to follow the lines on a dun-coloured tray cloth and embroider pansies in the corners of it. It was slow tedious work and to her it felt pointless.

Miss Caller also set her off knitting a scarf. If there was anything more tedious than the needles going back and forth, Catrin had yet to meet it.

Sometimes she rebelled because although she was allowed to walk in the nearby park Miss Caller was always with her so there was no conversation of interest and Roddy was always out in the evenings with his friends. He seemed to think this was an appropriate way to live but Catrin felt not much better off than she had when she had been able to come and go in Dolgellau and could ride and look after the horses and not spend her whole life learning how and when to speak and how and what to do. From morning to night the tedium was almost unbearable.

On Sundays they went to church twice. Catrin was even more bored then but she didn't dare to protest. She was meant to read nothing but her Bible, to sit quietly and take the odd brisk, freezing walk if the afternoon was light which it rarely was. All that was different was a huge meal in the early afternoon. She could have wept with boredom.

She hadn't realized that her brother was so religious and taxed him with it but all he said was that it was the right thing to do, they must be seen to be at church and he urged her go with him in the mornings and evenings. This was the beginning of his career, she felt, and she had to put up with it.

Roddy didn't allow himself to work or study on Sundays and she had the feeling he hated it all just as much as she did but here respectability was everything and he must be respected both as a man and the doctor he hoped to become.

In the evenings she went early to bed with nothing but a cup of tea to sustain her and then her mind became so active that she did not sleep.

He told her that she must try harder with her studies.

'You have a tendency to be idle,' he told her, 'it won't get you anywhere.'

'I didn't know that I was trying to go anywhere,' she couldn't help saying.

'You have to lose that accent and work at your lessons and stop saying things that you should not say. Miss Caller is not impressed. She says you don't pay attention.'

'It's just so boring.'

'Everything is boring,' Roddy said and she realized that boredom was the one horror she had not experienced until now. When she could do what she liked with her small life she had not felt like this.

'You don't seem bored,' Catrin said.

'I apply myself. If I'm going to be a doctor I must put up with tedious lectures and the kind of teachers who do not scruple to think that I will never get there and that I will never be good at it. I write long essays and read hundreds of pages and try to understand the diagrams and the ideas and how the human body works. By the end of each day my brain is befuddled and my eyes ache so much that I doubt I will ever get there.'

'You have friends.'

'Only other medical students. I don't have time for anything else and also we must cultivate one another in order to go forward with our work and in the end who I know will be as important as what I know so you also must be seen to be thoroughly respectable and obedient

44

to those who know better than you do about what your life will be.'

'It's easy for you, you know what you want from life. I don't know what I want any more.'

'You must learn to behave like a lady and to do what ladies do.'

'And what do they do?'

Roddy seemed stumped at that and also she could see that he was tired and yet in earnest so she tried to plague him no further. She began to persevere with all her studies so that he would be proud of her.

Gradually what had looked like nonsense on the page began to make better sense and once she had learned to enjoy reading life became a little easier. Most of the books in the house were Roddy's medical books but Catrin and Miss Caller were able to go to a nearby bookshop where she could buy history and geography books but best of all books of flowers and birds and trees with colourful illustrations.

Therefore she sat over the fire while the Edinburgh trees were bare of leaves and the streets were icily cold and learned about the seasons and the way that nature renewed itself each year. So by the time spring arrived, and it was much later here than it had been in North Wales, she knew what was happening and began to enjoy the new buds appearing, the flowers in the parks unfold and although there was a bitter wind across Edinburgh her life became less tedious.

She was worried about Roddy though. She thought the hard studying was sometimes too much. He coughed all winter and even spent a few days in bed but he had to study and he got on with it so that Catrin was glad when he stopped coughing as the weather became a little warmer.

That spring Miss Caller was taken ill. Roddy was convinced that it was something infectious and forbade Catrin from going to see her governess at home to find out whether she was getting better. But Catrin, having by then become fond of the girl who was not so very much older than herself, waited until he left the house and then, following instructions which the little maid gave her – they were on first name terms by then and the little maid was called Jinnie – she walked to the area where Miss Caller lived.

It was not far. Nowhere in Edinburgh was far. It had astonished her that the poor and the rich lived so closely and yet seemed to have so little interaction, but then she already loved it for its buildings, its hum, its humanity.

Miss Caller's home should not have been a shock to her but it was. She lived in the poor streets where the houses looked crushed together. Catrin had not thought, since her governess was always neatly turned out, that Miss Caller's family lived in what was almost poverty.

She had noticed that Miss Caller was always hungry for her meals, that she patched and mended her gloves, her skirts and hats were old and shabby and her shoes were well worn, but somehow Catrin had not realized that there was what was known as genteel poverty. She found it when she knocked on the door of the governess's home and a thin pale figure came to the door. It was Miss Caller's mother.

She fussed as though embarrassed and yet honoured and said how very very kind it was of Miss Morgan to go to such trouble and urged her inside. Much aware of the shabby state of her house, Catrin could see, she did not know what to do with her hands and wrung them. Her gaze darted about as though finding fault through Catrin's eyes at all she saw.

The fire was low in the sitting room and several children were seated at a big table with their pencils and paper. They seemed hard at work but making little progress as far as Catrin could see. Having only just learned how to make progress herself she felt bad for them in their worn clothes in a room where the fire gave out little heat and all of that was lost among so many people in the small room somehow.

There were no rugs on the floor, the house felt cold and damp and in places Catrin could see the walls had mould and cracked plaster. It smelled foisty and there was the acrid smell of overcooked vegetables, perhaps broth which had been heated and reheated and given out in tiny bowls to hungry children. They were all far too thin, their wrists and ankles protruded from their scanty garments and their faces were gaunt.

She insisted on seeing her governess and was ushered upstairs into a room which was filled with beds, a double and two singles. It was even colder up here, she could see her breath. Miss Caller was coughing and spluttering and apologizing and Catrin begged her to save her breath rather than trying to speak. She told Catrin when she could breathe that she should not have come, that her brother would not approve, that she might catch something. They did not know whether it was contagious.

Catrin was about to ask whether they had had a doctor and then realized her mistake. This family had not seen a doctor in many a day. They could not afford it.

'Nonsense,' Catrin said, brisk for possibly the first time in her life, 'I never catch anything.' This had a great deal to do with healthy living in the country but it was not so here. The fog, which was caused by smoke from so many chimneys, sometimes engulfed the streets for days. That plus the wind and rain hurling itself through the narrow alleyways didn't make for healthy living, she thought. And then she realized that she was starting to think like Roddy, like somebody who knew and cared about other people. It was a very strange and rather good feeling.

There were no servants and when she went downstairs,

ostensibly to leave, having tried to reassure the patient that she would be better soon, she found Mrs Caller in the kitchen making a meal with an onion and a few potatoes. Catrin saw instantly that she must help though Mrs Caller tried to tell her not to.

Firstly she went off to shops and bought food, then, being glad of having been taught how to cook years ago, she set to in their kitchen. She had called in and ordered more coal which would be coming that afternoon and for the first time ever she was grateful to have money which she could share with other people.

She made a beef stew with lots of vegetables and pulses. She had bought bread and butter and jam which would fill up the children until the stew was ready. She also bought apples and flour and sugar and managed to get the kitchen stove hot enough so that she could both let the stew bubble on top and put the apple pudding into the oven. The smell, Mrs Caller told her, was wonderful.

After they had eaten, Catrin sat the children down at the table and in a very-no nonsense voice, which she did not recognize, began to talk to them about birds and animals and how life went on in the country and they were interested because they knew little of it.

At first the children, being unused to her, did not understand that she was trying to further their knowledge while keeping them entertained. She told them about farm animals and about how grass grew and wheat and how the sheep ate in the fields and the cows gave milk and the hens laid eggs.

She spent all day in the poor little house, finding out that Mrs Caller's husband had died leaving her with nine children and no money and so the moment that her eldest daughter was employable she had been sent out as a governess. Her father had taught her. The second daughter, who had no interest in books and learning, was sent out as a parlour maid, much further down the social scale. She worked for rich people in a different part of the city and rarely came home. Her mother had learned to be grateful that other people were paying for her daughters' keep.

The third child was a boy and was an indoor servant at yet another house and spent his days hauling buckets of coal up the stairs, cleaning silver in a little back room which ran off the kitchen and fetching and carrying from outside to inside and back again. He was unhappy at his work his mother said, paid little and slept in the stables even in such bad weather. It was evident she felt sorry for her son rather than her daughters but his life sounded so dismal that all Catrin could do was sympathise.

Another boy was an apprentice who lived in and did not come home but he was not paid while he learned to make coffins and it was considered a most respectable trade but it made her shudder. Catrin thought it was all very hard. It still left five children who needed looking after. They could not go to school because any school nearby was not decently run, Mrs Caller said with a shudder. As to other schools they had not the clothes, she had not the money and they gathered here so that she could teach them what she knew while trying to cook and clean and bake and wash and now her daughter had come home ill. Catrin could see that the poor woman was beside herself with despair.

That evening Roddy had gone to some kind of social event so he had no idea that Catrin had spent her day at the Caller house. She knew instinctively that he would not approve so she simply didn't tell him but she found that she was looking forward to going back the next day.

Had he been amenable to the idea she would have asked him to go and see Miss Caller and perhaps he would be able to diagnose what ailed her, but she couldn't bring herself to do it because he would resist and also tell her she was not to go back.

She found a particular cough medicine that he had brought home. He was using part of the house as what he called a laboratory and was making up mixtures as a follow-up to his chemistry lessons. He had cured his own cough with it, he told her. He was pleased he had been able to produce a good result and so when he had gone the following morning she stole a bottle of this and dosed Miss Caller, who she now called Lucy, with it and she began to get better. Catrin was longing to tell him that right from the start it made a difference.

Flushed with success, Catrin read his books and alongside her memories of the fields and hedges and beaches of North Wales and how people there concocted their own cures she began to remember what they had made and what had worked and what had not and she found the whole idea very exciting.

She took food from her kitchen. Nobody could object and though she got several strange looks from the cook and the maids they were in no position to say anything. Indeed the cook encouraged her when Catrin explained briefly, saying softly that she had come from a poor family herself and would not begrudge a little sustenance to the children.

Mrs Caller was so grateful for the help that things began to get better straight away and Catrin was joyful at being able to make good things happen for the little family. She soon grew very fond of all of them. With the extra help, Mrs Caller did her washing and cleaning cheerfully and Catrin managed to get three of the children into a decent school not far away which would take them for a few pennies a week. With the children at school and only two to look after, Mrs Caller began to make pies and stews and soups and cake and soon the children started to fill out and look better.

Lucy's cough disappeared and within the week she was

downstairs helping as much as her mother and Catrin would allow. Catrin bought books and crayons, drawing paper and pencils and writing paper with lines to make writing easier for the children. Also, if it was a fine day she would take them to the park and on Saturdays they all went and played. They slept well now, full of good food, and they were cheerful.

Catrin helped Mrs Caller to make new clothes. She learned how to buy good material at a reasonable price from the nearby market and, remembering how she had hated embroidery, she began to love sewing because it had a purpose, to keep the children warm and cosy. Mrs Caller had been a seamstress before she married and was very good at such things.

Four

Sundays, however, were the days when Catrin stayed at home and she had begun to hate that day, going to church two or three times now, as Roddy seemed to think it essential, and then back to read the Bible. He had even begun reading out a sermon in the evenings. She didn't understand why he did this until she saw it was ambition that drove him.

The church they attended was full of rich people. She could tell by their neat clothing even if on Sundays it was muted. The cloth was fine cut and they were all healthy and Roddy was beginning to cultivate those he thought were the right people. She said nothing, she would not criticise him after he had done so much for her. She felt that she never would be able to repay him.

When she had been going to the Caller household for almost three weeks he came out of his laboratory in the middle of one evening and asked her about the missing medicine bottle. She had been studying various illnesses in one of his books and counting on the fact that he would not notice, but he came into the sitting room frowning and saying instantly, 'Where did you get that book?'

Catrin looked at it and tried for a surprised face.

'Ought I not to have read it?'

'It's not for general use,' and he took it from her and put it on the little table nearby. 'More importantly I have noticed that two bottles of those I have filled with that particular cough syrup have disappeared.' He knew, she thought, she could see by the way he looked at her.

'Didn't you notice that Miss Caller was not here?' she asked, eyes wide with innocence.

He hesitated.

'What is that supposed to mean?'

'She's been ill. I just thought the medicine might help and it did. She's much better.'

Roddy's frown deepened.

'You took bottles of that mixture without asking me?'

'It seemed a good idea. They can't afford a doctor. They are very poor, you know.'

'You went there?'

'Of course I did. She was very sick and her mother is widowed and has nine children. What was I meant to do?'

'It could have killed her.'

'That's very dramatic,' she said and smiled a little. 'You told me you thought that you had perfected it and tried it out on various people, including yourself.'

'Other students. Not other people. What if something bad had happened to her? Do you understand how the university would view it?'

'How on earth would they know?'

Roddy seemed stumped at that but he said,

'You must not go into my laboratory or take anything which is mine and you must certainly not take my books.'

'I only borrowed it. It's very interesting.'

'You aren't listening to me, Catrin.' He only called her Catrin when he was ill pleased and he certainly was now. 'You must not go to their house. We cannot be seen to associate with poor people or with servants.'

'Why not? Aren't we supposed to look after people less fortunate than ourselves? Isn't that the point of becoming a doctor? Or do we go to church to cultivate those who are rich?'

'You don't understand. I am nobody here. My father lives in what to them is some obscure little village in the middle of nowhere so I have to make my way and your way too so whatever is needed I must do and so must you until I can earn my own and your bread.

'I will never be able to join a decent practice unless we do the right thing. I am at the very bottom of the ladder here and it is a long hard climb to the top. If I have to be nice to other people in order to get there then I will do it and so will you. You are not to go into my laboratory or read my books or go to the Caller house again and

Miss Caller is not to come back. I will write her a note and send a servant with it,' and he swept out of the room.

He really did, Catrin thought, he was a nasty sideways wind, filling the whole house with venom. She would have to be more clever. She had money of her own which he gave her each month and had told her jauntily at the time that she could buy her own ribbons, set up accounts at the various shops and choose what she wanted. He would have her well dressed and cheerful always. Which meant that he wanted others to see her as his well-dressed, well-behaved sister.

So she used her own money to buy food for the Caller family, she bought material and gave them her time, but she was more clandestine about it. She made sure that he was never at home when she saw them and because he was now inclined to linger on a Saturday, suspecting her of disobeying him she wearily did not go. Also in the evenings when he was out with other students and friends she would come home mid-evening and sit meekly over the fire, giving her time to read history. She did quite like history though she didn't agree with most versions of it. The only women in it were queens which was a very poor show.

Lucy did not get another post but now they managed with the income which they had from her brother and sister who had both been promoted. Alec was now a stable boy, which was what he had hoped to be, and he had the ambition to be head groom. Lily became a personal maid at one of the best houses in the city and they were all a lot happier.

The children came back from school with various illnesses and Catrin, flushed with success, tried several remedies on them. She bought books with her own money so that Roddy would not notice and in the big book-shops where nobody thought about what she bought. The shopkeepers were grateful that she purchased the books which usually only medical students took. They were always weighty and she kept them at Lucy's home so that there should not be any confusion.

The young schoolmaster, Mr Green, called at the house ostensibly to tell their mother how well the chil-dren were doing, but Catrin could see straight away that he was very taken with Lucy and she was glad of the idea that the family's lives were so much improved.

Roddy came home unexpectedly one Wednesday and she was obliged to admit that she was still spending time with the family.

'There was a reason I told you not to, I have discov-ered quite a lot about their father.'

'Roddy, he's dead and he was a clergyman.'

'He was a drunk and an idiot and he brought his family about as far down as they could go. I employed Miss Caller because I wanted to help them a little but you cannot make friends of such people.'

'Well, they are on the way up now. Lucy has a gentleman friend, a schoolmaster, Mr Green, her sister is a lady's maid and her brother has a new job, while the other is about to finish his apprenticeship and go to work.'

'Have you no idea how far down the social scale from us they are? You cannot make friends of such people. And another thing. You treat the servants like equals. You must learn to put some distance between you and them. That girl who looks after you—'

'She's called Jinny and she's very nice.'

'She comes from the country, has a thick accent and is ignorant.'

'I came from the country, with a thick accent and was ignorant.'

'That is another matter. You are a gentleman's daughter.'

'He is no gentleman, not after the way he treated me.'

'He is a typical man of his generation. He was ashamed of you.'

'He could not have been a gentleman when I was a small child. He pretended I didn't exist. I lived with the servants so no wonder I feel more at home with them.'

'He was grieving for his wife.'

'So he treated his daughter badly? Do you think that is an excuse?'

*

59

'You have been reading my books again, the ones I need to study,' he accused her several weeks later.

'I don't use them when you are there,' she said.

'What do you want with such things?'

'I want to know more about it, that's all, about how people are made up and how they get ill.'

'Why? You cannot become a nurse you know, it's not considered respectable among people like us.'

'I don't want to become a nurse. I want to be a doctor.'

'That's absolutely ridiculous, Catrin, and you know it is.'

He went off to his study and slammed the door.

She still went to see the Caller family and it was good news. Lucy had found a position teaching a family of two little girls. Their father was an important man at the university and he certainly believed in education for girls. They were allowed to read whatever they wanted. Lucy was praised and well paid and the little girls were half French and they taught Lucy French.

Their mother came from Paris and Lucy was inspired by the French way of dress. There was nothing modest about Mrs Thorpe and she bestowed her older dresses on Lucy, saying that she was far too fat to wear them, so Lucy went about 'bedecked in finery' as her mother joyfully said.

Mr Thorpe said that he spent all his days putting out financial and social fires at the university and came home exhausted to the bosom of his family. He adored his daughters and his wife was kind to their governess.

It was a Thursday in June when Catrin came home twice and found that Roddy was there before her. The second time that it happened he came into the hall and said,

'You're still going to see the Callers, aren't you?'

'Why shouldn't I? They are my friends.'

'There is diphtheria in the city. You shouldn't be going anywhere.'

She stared at him.

'What a thing to say! And you, hoping to become a doctor.'

'Yes, me. Not you.'

'Why not me?'

He didn't answer for a few seconds and then said wearily,

'Don't be difficult, Cat, I'm tired. Please, just do as I ask,' and he went back into his study and shut the door very softly.

And then she understood. Yes, he wanted her to behave in a way that he knew would further his career but they were brother and sister and he had dreams which were not to be her dream. She did not know how to reconcile the two.

They had been apart for so many years and they had

lost all that time when they were growing up. It could not be replaced. All those weeks and months and years when she could hear his voice and see his smile and know that he had a special place in his heart for her, it was over.

She spent a troubled evening but did not see him again before she went to bed. She did not want to disturb him any further than she had done. He needed to study. He needed to get on.

She didn't go to see the Caller family the next day. They didn't really need her any more, she admitted to herself. They had money, four of them were in work and Mr Green was now Lucy's accepted suitor and he had a good living and kind parents. Catrin was full of hope.

That afternoon she had a note from Lucy that made her sit down on the nearest chair in shock.

Dear Catrin

You must not come to the house. Two of the children are very ill and we think it must be the diphtheria. We are so afraid. We understand that it can go through families like wildfire so we are determined not to bother other people or go near anyone. I will let you know when the children are better. Until then much love,

Lucy

Catrin's first instinct was to run to her friend but she knew how unwise that would be. Roddy would not want her to and she must not go out and mix with people for fear of bringing such a thing here.

She stayed at home and tried not to think about it, not to question him about what was happening. It would not help. Fred Sutherland, Roddy's best friend, who was also a medical student, told her more about it but he too insisted that she should not go anywhere. She would be spreading germs and since she didn't have to go anywhere it was wrong of her to do it so she sat at home worrying.

The next note a week later was so bad that she had to read it three times to make any sense of it and even then the room spun.

Dear Catrin
Jane and Adrian died this morning and Mr Green has caught it from his pupils. I cannot go and see him. Please don't come anywhere near. It is a dreadful illness.
  All my love,
  Lucy

Jane and Adrian were the youngest of the children and Jane was not even old enough to go to school. What about the others, they went to school and it seemed that this awful disease was ripping its way through the schools and homes of the city. When Roddy came home she told him.

'Can nothing be done?' she said.

'The doctors are doing everything they can.'

'But so many people cannot afford doctors. What do they do?'

He shook his head, didn't answer for a few moments and then he said, 'Every doctor I know is helping even those who cannot afford them. We take an oath as you know and we help people where we can but I am inexperienced and might make more problems than they have already so I can only do a little and study hard, Catrin. Try not to ask so much.'

Catrin's throat stuck as though she had swallowed too much treacle and it lodged there, thick and nasty and brown in her throat.

'I'm sorry,' was all he said.

She lasted another day and then could not wait any longer. She ran all the way to the Caller house and when she got there she saw by Lucy's face as she answered the door that things were worse. Lucy stood back.

'You shouldn't have come, you really shouldn't,' while the tears slipped down her face in disarray.

'I couldn't stay from you. Not now. Not when things are so dreadful. There must be something I can do for you.'

Lucy shook her head slowly and painfully.

'You've got it, haven't you?' she said.

'We are all ill and – and Mr Green—'

'Mr Green?'

'He died yesterday. I have just had a note from his sister.'

'Oh, Lucy, no.'

'He was in such close proximity – isn't that what they call it? – to the children that it was doubtless he would succumb, but he wouldn't leave them, he wouldn't let them go without what aid he could render. Please, Catrin, stay back,' and she closed the door with a firm little click.

Catrin stood there in the street and wept.

In the days that followed she and Roddy barely spoke. She tried to be patient and philosophical but she threw a medical book across the room so hard that it made a big dent in the wall. Now she was more determined than ever that she must try to make a difference. Roddy had a good many books and she knew he had finished with a lot of them so she began to study in earnest.

When she had read and reread them she began to take books from Roddy's study and if he noticed he did not say anything. She couldn't sleep or eat so she read until her eyes hurt, until her vision blurred, until all she could do was lie down and rest.

She and Roddy were alone, she had sent the servants back to their homes so that they should not get this dreadful malady and she was grateful that there were no interruptions. It was like her own private illness, she resented it so much and yet held it to her almost like a friend or was it the old adage, keep your friends close and your enemies closer? She was determined that in time all such diseases would be eradicated and people would lead longer lives and be happy.

Her mind showed her huge pictures of Lucy without Mr Green, her mother and the rest of the family trying to come to terms with the youngest children taken from them. At least the rest of the family did not die and Catrin had grown to think how lucky they were when whole families had succumbed to this terrible thing.

And then suddenly it was over, it was gone and it was as if the city gave a huge sigh and sat back, but the losses were profound.

She went to the Caller house and Mrs Caller opened the door and took her into her embrace. Catrin could not help but weep because the poor woman had lost two of her children, though she had struggled to feed them when they were alive before Catrin had helped and Mr Green had come along and fallen in love with Lucy.

'It is Lucy I feel worst for,' her mother said. 'She has lost the man who was going to be her husband and at least I have some of my children with me. Who is to know that she will ever marry now?'

Catrin didn't quite understand this but she could see

when she went inside that her friend had aged so much that she would be lucky ever to catch the eye of any man, she was so bowed down by grief. And since she had loved Mr Green how would she ever go forward and learn to care for somebody new?

'I wish that I could be a nurse,' Lucy said, 'but I will just have to get on with what I'm doing because I understand it without more training and am well paid.'

That Lucy could consider moving forward at this point was a surprise to Catrin and yet what else could her friend do? They still needed and probably would always need the money even though two of the mouths no longer needed feeding. Going on was the hardest thing of all, Catrin thought.

Five

Catrin plagued Roddy after that about her chances at the university.

'Why don't you want me to do it? Lots of women do.'

'Not lots. The odd one and most people want a man there when they are ill.'

'That is probably lack of choice,' Catrin said. 'If a woman was having a baby why wouldn't she want another woman there who knew what was happening, what it felt like and all the other illnesses that women have. What do you understand of the pain of bleeding each month?'

He blushed.

'See?' Catrin said. 'You don't even like to think about women as people, just as those beneath you who don't really matter.'

'Those things are natural,' he said.

'Try talking to Mrs Caller. She had nine children. Now she has no money and because her husband was the provider she is destined to poverty and she cannot even afford a doctor.'

Roddy was finally silenced.

'We do have the money, don't we?' she said.

'Yes we have money but only for essentials.'

'I need something to do, something constructive and this is what I want. Won't you at least let me try? We did agree that money was for both of us.'

'Not for this.'

'I think you are being unfair,' she said.

They didn't talk about it any more but he did allow her the books that she wanted and needed and sometimes now in the evenings he did not go out and they would sit over the fire and talk about what he was learning and she realized that if she went to university after several years of study she would be a long way behind him due to her lack of education but she was a quick learner. Lucy had taught her so much and she began to work hard so that she might stand a chance of fulfilling her dream.

She had to prove on paper that she was intelligent enough and learned enough to become part of this place and she did everything she could to make certain that she would earn an entrance there. She had dreams of them going into practice together and he becoming a great surgeon. She thought she would like to study women's ailments and then she thought of children and wasn't sure if you could do both but all she thought about were her studies.

It was more difficult to see Lucy when they both had so much to do and Catrin realized that they were now on a different footing. She saw herself as a potential doctor whereas Lucy was busy with the small children she looked after and did not have much free time. Also Catrin was aware that somehow part of the bargain was that she would see less of the Caller family. They were very quiet now and she knew how much Mrs Caller grieved over her lost children and how heartbroken Lucy was about Mr Green.

Roddy and Catrin now settled down to work hard. He was not happy with her idea of becoming a doctor and kept telling her that she had a long way to go and so in the end all she did was study until she reached the level that would mean she had a chance of getting into the university.

When she finally got there she was almost twenty-one but she had been determined and she felt the triumph of her achievement. Even then she had to work harder than the men just to prove that she could stay with them. Not that they were discourteous. Some of them looked surprised to begin with, others treated her like one of themselves. Her beauty did nothing for her here and she began not to care. She dressed as plainly and modestly as she could and went about with serious intent. She began to love this way of life just as much as Roddy did. They were for once in complete harmony and were able to help one another every day.

Roddy finished his education long before she did. But

having him so far ahead was a help to her because they discussed everything in their lives and she learned a lot from her brother and was glad of his knowledge and they had become best friends. They talked about the hospitals and the surgeries and all the varied work that he was doing and so when she came after him she was the better equipped to carry on. She got up with a song in her heart. He moved into hospital work and she became happy that she was following him and that they could spend their time discussing the problems that they met and the hopes that they had for the future, such as how eventually he thought he might specialize and how she wasn't sure whether she wouldn't just want to be there for everyone.

Jinny went off and married the man she had been going out with for so long. After that Catrin had another maid far more reserved and so in homage to the way that Roddy was treating her she did not make friends of the maids any more, though she hoped that she was still polite and kind and made sure that they did not have to work when they were ill, that they got plenty of free time to visit their families and that the better they worked the more they were paid. She liked running the house and Roddy didn't care for such things so she had it all her own way and turned out to be good at it.

No matter what they tried to give him, each winter Roddy was ill. A drug would work once and then not again and it seemed to her that each winter he was ill for a longer time though he would have nothing said about it and scoffed at her worries.

In the early spring of her final year before becoming a doctor she noticed Roddy talking to a family when they went to church. They had kept up the practice of going to church twice on Sundays and even the sermon which one would read to the other in the evenings. They dressed neatly and read nothing but the books they needed for learning and Roddy said to her when they walked home one summer afternoon, 'I have invited the Sutherlands to dinner next Sunday.'

He had introduced her to these people some weeks ago but she had forgotten them. Roddy had known Fred all the way through his studying and Fred seemed friendly and kind but his family were dull. Catrin didn't usually notice things like that. She had no time for friends. Fred's father was a clergyman. Mrs Sutherland was very quiet and rather serious-minded and Amelia their daughter was pretty and taking but she was also quiet. Roddy talked to them after church each Sunday and she would hover on the edge, being quiet and polite and smiling and saying nothing.

'Sunday dinner?'

'Yes, I thought so. Is that a difficulty?'

'No, of course not.' They always did have a Sunday dinner but they didn't invite anyone, they quite enjoyed it just being them. However they didn't have friends, just colleagues at the university. It would do Roddy good to have them there and she could afford to be generous.

It was strange. She knew that Mr Sutherland was important and that they lived in one of the most prestigious areas of Edinburgh but she was surprised to find Mrs Sutherland looking around almost in dismay at the home she had made so carefully for her brother and herself. She thought it was pretty and homely and though she wouldn't have thought it looked expensive or opulent it was very respectable, middle class if you liked, but nothing like the kind of houses she felt that they were used to.

Winter was far behind them and the weather started to soften. Catrin was glad of it though she did not want to have to entertain these dull people. The meal was just as usual, they had lamb with new potatoes, mint and peas and then a crème caramel which was Roddy's favourite. Nobody spoke during the meal and although she tried once or twice to make conversation nobody answered her. Roddy looked at her in dismay and Mr Sutherland talked about the church service they had been to, what he thought of the ideas and everybody listened and said nothing. Catrin was unable to eat very much even though it was her favourite meal and usually she looked forward to it.

'You read novels, Miss Morgan?' Mr Sutherland said

when they had finished eating and were drinking coffee in the sitting room. It was a beautiful day and she longed to go for a walk although she knew Roddy would expect her to go back to church. Had they been alone she might have suggested it but now she felt unable to utter a word.

Was this a trick question?

'Mostly I read the books for my studies but also I like to read about history and wildlife and places I haven't been to.'

That was safe, at least she thought it was.

'It's very brave of you to venture into an area which has always been predominantly male.' Could Fred have actually said such a thing to her? The way that he looked at her made her aware of herself as a woman but not in a good way, as though she ought to have been content with less.

'I hope to make myself useful,' was all she said, and then, 'When such awful diseases come to us such as scarlet fever and diphtheria I long to be able to help. I have lost friends and the small children of my friends to such things and there was little I could do.'

'You were very good,' Roddy said, and she had not thought he had noticed what she did. 'You helped with food and cleanliness and keeping the children occupied reading,'

She left it at that. She ached to say that she had wanted to be much more useful and when people were educated in science it was so much better, but wisely, she thought afterwards, she said nothing, drank her coffee and ate one of the tiny meringues Cook made for her especially. So much for not being close to the servants. She was good to them and they were good to her and always the food she and the cook had chosen was good and well presented.

She soon realized that she was jealous of Roddy's attachment to these people she felt they had so little in common with. She had not known that she wanted her brother all to herself. She didn't like the family and although they were civil to her there was no warm connection and it wasn't until she saw Roddy walking close to Amelia on the way back to church in the early evening that she got a huge shock. Roddy was in love with Amelia. How could he have chosen a woman so boring, so vapid, so unlike Catrin herself she didn't know and she boiled with indignation and hurt. Yes, Amelia was pretty in a lifeless sort of way. Her eyes were very pale blue and her hair was brown but had no shine on it. Her cheeks were white and she had thin lips which turned down at the corners as though she was constantly unhappy. She wore no ornament, she did nothing to enhance her looks and yet he was taken with the girl. Catrin was astonished and could not get used to the idea even though when they went to church after that Roddy always walked beside Amelia.

Also it seemed to her that Amelia's parents did not quite like the connection but were too polite to say so. Roddy had done nothing wrong, he was a man with a career in front of him. He was handsome, tall, well educated and well spoken and that was when Catrin realized that Roddy had more in common with Amelia than he would ever have with his sister. They had been too long apart and she had had no company whereas he had had a fine education and mixed with people of his own class. He had probably met a lot of young women just like Amelia though possibly not all as tedious and yet as far as she was aware he had fallen in love with no one before now. Did he resent his sister? No, she thought, in dismay, he did not think of her long enough to consider her at all. His heart was given to Amelia.

It was not so with Fred. He didn't openly dislike her but it became obvious to Catrin that the family endured her because their beloved daughter was taken by a man they did not particularly care for but had no reason to dislike and they loved her sufficiently to put up with the man and his very dubious sister.

Catrin saw in her glass how beautiful she was. Amelia could not compare but then she didn't need to. Amelia had Roddy's heart and his sister was merely a mild encumbrance. She decided that she would do her best to like Amelia and even her family since it now looked as though Amelia would become her sister-in-law. Catrin found herself more tired than she had ever known and in some ways just as alone as she had ever been. Amelia Sutherland had taken her brother from her.

The following Sunday they went to Charlotte Square to the Sutherland home for the first time. Catrin had prayed she and Roddy would not go there but she realized now that it was inevitable. This was one of the best areas of Edinburgh and the people who lived here were the richest but it was set to be a disappointment.

It was a cold day despite being August. Since Amelia and her mother wore no jewellery of any kind except for her mother's wedding ring, Catrin thought she would try to continue making the right impression. The church had smelled damp, her fingers and toes were cold and she knew that she would be grateful to get out of the rain which was falling sideways with a wind that whipped at your coat.

The hall was very dark. Nobody was there to help them with their outdoor clothes. Mrs Sutherland said that they thought it was only fair to give their servants the day off so no fires had been lit, she was offered nothing more than a glass of water which did not warm her and when they set down to eat it was a cold meal. Catrin was so hungry she wished she had paid more attention to her breakfast.

'We like to think the servants have time on Sundays to attend church, read their Bibles and think of their souls,' Mr Sutherland said in his dark, booming voice. 'We therefore do the same and eat sparingly.'

Catrin was inclined to say that she wished she had known this when she fed them, she would have made sure they had a potted meat sandwich each.

The meal was a slice of cold ham and a potato for each of them. There was no dessert and she could not help but think of the meal she had given the family when they had come to her home. Now she was mortified. They would be judging her skills with her house and servants and thinking badly of her.

There was church again. By now her boots were leaking and she could concentrate on nothing but the thought of a hot cup of tea.

In between the services Amelia and her mother got out their work boxes and began sewing. The men sat quietly reading their Bibles. Catrin felt lost. After the service she thought she had never been so glad to get back anywhere than she was to toast her toes over her bedroom fire and devour tea and scones but she ended up feeling guilty when these were brought to her room.

Ought she too to give her maids more time off, but then they had a half-day every week and were well paid and could have time off in the evenings if they asked, and since she and Roddy had nobody to stay and nobody to eat there other than the Sutherlands that one time she knew that she should not feel so guilty.

The maid who brought the tea was walking out with a young man as Jinny had been and at present she met him two or three times a week in the middle of the evening so she was hardly badly done by and when Catrin asked her politely what she thought Mary smiled and said that she was so much better off than a lot of lasses who were not allowed followers at all, never mind having so much time for themselves. She considered herself happy here and she saw her family and took money back to her mother who lived in an area not too far away. So Catrin tried to stem her conscience and enjoy her fire, hot tea and scones.

She came to dread Sundays, she resented these people and begged for a day off.

'We can't afford to upset the Sutherlands,' Roddy said. 'They are one of the most influential families in the city.'

'But they are so boring and they take no pleasure in anything.'

'I don't think Mr Sutherland believes in pleasure,' Roddy said. 'He thinks it ought to be enough to do one's duty.'

'I don't understand why you like them or want to cultivate them.'

'Because Mr Sutherland will help me achieve my ambitions and probably yours too so it will be worth it in the end,' Roddy said. Here Roddy looked down and then admitted,

'I have come to care about Amelia. I like her very much.'

Catrin stared at him. She didn't know until then that she wanted Roddy very much not to marry Amelia. Perhaps he would become tired of how boring she was and move on to another young woman more interesting. It was a blow and for him to openly admit it carried it forward into another sphere.

Encouraged by her silence he went on. 'She's everything a nice girl should be – demure, modest, she dresses neatly and never pretends to be anything she isn't.'

Catrin tried not to go on staring. Amelia was everything a girl should be? Presumably she was like the sisters of the boys he went to school with. Those girls who had no ambitions to be anything but wives and mothers. Catrin thought back to how Amelia raised her eyes so gently to Roddy, how she laughed at anything remotely amusing that he said, how she hung on his every utterance as though he were a god. No wonder he liked somebody who looked at him in that way.

At home Amelia was devout and kept her gaze low and muttered 'yes, Papa' to everything her father said while Catrin longed for her or somebody to disagree with him or to change the subject or for Mrs Sutherland to be other than a totally obedient wife and mother. Amelia deferred to her brother and father and now to Roddy.

Neither woman had any interest outside the home and

Catrin was bored with their conversation and that was also difficult because it was her only free day. She was deliberately excluded from the men's talk and felt she had no place to belong.

She and Roddy had talked about setting up a practice just the two of them since their father's money still came in regularly and there was no reason why they should not do whatever they chose.

It was the one thing she was glad of, that her father made it possible for her to do what she wanted to, even if he didn't know it, though he must be aware she was with her brother because Roddy wrote regularly to him and as far as she knew he would never lie. And yet the money arrived promptly into the bank each month and there were savings big enough for them to have the practice they wanted. It would be a good start and after that they would make money for themselves. She therefore tried to remain patient and let Roddy suggest in his own time that they would work together always.

Maybe when her father was proud enough of her to forgive her early life, she might even go home to Dolgellau and be accepted into his house as his daughter. It was her dearest dream though she never said so to Roddy.

Christmas arrived and it was a hard winter so that she dreaded even further the freezing house which the Sutherlands inhabited. She found them narrow and inward-looking, and she thought that Mrs Sutherland and Amelia did not approve of her.

It was a very long winter in Edinburgh. Catrin thought of how spring came differently in North Wales, how it was wet on the beaches and foggy in the mornings but the snowdrops covered the ground in February, celandines glowed in the grass and daffodils waved in the breeze. She longed for the place where she had been so unhappy. It was stupid, she knew, but she could not be easy here among these people as the cold bit into toes and fingers. She clung to the bedroom fire when she was able but Roddy became more and more eager to spend time with the Sutherlands and changed into someone she barely recognized.

Easter finally came though it snowed as it so often did when the first signs of spring were meant to be there. To them it meant fasting on the Friday, eating no meat for several days and lots of church services. She became so bored in their presence that she wanted to scream.

She had thought spring would never arrive and when it finally did she was not heartened as Roddy grew closer to Amelia and further away from his sister. Roddy was the only person she had ever loved. Perhaps she would never love anyone else and now he was lost to her, she was in second place and it was a very long way behind first.

On Easter Sunday afternoon she so badly wanted to go for a walk and since she would never be allowed while with the family to go out alone, Fred insisted on going with her. Once outside the house she left him and began to run and when they reached the park she ran and ran until she was completely out of breath and went to him where he was sitting on a cold park bench, watching her in some dismay.

'That's better,' she said. 'I sometimes have to get out and let off some steam and since Roddy doesn't like me to run I make a practice of doing so when he isn't there. He doesn't think young ladies should do such things. I wanted so desperately to get out and be free. I feel so nooled down.'

Fred frowned.

'What on earth does that mean?' he asked.

'Like I can't breathe the stale air of Edinburgh and here in the park is the only fresh air I ever get.' She couldn't help smiling here. She was so elated that she wasn't cautious with him and she realized as soon as the words were out of her mouth that Fred of course would not approve.

'You are a very strange young woman with very odd ways,' Fred told her. 'I can't believe that you really want to spend your life dealing with other people's bodily illnesses? Our profession is totally unsuited for women's brains and bodies and I think you need to behave in a different manner in public if you are not to set people against you.'

Catrin was furious.

'I certainly haven't worked so hard for nothing,' she said. 'Roddy and I will set up a practice.' Roddy had said nothing of late and she was becoming impatient. They were both qualified now. Why would they wait?

Fred looked like he couldn't believe this.

'What?' he said.

'Surely you knew that.'

'I never think of you as a doctor. I assumed it was a way of employing your time before you did what every woman does, marriage and children and a home. I have nothing against educated mothers but that is so that they can pass on their knowledge to their children not so that they can go into professions. In fact I did think that your brother and I would have a practice together. We have talked about it.'

Fred and Roddy were getting experience after finishing their studies by working for a doctor Mr Sutherland knew well. Catrin had assumed that Roddy would join her when she finished her studies both at the university and in the hospital. She had been so excited, couldn't wait to get started. Had she been wrong? Had she not heard her brother?

'He never said anything.'

'I think it is what he wants.'

'I want to work with poor people,' she said.

'I think you will find if you speak to Rhodri that he

never had any intention of including you. You wouldn't be an asset to a successful Edinburgh practice. Perhaps deep in the country it would be another thing but it would be foolish to leave here where he and I can do so much, especially since my family is here and can be of help and support. I don't know if you have observed but he and my sister are becoming close. It doesn't really suit our parents. My father was eager for her to marry a minister of the Church of Scotland but though we know a great many clergy she seemed to prefer your brother though I cannot think why, much as I esteem and like him. My father wanted me to be a clergyman but I was not chosen by God and now he feels that Amelia too has let him down.'

When she and Fred got back to the house Catrin could see that Roddy was looking very red faced and so was Amelia. Mr Sutherland, tall and inscrutable, greeted them with,

'We are to welcome Mr Morgan into the family, as I am sure you are aware, Frederick, and to Miss Morgan we offer the hand of friendship and hope that she will be very happy to come to us as our other daughter.'

The worst had happened, Catrin's heart sank. She felt that Roddy was marrying Amelia to further his career and she was sad that he had let such a thing get in his way. She knew that he was ambitious but to marry for that reason? She felt as though she barely knew him.

The thought of spending her life in their house where the rooms were cold and the food was cold and the religion was there always like an unwanted relative was so bad that she could not even bring a smile to her face.

Roddy stood there like a simpleton and he said,

'Now that Frederick and I are finished learning we will set up in practice and we will make it the best practice in Edinburgh.'

All Catrin's hopes died there. She must have managed to stammer out her congratulations to them and smile as though happy to go along with what was happening.

Later and it was very late when they went back to their house – Roddy so elated and she so cast down – she implored him to let her into this new life which so excluded her.

'I want to help.'

'You can help. You will have a proper family and so will I. Finally we have a place and Mr Sutherland is so important that in time I will be able to specialise and do all the good that I want to do and to have you there at home will mean so much to me.'

'What about our house? We will have to give it up and I like it so much. What about me going into practice with you?'

They had reached their house. Roddy took off his things and gave them into the hands of Ailsa, one of the maids. She tutted over how wet they were and she helped Catrin off with her boots and said she would take everything in by the kitchen fire.

'It was never more than a dream, surely. I shall need a proper practice,' Roddy said to his sister as they went in to the drawing room.

Catrin could not help comparing this cosy little house to the great freezing mansion the Sutherlands lived in, where every book was a prayer book, a Bible, a book of psalms, great walls of religious books which held no interest for her.

'I can't go and live there and give up everything,' she said, in a last attempt, but Roddy looked at her with his eyes full of love for the girl he had just left and she saw that to him the girl and the lifestyle were all one. He had found exactly what he wanted and he did not understand that his sister might want anything more. He was lost to her and so was everything she had hoped to achieve.

'It's our future, Catrin, we will have a family of our own at last and I just know that we will be happy.'

She went to bed and lay there in the darkness, staring up at the ceiling all night.

She tried to pretend that nothing was different. She needed to remind herself of who she was even more than ever, because it became obvious to her that if she fought for what she wanted she would lose her brother and she owed everything to him. Her self screamed that it was not fair, but if it had not been for him she would still be in Wales, nobody with nothing. Now although this was not how she had hoped things would work out it became clear to her that it was the only thing to do. Nobody seemed to notice what she did, they were all so concerned and excited about Amelia and Roddy's wedding which was to be in July that she had become unimportant. She would have to be glad of that.

She was expected to be at their house a lot but somehow she managed to say nothing even when she had been shown the dark bedroom which was to be hers. That demonstrated to her how little she mattered. She had never seen a monk's cell but she had an idea that it would be very much the same. It was at the back of the house, the black grate had not seen a fire, there were no sticks, no paper, no kindling. The room itself was brown with no carpet, just linoleum and there was nothing more than a tiny wardrobe, a narrow single bed and a chest of drawers because she was expected to think about finery so little.

There were religious pictures on the walls, all of people suffering and looking up to heaven as though for mercy. The paintings were dark and the figures stiff. She knew nothing about painting but it seemed to her that these were very badly done. When they stayed there now her morning hot water was always cold, with a tiny thread-bare towel as though the servants understood that she did not matter and therefore went to no trouble. When her morning tea arrived it was cold or did not arrive at all. She was given books, religious books, she was expected to study her Bible most days and Mrs Sutherland, with great pride, gave her a workbox which she said had been her mother's and in it was grey wool for socks, the four thin needles to knit them on and cotton reels in grey and black and brown such as she would knit for the outer garments for the men in the family as they sat over the fire at night.

What made life even harder was that Catrin became a doctor that summer. She had studied, she had worked, she had followed other doctors and even consultants around the wards in the hospitals and she had loved it. She knew very well that this was meant to be her life's work and it was to be denied her.

It took time to school her mind to accept that she must do what her brother wanted. She could not risk his future, his career, his marriage and how happy he was. Roddy was getting everything that he wanted. She was getting nothing. Nobody spoke of her achievements, it was not acknowledged. She thought that perhaps after Roddy and Amelia were married she might manage something better but for now she must bide her time.

Roddy had given notice on their house and they would be leaving it when the marriage took place. She wanted to hang on to the front door, to chain herself to the railings as suffragettes had done and refuse to leave, but there was nothing to be done. Very often now they stayed over at the Sutherland house and she felt that there was nothing she could do. Her summer was to be taught obedience and abstinence since the Sutherlands fasted on Fridays. In fact they could be said to fast always since there was no joy in their food. Whether their cook was not very good or whether the poor woman had wilted under lack of enthusiasm for any of the joy that Catrin had always thought should be in food she didn't know, just that the bread was hard and black, butter was non-existent, there were no cakes or biscuits, no chocolate, no alcohol. No whisky. At one time she and Roddy had sat over the fire talking of their plans for the future and drinking a couple of tots before bed. They had been happy then. At least she had. Was Roddy unhappy until he saw Amelia? Perhaps he had been and she was so full of her own plans that she did not understand. He certainly did not care how unhappy she was now. She was someone who didn't matter.

She was a woman in the household and spent most of her days sewing and knitting and reading her prayer-book, never wearing anything except black, never going anywhere for pleasure. Even the park which she had loved running in was out of bounds. Ladies did not run. Ladies were quiet and meek and did their needlework. She felt as though she had died and been left like the

Catholics believed, in purgatory, for the ghastly mistakes of her life. She was worth nothing.

There was to be no honeymoon after the wedding of course, perish the thought. They were to be married and then to have a weekend in Dundee and come back and set up their lives. They even had a separate bedroom each, which was usual, but Catrin could not help but think of how wonderful it must be to roll over in bed after a bad dream and feel a living breathing warmth, someone's back to snuggle against, someone there who was yours.

It was therefore a shock to her to come back into the house a few days before the wedding and find raised voices in the drawing room. She was spending a lot of time packing up what she and Roddy owned. She had been busy that morning putting her pretty dresses into a large box which would in time be given to the more deserving, that was how Mr Sutherland put it. The books she had bought and loved were also not to go to Charlotte Square. No decent piece of jewellery was to follow her there. In secret she had put aside books and jewellery and the dresses she liked best but how on earth she would get them over to the house she was not sure and even then she had the feeling that they were bound for the attics.

It was late afternoon, had rained hard and she was thinking of a cup of tea and a scone while she still had a cook who thought that scones were baked to be laden with cream and raspberry jam and she was looking forward to it, coming out of the rainy street. She would soon sit by her fire, and it would not be long before she had no fire to sit against so she knew that she must make the best of it.

She stopped just inside the door, listening.

'What is it?' she asked Ailsa softly.

'I don't know, miss. Going at it hammer and tongs they have been. Cook and me tried not to hear because it's so loud but it was scary so we stopped in the kitchen and you can't find out much from there.'

Catrin was starting to think that an advantage. She stared at the drawing room door which was only just ajar. The three men were quarrelling. They did it a lot, talking of ecumenical differences and Mr Sutherland quite enjoyed a good fight as long as his point of view prevailed but this was different. It was real anger and she had the feeling as she drew nearer that there were insults.

'To think that we had to find out in such a way,' Fred said, obviously trying not to shout, his voice quivered.

'I have never heard of this man,' Roddy said.

'He's certainly heard of you. His father owns mines in North Wales. He understands that your family is everything it should not be, and your sister is everything she should not be. Why did you not acquaint us with such things?'

'I didn't think it was relevant.'

This discussion had obviously been going on for some time. Her brother might just as well have said 'because it was none of your business', such was his flat tone. In anger Roddy was the opposite of most folk, he got quieter and quieter.

They had found out about her, about her child. She wished she could run from the voices which all started up together now and she heard a lot of things she would not have wanted to hear, such as that she was a whore. She had never heard Mr Sutherland say such a word before. Also he said that Roddy was deceitful and a liar. That Amelia would never be allowed to have anything more to do with either of them, that she was heartbroken and The Morgans had done that, had been artful and unchristian and neither of them should be allowed on this earth.

As she stood mesmerised in the hall, the drawing room door was flung back so that it banged against the wall and Mr Sutherland, looking like a bonfire, strode red faced into the hall. He glared at her.

'There she is, the strumpet,' he said.

She waited for Roddy to defend her but it seemed that all the fight had gone from him. He had managed to keep down the embers of his wrath and now she saw him with his head bowed.

Fred was saying his piece and he had so obviously been rehearsing it as they spoke.

'You will never practise here or in any other part of Scotland, my father will make certain of that. You and your sister are now outcasts. We will never utter your name again,' and with a movement that would have done a bad actor proud, Fred swept through the hall and out of the front door with his father like a nasty east wind close behind him.

This was followed by possibly the longest silence in the history of mankind. Catrin no longer wanted her tea and her scone, she no longer wanted anything but that the earth should swallow her up. For a lifetime it seemed nothing happened and then Roddy came out of the room, eyed her and said,

'You've ruined me,' and then he ran lightly up the stairs and slammed his bedroom door.

Six

The following day it was almost a relief to have something to do. It was a lovely day but neither she nor her brother left the house. Roddy did not leave his room and neither of them ate anything.

The guilt crashed about her. All her brother's plans were in pieces. Whatever were they to do now?

Nobody did anything, nobody spoke. Everything had stopped. In the end they only did something because the tenancy on their house was fast running out and so Catrin went on with packing though a different kind of packing it was now. She had no idea where they would go or what they would do and her brother was no longer speaking to her so she could not ask for any kind of counsel. There was one thing to be thankful for. She packed up every piece of jewellery she owned, she packed all her clothing and all her books and she felt a little grim satisfaction in this.

There was the income from their father but they would still need to be practical now they were starting from the beginning again. They needed to make some money, though how they would do it now and where they would go she could not tell.

She felt smothered in her brother's silence. This was all her fault, there could be no doubt about it. He was right, she had made a bonfire of his chances, his life, his marriage, his career. He had begun to think of specialising and had talked to Fred about it, who was very enthusiastic, and had thought that they should both become great surgeons and change the world.

Well, the world was certainly changed. She paid off the servants and after that she and Roddy were alone in the house. For some reason in August there was perpetual rain, as though June and July had had too good a time of it with all that sunshine and August had to make up for it. No doubt the farmers would be pleased was all she stupidly could think.

And in the end he came to her and said so softly that she had to listen carefully,

'I have been making enquiries as to where we can go but word has spread and we are not wanted. We may have to go south to escape the talk, we may have to go back to Wales. I have found nowhere that they want us. There are places for me but not with you and a lot of places where a woman doctor is nothing but an encumbrance. So far I have found nothing. How we will live in the future I have no idea.'

Catrin wept hot tears into her pillow every night.

*

It was almost September and she was starting to think that they would never find anywhere to go and then there was an opportunity and such an opportunity as they would never have wanted.

'I think this is the place where you went and had your child,' Roddy said, flatly and not meeting her eyes. He had not looked once at her since things had gone wrong.

'Oh no.' She could not help the unfortunate utterance.

'It's the only chance that we have,' Roddy said. 'They want two doctors because there is nobody within miles and it is very isolated.'

'I don't want to go back there.'

'I thought you did.'

'I did and then I didn't and you know what I mean. It would be so very hard.'

'I know,' he said. 'But we have to leave here. The whole city is talking about us and the Sutherlands feel betrayed and besmirched because we lied to them.'

'We didn't lie.'

'Lied by omission,' Roddy said.

'Can we not wait for something else?'

'We might wait for a very long time and bad news travels faster than good. We ought to go now and far enough away so that we can manage to meet something new and different.'

'Somewhere in the south would be better.'

'I have tried in many different places and the only

positive thing to come out of it is this. We have to do something, we have to go somewhere. Are you completely against it?'

'If it's all we have then no of course not.'

'We did have family up there at one time but further over near Hexham and they are long since gone but we have to give it a try.'

In the end, because they could not go anywhere in the city without being stared at, they made themselves pack up and leave as soon as they could. They had little to take with them but clothes and books. Catrin was glad in some ways. At least she did not have to drag with her reminders of what might have been. Nobody would know them in that desolate place. She tried not to think how she had let everybody down in a way that she could not have helped. She felt responsible, she felt guilty.

She did attempt to give an abject apology to her brother but all he would say and bitterly was,

'Perhaps you should have thought about such things before you went ahead and behaved in such a low and disgusting manner.' Roddy stopped there as though he could hear how unfair he sounded, how unjust. He paused and then he said,

'I didn't mean that. I understand that you were not much more than a child and like most girls had been told so little that you got it wrong without being aware but . . . but I feel as though the cost has been huge, that

I could have been such a good surgeon, fulfilled all my ambitions and have with me the only woman I have ever loved.'

In the end Catrin was relieved when the train taking them south set off from Waverley Station. She hoped never to see Edinburgh again.

There was one part of her that didn't want to go back to that dreadful isolated hilltop town. The other part of her had always wanted to, to search for the child that she had lost. She had always been convinced that the child lived. So many orphaned children died but in a lot of cases they were taken by childless couples. She had done some reading on the subject and knew that babies were most popular of all. Yes, her child would be fourteen. Would she be anything like her, and would she recognize her if she saw her again?

She had argued against this. Many couples from different areas and some from different countries adopted children and they never went home because it was not home to them at all. They did not remember it. There were records of course but she had the feeling that in a lot of cases these were destroyed, possibly on purpose, otherwise through neglect.

Now that she had no option she was longing to be there. She didn't say anything to Roddy because they no longer talked about anything. They had to cling together because they had no choice.

They sat on the left-hand side of the train, Catrin knowing that as the coast came very close to the railway line there were wonderful views of the little villages, the small stone houses and the waves crashing up the beaches on the way to Newcastle.

From there they went to Durham, from Durham to Crook and after that it was a short uphill ride. She remembered nothing of it but how hopeful they had been on the way to Edinburgh. All that was gone.

It was almost October and when they finally reached their destination the stationmaster helped her and Roddy with their trunks as they got down from the train. The Station Hotel was up a slight incline but only a few minutes away. The building was painted in big squares of black and white. By now the evening was dark and all she could make out were shapes and shadows, the roads, the pavements.

She could not see where the surgery was. They would be spending a few days at the hotel until the place could be made right for them. They had been told that the building was perfectly usable even though there had been no doctor in it for many a day. The parish council was just glad that the doctors Morgan were willing to start up a practice, were grateful and they sounded enthusiastic, at least the letter did.

Her heart raced and bumped and did terrible things because of the horror of her memories or her excitement now. The Station Hotel was not a big place, it had five bedrooms, but then why on earth would people want to come to such a place except that it was on the main road to Scotland for those folk who drove in whatever way she could not imagine.

It surprised her to find that all the rooms were taken and she was glad that Roddy had had the foresight to book ahead. She could hear the wind howling across the fell and it made her shudder both with the awfulness of the past and her trepidation about the future.

She tried to reassure herself because Roddy was with her but he was so quiet that she didn't want to say anything.

The first thing she noticed was that the Station Hotel was not right beside the station but just a little way up a slight hill. It was spotlessly clean but she didn't want to be there and that coloured her judgement. Men lined the bar in both rooms that she could see into. The air was thick with blue cigarette smoke and fumes from the fires and there was a smell of warm beer which made her feel slightly nauseous. Men sat at round tables playing dominoes. They were accompanied by skinny dogs with long legs who lay about enjoying the warmth. There was a dart board further over in the first room she saw into and another group of men were gathered around it.

As she stepped into the first room unsure of what to do, conversation halted. The room was bright with lamps and probably she looked good and it was not a place any woman would have gone into without a real excuse. They stared collectively.

'Wrong room,' Roddy said, slightly apologetic, and then they were back in the dimness of the hall.

As they stood, a large woman appeared from the back of the building.

'Good evening,' she said.

Roddy said that he had booked two rooms and she acknowledged this and called on a slight skinny man to carry the bags upstairs. The station master had promised to send them the heavy luggage later.

'Oh aye,' she said, 'you'll be the new doctors. You're very welcome, I'm sure.'

It was not a Scottish tone but had similarities and the woman had a deep, thick voice with short vowels, brown like chocolate.

Upstairs Catrin was left to herself in a room with a good fire and everything was clean and neat. After she had washed her hands and face she went downstairs and ate with Roddy in the little dining room. The meal was good, pot pie, suet crust, beef, onions and potatoes in thick gravy and a pudding of rhubarb and custard, but she was now longing to see the surgery and although when she went to bed she slept fitfully she could hardly contain herself. What would it be like and how would this place have changed since last she was there?

The man from the council was at the hotel by nine to show them around the surgery. He led them back down the hill. It was beginning to sleet and she shivered against the cold. She was surprised how busy it was with houses and shops next door to one another. Women wore headscarves and thick boots and coats and gloves and mittens against the cold. Small children were with them, one or two little ones crying no doubt because of the temperature. There was a gathering of old men smoking and standing against the street corners, but as the sleet grew worse they disappeared into the houses.

She convinced herself that the only people out were those who needed to be and that normally the place would be even busier, nothing like she remembered it but then she had not been allowed out and was hustled into the huge building where she stayed and then out again to go home.

Mr Ferguson, the council man, said of the last doctor, 'He was soft. Couldn't stand the weather. I hope you folk are made of sterner stuff. Being Scotch of course you will be used to it.'

Neither Catrin nor Roddy chose to disabuse him. It could not matter to him where they were from.

They seemed to walk a long way but it was just that Catrin was looking about her. They went back down the hill, past the station and turned into a road on the left-hand side. At the big house on the end Mr Ferguson walked in and they followed. There was a garden of sorts out front, long grass to right and left of a path which led up to the front door with windows on either side. It was a much bigger house than the others in the street. It had an imposing porch with tall pillars at either side as though to distinguish it from the others but it was still part of the terrace to the left. To the right it had a side garden. She was glad that there was outside space. It was always useful.

Mr Ferguson had several goes at unlocking the door until Catrin grew impatient. It was stuck.

'It's the weather, the cold and damp,' Mr Ferguson said and pushed hard until finally the door gave with a shudder that showed it had not been opened in some time.

The first thing Catrin noticed was the smell of mice, sweet and acrid all at the same time. Dirty little creatures, she thought. The second after that she decided that they could not live here at least not to begin with.

'It's filthy,' she said in dismay without thinking, as she saw the doors to the rooms were open and curtains were half falling to the floor in one room and windows were rotten. The other room had no curtains and the dark autumn light was pale there.

'It could do with a brush,' Mr Ferguson allowed. 'It was meant to be done before you got here.'

It was the nearest she was going to get to an apology, she thought, irritated that nobody had tried to get the place ready so that they could start work. It would be a week or two before this place could be habitable and in the meanwhile she and Roddy were paying to stay at the hotel when they had decided to save everything they could for their new practice.

In the rooms were various pieces of broken furniture. Soot had thrown itself across the floorboards in one room, doubtless the rain with a good wind behind it.

Catrin felt like crying with disappointment. This was a surgery? Out the back was a yard with a broken gate and then an unmade road with coalhouse and lavatory. Wisely, she thought, she did not go near these.

'The chimneys need sweeping,' was Roddy's contribution to the conversation.

'I daresay,' Mr Ferguson said, handing him the keys. 'Well, I'll leave you to look over the rest of it. It will be all right when it is cleaned up and in the meanwhile I daresay you will be comfortable at Mrs McNorton's,' and off he went, slamming the outside door to make sure it shut.

Roddy looked appalled. There were two rooms upstairs and a pantry beside the kitchen. The kitchen range was very old and the oven handle had dropped off. Roddy walked around and in the end he said,

'It needs a fairy godmother,' with a hint of wry humour.

'It needs pulling down,' Catrin said.

'I think as a building it will be sound. I don't under-stand how this was ever big enough to be used as a surgery while he lived here. The man must have had no privacy and if it was as bad as this and he had to deal with it all himself no wonder he left. No pharmacy, no rooms for seeing people, no waiting room. I'm surprised they think they need doctors if this is all the welcome we are to have.'

It was the longest speech he had made since things had fallen apart in Edinburgh and though he was being practical it filled her with relief. If they could just keep going, day to day things would get better and here at least she would be able to see the place where she had been sent and perhaps come to better terms with what had been done and she would go to people who might be able to help her to find her child. Suddenly she felt better, hopeful. This would work out. She would do her best to look after Roddy in every possible way and try to make him happy and comfortable and her heart began to lift. After all she had now got what she had most wanted. She was a doctor and this was a fresh start.

'I think I'm going back to Mrs McNorton to see if we can get things done. She seems like a capable soul,' she said.

At that moment a young woman appeared at the out-side door with a baby in her arms.

'Would this be the new doctor?' she said, looking hopefully at Roddy. 'I'm so worried about my baby. She's hot and fretful.' The woman was on the verge of tears, Catrin saw.

'I could go back to your house with you if you like,' Roddy offered and he took hold of his black bag, for it never left his side, and the young woman, awestruck that he had offered her a home visit, immediately led him back down the garden path and into the road.

Catrin went and had a look around the town and could not believe it was the same place that she had been all that time back, but then she had only seen the house where she had been imprisoned so what did she know?

She thought that the Hilda House, where she had stayed, was at the top of the street where she and Roddy were about to set up the surgery but although part of her longed to see it she was afraid, though she didn't know of what, so she turned the other way which led into the main street. In time she would go there and from there she would do everything she could to find out what had happened to her child. In the meanwhile there was life here, it was a real village. It took her but a few minutes to get back to the Station Hotel and ask her landlady for help. She had not been mistaken. Mrs McNorton clicked her tongue and said,

'Those men from the council, they are no use. If they had got themselves organized you would be able to get straight on with your work. Now look. Always leave it to a woman, that's what I say. I daresay Mrs Clements who does my rooms would come and help. She's looking for more work.'

Mrs Clements also when told of the dilemma shook her head over the stupidity of men and since Mrs McNorton offered her cleaning products and cloths and a bucket and mop she accompanied Catrin back down to the surgery house.

'Dear Lord, will you just look at it,' she declared when she stepped inside and the first thing she did was to go into the backyard and find paper, sticks and coal to light the kitchen range for hot water. 'You might go to the hardware store. That's what I would do. I daresay Mr Barron will help you out with decent furniture and beds and linen and you will be needing pillows and blankets and a whole load of other things which come to mind. Since you'll be buying so much his lad will maybe come and take out all this furniture which needs getting rid of and bring in the new and I will try and scrub the rooms before then and I will call on the sweep. He lives a couple of doors down and if he isn't busy he might set to before I go to too much trouble so that we don't have a bigger mess.'

The hardware store was halfway back up the street, beyond the Station Hotel. Mr Barron wore a very businesslike grey coat over his clothes, the better to be taken seriously, Catrin thought, and was only glad that she had enough money to make the place habitable. There was little they could do at present with how small it was. They would be living at the surgery with space only upstairs and since they needed two surgeries the kitchen would be all their private space and even that would need to be the pharmacy.

Mr Barron's lad, Rusty, had a horse and cart and was so enthusiastic about shifting the stuff as he called it that Catrin could have kissed him. Rusty was no doubt named for the shock of bright red hair which topped him off like a huge carrot, she thought. This later turned out not to be true, his proper name was Russell but she liked the idea of the carrot better.

He went straight off to the house and she ordered beds, mattresses and bedding, crockery, cutlery, kitchen knives and Mr Barron said he knew where he could lay his hands on some very decent second-hand furniture for her dining and sitting rooms. If Mrs Clements would measure up, his wife would run up some curtains for the main rooms. Catrin said that what she really needed was two tables and four chairs for the surgery, one for her and her patient and the same for her brother. She also needed a lockable cabinet, which would live in the kitchen and be there for the medicines.

Mr Barron seemed to think that all his chickens had come home to roost such a big order did the new lady doctor give him. He made a huge list with a flourish of his pencil which he stuck behind his ear when Catrin finally ran out of needs for the surgery house and even then he said she would need pots and pans and 'stuff like Yorkshire pudding tins for the oven'. Catrin thought Mr Barron was perfectly right in all he said. What was a home without a Yorkshire pudding tin?

When she got back Mrs Clements had the kitchen fire burning. There was hot water in the boiler and Rusty was already carrying out the broken furniture, whistling as he did so. The sweep had been and Mrs Clements had tidied up and then begun on the rest of the house.

Rusty was a helpful lad and enthusiastic. He showed Catrin where the coalhouse was and even filled and carried buckets of coal into the house and he brought kindling and matches from the shop and helped Catrin to light more fires and Mrs Clements scrubbed floors and wiped down walls and all the time she tut-tutted about folk who let houses get into such a state. She sang hymns as she cleaned. 'Now Thank We All Our God' rang out as she opened the newly polished windows. The sleet had stopped, the day had cleared. Mrs Clements went on to 'Love Divine All Loves Excelling' which she told Catrin was a favourite at weddings. She was indiscriminate and later there was 'Away In a Manger', and 'There Is a Green Hill Far away'.

The house began to smell of lavender polish – how

that happened Catrin didn't know since there was nothing much at present to polish but she didn't care – and bleach. Was there anything better than the clean smell of bleach? Mrs Clements scrubbed the upstairs after Rusty had gone off with the awful beds and mattresses and Mrs Clements had got him to measure up for curtains. Rusty was a happy man, Catrin had tipped him handsomely for all his work and he told her that if she needed more things doing he was the man to help.

The surgery house would need its privacy so Mrs Clements went away to her dinner at midday and said she would call in at Mr Barron's shop and see if Mrs Barron would make the curtains as swiftly as she could and whether the shop had any good sharp knives because there wasn't a decent one in the house and there was no use in trying to chop vegetables without. Mrs Clements seemed eager to shop and cook and Catrin felt much more enthusiastic with a woman like this to help.

The fires were now going properly as Mrs Clements said and Roddy returned, having sorted out the baby's problems and helped several other people on his way back. It felt like good progress to both of them and to her relief he was beginning to thaw. They were speaking if only for necessity but he had calmed down. She was very careful in what she said and did and he offered her the same respect. Perhaps in time they would get beyond what had happened to them, perhaps even beyond blame for her but the shame and guilt burned in her every time she thought of what she had done and how it had ruined Roddy's relationship. Her own thoughts were tinged with relief but she tried not to dwell on these positives. They had been so dearly bought. She kept thinking of the Sutherland house and shuddered and also now she would have the chance to fulfil her biggest dream. Things rarely worked out as you wanted them to and both she and Roddy were paying for her mistake but life marched forward and sometimes you had to increase your pace to keep up.

That night, back in her room at the hotel, she slept, full of plans for the future, but her sleep was awakened by noisy banging on the door. Mrs McNorton said as Catrin went and opened the door,

'We've got a lass on the doorstep who won't go away and I didn't like to disturb the proper doctor, he needs his sleep. Will you come down and see what you can do?'

Swiftly tying on her dressing gown and not saying that she was a proper doctor, she went down the stairs. It was a bleak, cold night and Mrs McNorton had not thought to offer her unwelcome guest a place in the hall so Catrin was obliged to usher her in. She could see what the problem was straight away. The girl was hugely pregnant and very undernourished.

'She can't stay here,' Mrs McNorton said as she held the oil lamp carefully in both hands. 'I run a respectable business here but she's been banging on the door fit to wake the devil and I can't have my guests kept up like this.'

Catrin ignored her and led the girl into Mrs McNorton's front parlour despite her landlady's protestations.

'Scandalous,' said Mrs McNorton as she put down the lamp and disappeared into the back of the hotel but the girl was in a lot of pain. Catrin wanted her made comfortable, she would need all the strength she could muster. She called Mrs McNorton back and saw the woman's reluctance but ploughed on.

'She could do with a bed,' Catrin said.

'You aren't putting a lass like that in one of my good bedrooms. It's Audrey Wilfrid and she's no better than she should be.'

'I'm married,' the girl gasped. 'I'm respectable all right, it's him that isn't.'

'He thought he had to marry you. God knows whose bairn it is.'

'This isn't helping,' Catrin said. 'Go and get my brother, please.'

'Bring a man into this lot?'

'Please.' Five minutes ago he had been a proper doctor, now he was just a man. Mrs McNorton had a way of belittling people which could never have been bettered, Catrin thought.

Off the landlady went and Roddy came down. Catrin

asked him to carry the girl into her bedroom and Mrs McNorton could bring something clean to go on the bed in case they needed it, Catrin said. Mrs McNorton came back with newspapers which Catrin decided would have to do to go beneath the mother-to-be.

Her brother dosed the girl with morphine to kill the pain and she began to breathe more easily.

'How long have you been in pain?' Catrin asked.

'Two days. We didn't know anybody was here. We didn't know we could have help.'

'You are lucky then,' Roddy said, smiling at her just a little. 'Here we are, all ready and waiting.'

'Is this your first baby?' Catrin said.

'I lost one just after we got wed,' the girl told her. And there was probably the reason for Mrs McNorton not being very keen on the idea. Nevertheless two hours later the baby was safely delivered and Mrs Wilfrid's husband was pulled out of bed, complaining that he was on shift and had just fallen asleep.

'We can't be having goings-on like this on my premises,' Mrs McNorton said. 'How soon are you moving out?'

'As soon as we possibly can,' Catrin said but to Roddy and in private later.

The plight of the young woman and Mrs McNorton's reaction made her uncomfortably aware of her own circumstances. She tried not to think too much but being here made things come to the front of her mind, whereas in Edinburgh she had had days and even weeks when she didn't think of her young life.

It was another week before everything was installed at the house with Mrs Clements dividing her time between the Station Hotel and the surgery, and Catrin was just grateful for a bed of her own, with a new mattress, clean sheets and a little peace so that she could sleep.

The Station Hotel had been rowdy in both bars. Saturday night was the worst and Mrs McNorton said how grateful she was that Doctor Morgan was there – only Roddy was allowed this courtesy – as after a fight in the street he went out and stitched several heads back together. He liked stitching so he came in rather full of himself, Catrin thought. 'And good practice for your bandaging,' she said, he hated that.

'We need a nurse. We need a chemist,' she told him.

Sunday was comparatively quiet. They went to church in the morning though Catrin said, 'I feel that I had sufficient of church in Edinburgh.' She felt awful after she had said it but Roddy did not reply and she felt that they were at last bringing their friendship forward just a little. She hadn't meant to say it, wished that sometimes words didn't just tumble from her before she had thought of their impact upon her brother.

He ignored her. She liked the church. It was as new as churches in that area got, hastily refurbished when people came here to work and had rather a fine lot of stained-glass windows which Catrin spent the half-hour sermon watching. It was too nice a day to be inside and she had a lot to do trying to get everything set up back at the house. This was a waste of time, she felt sure.

It proved not to be. The vicar, John Bainbridge, was tall and thin and sociable and both he and his rather stout wife, Susan, assured both doctors that they were more than welcome and they found themselves at the old vicarage drinking tea and eating cake and making enquiries about chemists and nurses. John and Susan knew lots of people in the district and Catrin felt they could be of help.

In church and after it people craned their necks. They most probably hadn't seen many women doctors. Others would just be grateful that they had one doctor, never mind two.

Catrin had contrived to make a Sunday dinner the week they moved. She was out of practice at such things but it was adequate. They had so little space and eating in the kitchen was something they were not used to. They needed a much bigger place than this. Catrin had taken to thinking of the place where she had been her most miserable. When she could she was going to turn it to good use and produce much better memories for herself.

*

Just beyond the town on the top of the fell there was a big pit and there were a number of hastily built houses for the pitmen and their families. There was also a steelworks just down the bank from where the surgery was and all the trades that a small town needs to look after the people who flock there to work.

Right from the day the surgery opened – and that had to be as soon as they could possibly manage it – people crowded in. They had been without a doctor for many months. Also the farms surrounding the town were occupied by growing families.

There were a number of good things about being up on the felltops. The air was fresh and pure, the winds blew straight through the streets and whirled any rubbish away. It rained a lot and it was icy right from the beginning. Catrin and Roddy loved ice. It killed germs.

She also noted that the pitmen's wives were ultra clean. Daily they fought their battle, going out early to hang up their washing so that sometimes it was stiff with frost when they collected it back in again. If anybody was ill on Mondays the women tried to put it off because Monday was always washday, no matter what the weather was and they were busy all day and had no time for those complaining of their ailments.

Catrin grew to prefer Mondays to other days whereas on Sundays when she and Roddy hoped to have a few hours to themselves it rarely worked out like that. Since they were living at the surgery people were given to calling day or night without regard for the doctors' meals or sleep.

Great queues formed in the hall and the front garden and between them they could barely finish the surgery before noon. Then there were house visits to be made and another surgery in the early evening.

At the first opportunity she had, she walked up to the Hilda House and since the outside door was unlocked she went in and looked around. In vain did she try to work out where she had been kept, where she had given birth, the corridors she had trodden and the ceilings she had looked up to in the darkness. It hid its secrets well. It would make a good hospital, she thought. At the moment, at least if they could use part of it, it would do away with the problem of not having sufficient space, but if the surgery house had been a slight problem this would cause a lot bigger headaches and it would need money. When the surgery was finally over that morning, and it took two hours, she led Roddy up to look at it and he shook his head.

'It would take an awful lot to make it so that we could use it.'

'If we could have just part of it we could have the house to live in and this as the general practice place. Why don't you go to Mr Ferguson and ask him about it?'

'Why don't you go? I think you could persuade him

more easily,' Roddy said and she thought that perhaps her brother was right. So when she had done the morning surgery the following day she made her way up the main street to where the council offices stood and there she asked for Mr Ferguson. He stood up and greeted her politely.

'Miss Morgan, how are you? I hope you are settling in well.'

She didn't like to spend her time correcting people so she let it go that he did not call her doctor. He offered her a chair and she explained the problem to him. He pursed up his lips and said,

'Yes, I know the building you mean. I have a feeling that the town itself now owns the building but it cannot be used much because it's so very big.'

'Do you know anything about what it has been used for?' She tried to keep her voice normal but she could feel it quivering.

'I have no idea. I don't know anything about it and as far as I am aware there are no records here at the council offices of births, deaths and marriages or anything else which might be of help. This place has been nothing but a ghost town for years.'

Here she had an idea and went on calmly, 'It might help if we knew more about who had lived there in the past and what they had done. My wish is that my brother and I might have a small hospital there.'

Mr Ferguson was silent and when he recovered his voice he said in a surprised manner,

'As far as I am aware the place is completely empty and has been for a very long time. I fear that even a small hospital would take a great deal of money.'

'It would also be an important asset,' Catrin said. 'The town here is quite big now and there are a good many people. Sooner or later they will all need a doctor. A man who is ill cannot work and a woman who is ill cannot look after her husband, children and home and when children are ill everything stops.'

'The boom, if you can call it that, has only been during the last few years when the pit was opened,' Mr Ferguson said. 'Sharp sand was discovered and Consett iron Company is only a few miles away so that the foundry is also here because of the resources. As soon as there is work people come. When I was a boy I lived in Crook and this place was empty.'

She wanted to ask him if he remembered the orphanage being a place for unmarried mothers but she couldn't. He would wonder how she knew that and why it mattered.

'There is never sufficient money for everything. We are trying to build better roads. As you can see many of the back streets are unmade. We are trying to put bathrooms into street houses and provide education and running water and electricity. Times are moving forward quickly but this area has only just begun to prosper and the money has to come from somewhere.

'You could go to the local businessmen and see if they would be prepared to make a contribution towards the hospital or if they would like their men to pay a small amount each month towards the cost of keeping you and the doctor here. I know that you charge when people come to see you but I'm sure that would help if they would do it.'

So far few people had offered to pay either Roddy or herself and she was already worried about finance. Their father's contribution had been big in the beginning but it had not increased, Roddy had paid out a good deal so that she could follow in his footsteps and their income was getting smaller and smaller as they went on spending money and not making it. Their father had not seen fit to increase the allowance. She thought the payments were at his discretion and she didn't know whether they would go on if he died or decided he had something better to spend his money on. It wasn't easy.

They had had no contact with him since they had run away from North Wales together and she had been surprised that he went on paying the same amount. Did he know or care that she was now a doctor?

Mr Ferguson came good on his word that he would look into the idea of the big house and said that the council had decided they could use the building as they liked because it would benefit the whole place. He gave her the keys and initially she felt strange about being there and if she would remember anything more and if it held such horrible memories for her that it would invoke some kind of ghost but it was nothing beyond a shell and as she and Roddy walked around it she was close to despair at the amount of money it would take to put it right. It had seen no person, had had no fires in many years. The wallpaper was stripped off in places so that no room was neat, the cobwebs ran from the corners and across the windows, some of the tiles around the fireplaces were cracked or loose, several windows were broken so that the wind howled through, doors were hanging off, dirt was thick in the hallways and the rooms had not even a single rug on the floor.

The bathrooms had no water, the kitchen had no water, there was an old stove and nothing more. Somebody had removed every stick of furniture.

She felt heavy-hearted when they went outside. Roddy said nothing. The big gardens right around it were a wilderness. Stone walls had fallen down, gates were lying in the long thick grass, the fruit trees in the orchard were old and gnarled. Beyond the walls and fences blown down stood the fell, how dark and grim it looked to her now.

How they would ever afford to bring the place up to a reasonable standard so that it could be used as a surgery, never mind a hospital, she could not imagine. How to make it sound and get the chimneys to work, fires to burn when they could barely afford coal, beds and chairs and tables when they had so little money left, how to get the water running, the floors clean and even a mat to put upon any of it, keep it warm and dry and staffed neither of them had any idea but there was space here and they needed that most of all.

There was a part of her that determined to make it into a place which would be the very opposite of what she had endured there. It existed now only in her memory she could see but if she could turn it into a hospital it could be something very special, St Hilda's Hospital, and babies would be born there and their parents would take them home and she would feel a huge achievement that she had done such a thing.

Seven

Catrin found that the patients who came to see her were women and children. Men would not have thought of such a thing so Roddy was taking charge of the few men who bothered with a doctor and seeing those who specifically asked for him and most of them did.

It was now almost Christmas and the first snow fell. Catrin did not welcome it. The days were short and dark and she felt cold all the time.

On the Thursday before Christmas when she was glad to get her surgery over with five minutes to spare, a tall man loomed up in the street and very politely asked if he might have five minutes of her time.

There was something about him which Catrin liked. It was breeding, she decided. That sounded awful, like he was something to be shown off, but he was tall and slender, about her age and carried with him a certain air which she put down to grace. His clothes were old and worn but of good cut and cloth. She asked him to sit down and liked his friendly gaze and warm blue eyes. It was cool in the room despite a fire but it was the best she could do.

'My name is John Reed. I almost didn't come, I'm not sure I need a doctor. I just don't know what to do.'

'Anything you say is confidential and if I can't help you I might know somebody who can.'

He let the silence fall for several moments and then he said,

'My father died last autumn, more than a year ago. It was a hunting accident. He tried to make his horse take a very difficult fence and kept urging the poor beast forward. The horse knew better than he did unfortunately because the horse took the fence, missed it and fell back on top of him and he was killed.' There was a pause and then he said rather bitterly,

'The horse had to be shot. It had broken its back. Such a good horse too.' As though he was more upset about the horse than about his father, Catrin thought with concern. He seemed glad of the silence and let it go on for a few moments while he thought of what he wanted to say next. Catrin didn't prompt him. He would tell her when he was ready.

'My mother broke her heart when he died. God only knows why, he was difficult and neglected the estate. We had three houses, one on the river in Durham, one on the coast in Northumberland and both those had to be sold because of his extravagances. He drank and gambled and – he liked women. He would go to London for months on end and we would never hear from him and then he would come back and badly treat her. I don't mean that he hit her, it was just that he had no thought for her, or us, or regard for anyone and he was always telling us what to do and complaining about everything. The house rang from his shouting and when I was younger I often hid so that I wouldn't have to have anything to do with him.

'He was master of the hounds for years and that was a very expensive role, but he neglected the farms and the estate. He sold all the paintings, and the decent furniture. In the season he hunted five days a week and would invite a lot of people to stay at the house so my mother was always having to put on parties and look after dozens of guests.

'She learned to hate it all but she never learned to hate him and now I'm afraid that she is going to die because she hasn't learned to live without him and his bullying and his – his ignorance and—'

Here he stopped abruptly and then he sighed and took in his breath and he said,

'I didn't mean to say any of that. I'm sorry. It's just that I don't seem to be able to coax her to do anything. It's like she's given up. The one thing I was glad of when he died was that she might have some kind of a life, some sort of freedom, but although she isn't so very old she feels it and looks it.' He wasn't meeting Catrin's eyes now but gazing at the wall and then at the floor. 'Might you be able to call in and see her when you are not too busy?'

'How long were they married?' Catrin asked.

'Thirty years.'

'I'd be happy to come,' Catrin said and then he looked so hopefully at her that she had the feeling he had thought she would imagine he was wasting her time.

'What about tomorrow morning after surgery, unless there is an urgent need to see someone? Half past ten?'

'Thank you so much. We live not far on to the fell. You'll know the place when you set eyes on it. It's falling down and the old sign says Castle Hall.'

'That's Sir John Reed,' Roddy told her when he got back after his own surgery.

'Is it? He didn't seem like that.'

'Like what?'

'Well, lordly.'

'Don't you find that the most decent people never do? You liked him?'

'Yes, I did. I have the feeling he has had nobody to talk to.'

'He'd have death duties to pay too. I think it can be very costly.'

'He says the house is dropping to pieces,' Catrin said.

*

There being no more urgent call the following morning Catrin picked up her bag and set off across the fell. It was a cold, blustery day and she thought that she could smell more snow. When you had lived in Edinburgh for any length of time you recognized that smell. Yesterday's snow had lingered and provided a neat carpet for the pavements and roads. From a doctor's viewpoint it meant accidents as people slipped and skidded but it also gave a cold, healthy feel to the day. She could see her breath.

The views up there were spectacular for those who loved desolate places. There were a few grey stone-walled farms but the fell went on for miles before dipping into the valley where the road went on to Durham City.

The stone house was set back. Catrin stopped to look at it. It was a beautiful building and very old. It had three storeys and many windows, all of which glinted in what light there was. To the sides and presumably at the back were gardens and in front were trees and perhaps in other places to shield the buildings from the wind which constantly swept the fell.

Catrin barely had time to knock on the front door before he opened it. He must have been waiting for her.

'Sir John. Good morning.'

'John, please. Do come in and thank you, Doctor Morgan.'

There were three yellow Labradors lolling before the hall fire. John Reed's version of poor was not quite the same as other people's, she decided. If he could provide a fire in the hall and feed his dogs he could not be that badly off but she would have done the same and they were in a coalfield though she thought the fire burned wood from the sweet smell.

The house was very clean but the carpets and curtains were ragged and frayed and only one lamp burned in the hall. The stairs were wide and the risers narrow so that they were easy to climb. Catrin dreamed that women in gorgeous frocks would have come down these stairs to dinner in the old days when people had money and did such things but did it ever happen in such out of the way places? It was so far from anywhere. There was something about it that whispered of loneliness, unhappiness. There was not sufficient money, John had spoken honestly, and it was a shame. It had been and no doubt could be lovely again.

The landing was huge and went off in various directions. He led the way into a big bedroom and there was another fire. In the middle of a huge oak bed a tiny woman lay, her eyes closed, her thin hands on top of the covers.

'Johnnie, is that you?' she said in affectionate tones as she opened her eyes.

'I've brought Doctor Morgan to see you.'

'I have told you a dozen times. There's nothing wrong with me. I don't need a doctor.'

She opened her eyes even wider.

'A woman doctor. Oh my dear, how very enterprising of you,' and she beckoned Catrin over to the bed. 'And how beautiful you are.' Her thin hands were brown with age spots and wrinkled with lack of decent food. The blue veins stood out prominently. But it was her face which impressed Catrin. She had been and in some ways still was a very beautiful woman. Though her hair had turned white it was clipped up away from her neck and although her blue eyes were dimmed perhaps with short sight but certainly with sorrow, she had high cheekbones and an accent that people called cut glass. She had a friendly smile and she took both of Catrin's hands and smiled so sweetly that Catrin wished she had known her own mother so much better. What a loss it was to have no happy memories of her. She sat down on the bed and smiled back at the older woman and was pleased that she might be able to help.

Lady Reed had a twinkle in her eye.

'Mother—' John reproved her

'Oh well, I couldn't help it. You are most welcome, my dear.'

John went out and closed the door.

'Johnnie is a dear boy but he does fuss so,' his mother said. 'Where are you from?'

'I was born in North Wales but I studied in Edinburgh.'

She sat in an armchair close to the bed and smiled at the patient.

'I used to go to Edinburgh when I was very young. I had an aunt who lived there and she kept the best society. What fun we had in those days.

'And now you are come to us. How very fortunate we are. We have lacked a doctor for many months. I'm very glad to see you, my dear, because I have few visitors but really there is nothing wrong with me. I'm just very sad. My husband died more than a year ago and I miss him so very much. Johnnie was our only child. We were so upset when I didn't have any more children and I'm afraid Johnnie was a disappointment to his father. I think sons always are. So much is expected of them. If we had had half a dozen children it would have been a lot easier for all of us but it just didn't happen. Then there was Anne of course.'

'Anne?'

'My husband and Johnnie found her, as far as I can remember. It must be eleven or twelve years ago, wandering around the moor in thick mist. We had no idea where she came from and still don't but she is such a comfort, such a dear. A very capable girl. My husband didn't really like her because she was not his but just for once I put my foot down and I haven't regretted it for a second. She is just wonderful.'

Catrin's heart lifted. How many times had it done so in the past, that something would happen, that she would see her child again, that the child was not dead and not lost but had found a home where she could grow and be happy.

'I understand there was an unmarried mothers home there,' she said with a slight catch in her voice.

'Yes, we thought that perhaps she had been adopted and then – well, we didn't quite know after that. Presumably if someone had taken her she would not have been lost on the fell unless there had been an accident. John made all kind of enquiries at the time, not least because his father was very upset at the idea of having a child here who wasn't family. He was always big on family, you see. There was nobody like the Reeds. They're a very old family you know. They were here during the border raids when the reivers came down and took cattle and silver and anything else they could find. It sounds awfully romantic and my husband was very proud of his ancestry but it couldn't have been like that at all. Whatever, he wanted sons and I could only manage one and then Anne came along and he would never have that she was one of us, but I wouldn't let her be turned out and Johnnie backed me. His father called him soft for housing an orphan or an illegitimate child but we did keep her though he would never have her anywhere but in the kitchen unless she was doing housework.'

It reminded Catrin very much of her own life and she already felt sorry for this girl, whoever she was.

Catrin's mind was going mad but she stilled it. She

had a patient to attend to before she let her thoughts go wild about the girl.

'Do you feel less sad now than you did when he died?'

'Do you know, I don't. People think that you get over such things in a matter of weeks but that's those who haven't been through it. I keep remembering the happy times when we met in London. I had an awful shock when I came here. I thought the estate would be woods and fields and lovely little villages such as we had when I was a small child and lived in Hampshire. Instead of which I got this.' She laughed shortly but it was clear that she had little affection for the place and why would she?

Catrin said, 'I think grief is a difficult thing and we all grieve at a different rate. Just keep warm and try to eat and perhaps get up and sit by the fire for a little while each day if you can manage it.'

'Johnnie has offered to carry me downstairs but I haven't managed it yet. I feel like nothing has changed here in this room.'

'Even for an hour, just to look out of a different window would do you good.'

'There's nothing to see but fell. When my husband went to London so often without me I wished I could have gone but he had his own friends there and I was never wanted.'

'It seems to me that you are very wanted now. I think it took quite a bit of courage for your son to come and see me and ask me to come here so perhaps think of him and see if you can try to eat just a little more and go downstairs.'

'I will, Doctor Morgan.'

'I will come back in a few days and see how you are or sooner if you decide that you need me. A note would do. Could I bring you some books or do you have a huge library?'

To Catrin's joy there was a small library in the town halfway up the main street. She hadn't much time free but reading was such a joy for so many people.

Lady Reed smiled.

'The library here is enormous but I fear that the books are in German,' she said.

Catrin went slowly down the stairs and John Reed must have had remarkable hearing for he came out of the kitchen and beckoned her with a wave of his hand. The kitchen was cheerful. She could smell coffee and cake and as she went into the room she had a shock. The girl turning from the stove looked vaguely like her but not so that anybody else would notice. The girl had green eyes. What colour had Joe's eyes been? What had he looked like? His cowardice had changed her ideas of him and she could recall nothing since she had tried to put him from her mind. He had let her down in a huge way. Perhaps things would have been different had he been there for her. Perhaps they could have married and kept the child. She dismissed this idea, knowing it for stupidity. None of this had happened and yes, the girl had hair almost the same colour but nobody would take her for Catrin's child. She was glad and sorry for that but wanted to take the child into her arms and claim her. Frustratedly she realized that she couldn't remember Joe's face and mannerisms and no matter how hard she tried afterwards that day she could not bring to mind anything more helpful.

'This is my sister, Anne.'

The child was so mature, not at all like a fourteen-year-old, or was she? Perhaps being here and having experienced what must have been a strange family life had made her older than her years.

Anne asked her to sit at the big white well-scrubbed kitchen table and poured tea from a large brown pot and cut carrot cake. They were obviously anxious and bombarded Catrin with questions and both pairs of eyes looked at her so very worried that she could tell how much the white-haired woman in bed meant to them.

'She is grieving. It takes time.'

'Even if you didn't love somebody?'

'Johnnie, she did love him,' Anne insisted.

'Why? Why in God's name would anybody love him?' John said. 'He was a rat.'

'I think it could be a matter of pride,' Catrin said. 'Can women not love somebody who is unworthy of them? I think they often do.'

'He was unworthy of anybody loving him. He didn't love Anne or me.'

Catrin couldn't bear to watch the look on the girl's face so determinedly she regarded him. Did children ever get beyond not being wanted? She had a horrible suspicion that they didn't.

John looked straight back at Catrin and said, 'What can we do to help our mother?'

'I will give you something to help her sleep. She looks to me as though she hasn't slept in a very long time.'

John went outside with Catrin and he obviously had something to say.

'I don't understand why my mother can't enjoy life. It's the first time she has had the chance all her adult life. She was very young when they married and she has had nothing but bitterness and sorrow. We don't have the kind of money we used to have but I think there is enough for her to lead some kind of life. If I could just get her dressed and out of the house it would help.'

'If you can get her dressed and downstairs and enable her to eat something which will nourish her properly I think you might see a change in a relatively short time. Of course winter is always the hardest part of the year for illness but spring is only weeks away if we can look at it like that. If she could sit in the garden by then I would be pleased with her progress. You must have some good memories of your father,' Catrin said. Having so few good memories of her own father she always hoped that other people had done better.

John hesitated and then he said bitterly,

'Oh yes, because he thought I was going to turn into him. He taught me to ride. He insisted on me going hunting when I was a small child. It put me off for life and the only thing he was proud of was that I was an excellent shot. Once he understood that I was nothing like him he made sure I didn't have the things I most wanted. An education, a lot of reading. All the books in English were burned on his orders.'

'What did you do?'

'I learned German,' he said with a hint of a smile. 'I borrowed a book that taught me German and I out-witted him, possibly for the only time in my life.'

'Very useful,' she said, smiling back at him.

'You can't begin to imagine.'

'Your sister is a lovely girl.' Catrin couldn't help but say it. She wanted to talk about Anne for the rest of her life and most of all she wished and wished that this child could be hers.

'I never think of her like that,' he said ruefully. 'She has never behaved like a child. She hasn't had the chance. Our father would shriek at her if he saw her even in the hall and she would run into the kitchen and hide. I think she was almost glad when he died and, to be honest, so was I. It's a much happier household without him but to say such things makes me feel guilty and I feel unworthy to have this place and not be able to rescue it. I wish I could somehow come into money. Now that would be useful.'

Catrin agreed and they smiled at one another before she left.

Catrin told Roddy all about this after evening surgery.

'They sound interesting,' he said.

'The old lady makes me worry. She seems to have given up. I don't suppose John Reed sleeps very well in case she dies. I wish I could have some time on my own with Anne and find out what she is really like. She has had such a bad time.'

'It happens to an awful lot of children.'

'That doesn't make it any better,' Catrin said.

'I think the fact that Lady Reed and John were so good to her would make all the difference. You had no one and a childhood which forced you into being a woman long before it should have done.'

Catrin didn't sleep very well, trying over and over to remember whether Joe had green eyes but she couldn't persuade herself. She had the feeling that his eyes were like brown velvet. She brought herself up short there, he had been a horrible selfish lad and had thought nothing of what he had done and of how she had suffered. In her mind she gave him beady black eyes and nasty scars in nasty places. It made her feel a little better.

'I hear you went to see Lady Reed,' Mrs Clements said as she washed the kitchen dispensary floor. Mrs Clements always knew everything. She insisted on washing the floor daily as she was concerned about people walking in and out, the germs, the drugs and all the bottles and mixtures, never mind that food had also to be prepared and eaten in there. 'Poor lady, she had a dreadful life with the squire. I remember him young. He looked just like John does now, very handsome and tall and with that taking air which all the family seems to manage. He was the very devil. A lot of people were pleased when he died and just wished it had happened a lot sooner. That place was prosperous once. Now Sir John is left with half a dozen farms which are good for nothing but sheep, that great big house falling to pieces and no money.'

Catrin couldn't stop thinking about Lady Reed and her awful life. The local people did not call John squire and in a way it was a compliment to him since his father had done nothing but spend recklessly until there was little left.

Perhaps Lady Reed felt her time on earth was done and yet she might be only fifty. That was not old to die when there was nothing physically wrong with you. But her husband was gone and she could not relate to anything new. In a way he had subsumed her until there was nothing left beyond a husk. She felt guilt and shame that she had married the wrong person who made herself and her son unhappy all their lives.

Catrin determined to see the owners of the various works. She did wish that Roddy might go but he was busier than she. For some reason many of the women preferred to take their sick children to see a man and the men never came to her. Some of them would not go to a doctor at all so she and Roddy had to be pleased when any of them turned up at the surgery, shamefaced with eyes cast down in case anybody saw them in their supposed bodily weakness.

So it was only when women were ill that they came to see her and to her delight lots of them, despite their many children and tiny homes, did not ail much at all. The air was the purest that she had ever breathed, the luckier ones had big back gardens and many had allotments where they grew potatoes, cabbages, leeks, parsnips and carrots. They had rows of gooseberries and black, red and white currants and raspberries. Rhubarb would flourish under old buckets. Their diet was rich with local meat, broth with ham and pease pudding to keep out the cold and fresh eggs, cheese and milk from the nearby farms.

The children wore thick clothes as they ran to and from school and they were out playing in all weathers, frost killing what germs they might have gathered. They would wear mitts and hats and scarves which their mothers, grandmas and aunties would knit for them. They all had thick overcoats and stout boots. Because employment was high there were few poor people. It was a place where family looked after family and often the grandparents would live next door or at least in the same street. Visits were made daily aiding one another in comfort and kindness.

Presumably the employers paid them fairly or what they thought of as enough but people did not like paying their doctors, Catrin and Roddy had soon discovered. They would give jam or eggs but when it came to fees they seemed to take it as an affront that they should be ill at all or that doctors were really necessary. They tried to mend themselves or get their neighbours or wise old men or women before they would admit that they needed more skilled mending, so there were a lot of places that medical income did not come from and it had become a daily worry. In particular there was a woman who helped with childbirth. Catrin knew that this was common and understood the need but this woman had a reputation for drink and slovenliness and it worried her, but then she could only go when asked and that did not happen often. Calling in was something the neighbours did, not the local doctors.

First of all, Catrin went to the big pit which stood on the edge of the village, not far from John Reed's farm. It was called Castle Bank Colliery and was named apparently for Dan's Castle, Dan had been a pitsinker. Or maybe not but it pleased Catrin to think so.

It was a big pit for the area and employed seven hundred men. Catrin knew something about mining because where she came from there was coal and gold mining and there were slate quarries so she was not surprised or intimidated by the huge wheel, the outbuildings and the general business about it all. She therefore walked up to the edge of the village. There had been a building on the site of the Hall since coal mining began according to Mrs Clements and because there had been coal found here since the fourteenth century, things obviously went way back.

The pit offices were not exactly comfortable, she thought as she reached them, just a couple of wooden shacks from the outside. She went in and found a middle-aged woman sitting at a typewriter behind a desk, bright eyed and wearing a twinset, pearls and a tweed skirt, her hair stiffly permed and grey.

'It's Doctor Morgan, isn't it?' she said with a welcome smile.

'Good morning,' Catrin said and tried to think of the manager's name.

'You wish to see Mr Dunstan of course,' said the secretary.

'Thank you, ' Catrin said gratefully. 'Do I need to make an appointment?'

'No, no, he is for once in his office. If he had been underground you might have had to come back. Just give me a moment,' and she disappeared into the office behind hers, coming back very soon.

Catrin was therefore ushered into the pit manager's office and saw a man of about her own age, who greeted her politely and asked her to sit on a rather unsteady dining room chair across the desk from him. Obviously Mr Dunstan did not spend money on furniture, she surmised and hoped he was less miserly about other things.

The office was plain but neat, files behind cupboards, no papers left about, just a pen and some drawings on the man's desk.

'Ah, one of the new doctors,' he said.

Catrin did not take to him. He had an air about him which was almost defensive, that he must keep people away somehow. He had hard dark eyes and a thin mouth set into a line.

'It's good of you to see me,' Catrin said.

'What can I help with?'

'As you know we are just setting up here and are hoping to use the big house in the village, the place which used to be Blessed Saint Hilda's orphanage, as a small hospital. There is no hospital anywhere nearby and it would be a great asset to the village if we could offer help to whatever comes along. You have a big workforce, Mr Dunstan, and sooner or later they will all be in need of medical help.

'We would like to be able to do as much as we can. At the moment there are just the two of us but we would hope in time to be able to pay for a chemist and a nurse to help. This all takes money. We wondered whether we might look to people like yourself for support?' She smiled winningly at him but Mr Dunstan did not smile back.

He sat back in his chair and surveyed her levelly.

'I see,' he said. 'I thought the usual practice was for people to pay their doctors for treatment.'

'That would be wonderful but it very often doesn't happen and we can't live or expand on eggs and black-currant jam, I'm sure you understand.'

'They could manage it from their own pockets if you were just firm in your demands for payment.'

'You would be surprised,' Catrin said. 'We cannot withdraw service, nor would we choose to because some folk can't or won't pay. We take an oath to assist whenever we are able and some of these people have very big families.'

'That is their choice.'

'Really?' This was a novel view as far as Catrin was concerned. She could think of a great many tart things to say but was too wise to utter them. She was however starting to dislike Mr Dunstan. She hadn't realized until then that she very much wanted to like him because he could be a lot of help if he chose but he wasn't and it was a huge disappointment to her.

'I don't think I would call it that exactly,' she said.

'They don't have to marry.' Was Mr Dunstan married? She knew very little about him and wasn't sure she wanted to know more. He was almost hostile.

'Most men marry, surely,' Catrin plunged on, regardless. 'They need a helpmeet to look after them and their children and their homes so that they are able to go and work for people like yourself. It is a two-way street, I would say.'

'Are you married, Doctor Morgan?'

This was getting worse.

'I have not been that lucky yet.'

'Then I wish you well in the future,' he said and Catrin felt obliged to get up and leave his office. She was fuming.

'I made a mess of it,' she told Roddy that night, dismayed and thinking back at all the things she could have said that might have sat better with Mr Dunstan and persuaded him.

'He sounds like an idiot,' Roddy said loyally.

'He must be very clever to run such a big affair and it is his own.'

'We can try again later,' Roddy said.

Catrin knew there was no point in going over their bills, they were only too aware of spending money they didn't have but it was necessary at this stage and they needed the extra room at the Hilda House if they could just get it going.

Catrin therefore didn't hold out a lot of hope when she made her way down the bank to the steelworks manager's office. The manager was a much older man, she had seen him about in the street from time to time, he lived almost next to the works and made his way up the slight bank and along the road to his pretty detached house which looked out over the fields down toward the dale. He was about sixty she had surmised and she had it in her mind that older men were even more curmudgeonly than younger ones.

The foundry was a place of interest to her since she hadn't seen one before. There were various buildings and she passed a man with a wheelbarrow, others going in and out of the office, a lot of sand on the ground and an impression of warmth. Mr Swan was in the works, his secretary told her and since he could be there for some time would she like to go inside and see if she could find him?

She hadn't thought she would be allowed to do that and was urged to be careful. It was very warm inside the huge building. Overhead a crane worked and men were gathered in groups doing whatever they did. Some greeted her cheerily or if it was very noisy touched their caps in acknowledgement of the doctor. She thought that was nice and smiled at them.

Mr Swan was unmistakable. He was not very tall and he wore a suit and a trilby hat. She went over to him and he stopped talking to the other man and told her he would be with her in five minutes. Indeed she was just making her way outside when he caught up with her. They walked together into the office and Miss Waskerley, his secretary, brought cold drinks to Mr Swan's office. Usually in such circumstances people offered coffee or tea but she was given a brimming glass of Fentimans ginger beer and it went down a treat, as the local people said.

'Nice stuff,' he said, 'it keeps cool in stone jars and is just right after a warm morning in there,' and he nodded back at the works, smiling. Catrin loved an enthusiast and it was obvious to her that Mr Swan was very proud of his foundry.

She explained her problem and he said, immediately, 'I am grateful to you and your brother for coming here. We have lacked a doctor for many a long day and a small hospital would be wonderful. Of course I will help. In industries like ours we try to be careful and have few accidents but in mining it is sometimes another story. I'm sure Mr Dunstan tries his best but they do occasionally happen.

'Also if a man is ill he can't work and then I lose money. You might ask others to donate. I think you would be surprised how many shopkeepers and small business people would encourage you financially. Even if they can only give you a few shillings a month it would add up and make a difference and buy bandages and beds and try to keep you and your brother in food and fuel.'

'I think his enthusiasm is helped by the way I went to his house earlier in the week,' Roddy said later, 'as one of the grandchildren injured his ankle when he was visiting. They have a lovely house with a big garden.'

Catrin approached shopkeepers, grocers, the local blacksmith, the milliner, the dressmaker and the hardware store where Mr Barron was very generous since she had bought so much from him and was aware that plans for the Hilda House would bring him further income. Those who knew her were more open-handed but she had one or two surprises. When she went to the school the teachers both gave money. They needed to stay well and they wanted their pupils to stay well for the sake of their education but Catrin was grateful to Miss Irons and Mr Stapleton for their generosity.

The publicans were also keen because they made a lot of money out of selling beer and the Station Hotel also offered a contribution. Women who had children always paid and usually before they left the surgery. Farmers varied. One man who had no children and lived alone gave her more money than another farmer who had seven children so she didn't know what to expect.

She and Roddy spent money on nothing but necessities, were able to order beds and bedding from Mr Barron, drugs, equipment and bandages came from a supplier in Consett, where the huge ironworks stood, and another in Bishop Auckland, which was just outside Shildon, the home of railways and they managed to keep things going, but it was all a struggle.

Mrs Clements had enough to do so Catrin scrubbed floors and wiped clean walls, made meals which cost as little as she could manage and the washing was mountainous. Rusty, Mr Barron's son – Catrin had got to know well as she paid him for every little job he did and he was reliable and Mr Barron had taken to bragging in the village that the doctors could not do without his lad, he was so proud of him – set up a washing line out the back where it would catch the wind which blew over the fell and on fine days Catrin was rather pleased with her white sheets and pillow-cases blowing like sails even though on more than one occasion she had to run across the fell to catch several of Roddy's shirts which threatened to be lost somewhere in the Deerness valley.

One of the local farmers even donated a horse. Catrin had ridden since she could walk and was very pleased and impressed. It would make life easier for the outlying farms so it was she who went to these in all weathers though she had to be careful of ice and snow. Luckily there had been no deep snow or thick ice yet. It was to come. Women seemed to go into labour on wet days in the middle of nowhere and there was the odd accident on the farms. The horse was a fine one.

'Oh, Mr Benson,' she enthused, 'what a gift.'

'Aye, well,' Mr Benson excused his generosity. 'I thought you might have need of her. This is Cymbeline, she's a grand mare.'

'Cymbeline?' Catrin could not help but ask.

'Aye, lass, as in Shakespeare, tha' knows,' Mr Benson said.

Cymbeline and her fellow horses were stabled just behind the Hilda House where Mr Benson owned a good many acres so Cymbeline didn't even have to move away from her family to belong to Catrin, or on loan Catrin always told herself. Mr Benson's stable boy was in charge of cleaning the stall and feeding the mare and general looking after so all Catrin had to do was let him know when she wanted the horse saddling and off she went. She very much enjoyed discovering the local landscape around the village.

Eight

There was soon a new problem. Roddy came out from his surgery at the Hilda House and home for his tea and he said, 'We're only going to be able to run one surgery at once.'

'Why would you do that?'

'Because I'm getting a lot of young women coming to me and I can't see them by themselves in certain cases. I'm having to ask Mrs Clements to come in and chaperone them while I examine them. She doesn't like it and I don't blame her and I don't think they like having her there because although she's a lovely woman she does have a tendency to gossip.'

That was true. Catrin sighed.

'So until we can afford help I'll have to be with you when you have female patients who need examining,' she said.

Roddy was not being too sensitive, Catrin thought. When she looked at her brother she could see how attractive he was, tall, slender and dark, just over thirty, the right age to marry but he was aware that they did not have any free money and marrying was an expensive business. He singled out nobody. He treated them all alike. Did he still think so much of Amelia Sutherland? They never talked about it so she was unsure but he seemed happy. She did hope that he would find someone he cared for. She thought a wife and child would make him complete.

So when he had to examine a woman Catrin was always there. It made more work but it also brought out a new aspect of her brother that she had not considered.

'I think they find it easier when we are both there,' he said, 'Getting people to confide in you is useful.'

'Doesn't it also bring in those who waste your time?'

And then he surprised her.

'I never feel that helping these people is a waste of time. Some people are lonely. Some are afraid they will die. Some are too scared of dying that they don't come to the surgery. I want them all to come. I want every ache and fear in the waiting room so that I can lessen their pain and suffering of whatever kind even just a little. I get so fed up of all the things we don't know. I hate how defeated I feel when somebody dies young. I want them all to live to be ninety, hale and well and in their right minds and then to die in their sleep.'

He stopped there and began to smile at his own enthusiasm and she was grateful to see that he found happiness in success.

*

There was a rich young woman nearby who liked Roddy and she kept coming back to him with what he felt were imaginary illnesses just so that she could see him. It became known that Lily Bell was after marrying the doctor. Therefore Mrs Clements or Catrin spent a good deal of time with Roddy in the surgery because no matter how often they tried to get her to see Catrin she refused and left Roddy nowhere to go.

Lily's family had owned pits in the area and she was an orphan. Lily had inherited a fortune. The fortune had become magnified in people's minds, Catrin had the idea it was nowhere near as large as people said. She had never had a lover, she had never had a follower and though a dozen men of different kinds had tried to court her Lily would have none of them. She had taken a shine to the new doctor, it was said with pride and some curiosity.

Lily was very Irish-looking with a pale skin, deep blue eyes and black hair. She was a tall, rosy-cheeked, silken-faced woman and Catrin didn't think Lily had ailed for a second in her life. She had the idea that Lily was unaware of how often she tried to see Roddy, she was so in love she couldn't bear not to spend day after day in his company.

She lived alone with servants in a huge house just before the banks went down into Weardale. She must be lonely. She never went anywhere until the first time she came to see Roddy, thinking that she was ill when in fact there was nothing the matter with her. Until now everything was delivered to her home and she never saw anyone. It was rumoured that she sat over her fire in the living room and rarely ventured out of doors. It was the first time a lot of people had seen her when she rode a fine grey horse to the surgery and asked for Roddy's time.

To begin with he said nothing and Catrin didn't want to bring up the embarrassing subject of Lily Bell but when they had a little time off at Easter they went to church and she was there. People stared. Roddy's face was as red as the tulips that flourished in the graveyard and he tried to look straight in front of him rather than at the floor in case someone noticed.

They were having their Easter meal at the vicarage so he could not escape. Lily Bell didn't even look at him and she left after the Sunday service but Roddy was silent and Catrin could see that he was fuming, not at Lily, nor at himself, nobody had done anything wrong but it was just so difficult for him.

In the middle of the afternoon they walked home glad of the sit down by the fire.

'I feel very sorry for Lily Bell,' Catrin said. 'I know you are upset about it but she hasn't actually done anything wrong. Lots of people prefer a certain doctor.'

'I don't want to talk about it.'

'You must be the only person in the place who doesn't.

Why don't you marry her? Her money would make a wonderful hospital for us.'

'I do hope you are teasing me.'

Then Catrin felt clumsy. It was not fair to tease him when they had had to leave Edinburgh because of her mistake.

'I'm sorry. I keep forgetting.'

Then Roddy smiled and she thought it was a good smile, the first she had seen since they had arrived.

'Well, I am not talking myself into marrying Lily Bell.'

'She's very beautiful.'

'Do you know it astonishes me how people go on about beauty. Men see different things. I don't even like her. She is so odd and pushy and looks like she's going to burst into tears.'

'Maybe she has cause.'

'I daren't encourage her to tell me anything more than she already has. I wouldn't care, I've rarely seen a young woman who is physically fitter.'

'What about her mental health?'

'Now there you have me. I can't work out what it is.'

'Roddy, I wouldn't—'

'I just want to be able to work and to be left alone.'

There was a short silence when he got up and put some coal on the fire.

'Why don't we have some whisky?' Catrin suggested.

Her brother had had his usual yearly cough which had

lasted for weeks and she had the feeling that whisky would be good for both his head and his cold.

'Now that is the best thing I have heard today,' her brother said.

Was the weather here bleaker even than in Edinburgh, Catrin wondered, or was it just that somehow the city buildings sucked up the wind which howled down the narrow streets and there was nothing to stop it from sweeping across the fell? They had no fires in their bedrooms, they could not afford to spend money on more coal.

The calendar told her it was spring but there was no appearance of any such thing here. Ice froze in the water jugs in the bedrooms, water froze in the kitchen taps and everything became harder to achieve. People kept falling on the ice and Catrin and Roddy spent a lot of time setting broken bones for people in pain and also attending a lot who had influenza, mostly older people. Catrin was just glad that Roddy, though he had spent a couple more days in bed, got better after that. She was grateful for the clean air here. They lost several elderly patients and it seemed to Catrin that Roddy took it personally.

'Mr Roberts didn't make it,' Roddy told her, stamping his boots free of snow so that he would not make the hall floor too wet. He sighed.

'He was eighty-nine, Roddy,' his sister reminded him.

'Now Miss Roberts will be alone. You will call in and see her when you can?'

She didn't like to tell him that Miss Roberts was ninety-five and that Catrin had called twice that week while the poor woman grieved over her brother. They had had no one else since their parents died. Loneliness seemed to be one of the biggest killers here, Catrin thought. Miss Roberts would be lonely now so she called in and asked the neighbours to look after her but Miss Roberts was a very independent old lady and it wasn't easy to do anything for her.

Their father had been a very influential man and they were prosperous but Catrin knew little of the family. They had a big Victorian house just outside the village on the road to Sunnyside and Mr Roberts had long since retired. He had been a judge in Durham City and liked the quiet of the countryside. Miss Roberts was unfailingly warm and polite. She could no longer walk to church or sit in a hard pew but the vicar went to her and she was known to provide money for summer picnics for the local children and Christmas toys. She gave Catrin a hundred pounds. 'For the new hospital', she said.

'Miss Roberts, that is so generous of you.'

'Not at all,' the old lady said with a light in her eye, 'you never know I might need to use it in the next few years. Now give me a kiss, my dear, and go back to your real patients.'

Catrin kissed the old woman's wizened cheek and went gratefully back to her evening surgery.

Catrin called in to see Lady Reed every week but there was little she could do. You couldn't force people to eat and since the poor old woman wouldn't get out of bed everything had to be done for her. Catrin had tried to talk herself out of the idea that Anne was her child, she was far too old for her age and had had to face things such as children shouldn't have to and Catrin felt anguished for her and after all she was not much more than a girl. She wished she could have spent more time there but she was busy and it would have looked bad. John was never there. He was always out repairing cottages, chopping wood, seeing to the kitchen garden, and when the cottagers were ill Catrin would meet him there.

She began to wish that Lily Bell had taken a fancy for John Reed, it would have made life so much simpler but of course it never worked like that. He had no time for anything more in his life, in fact he had no life. He gave it every day to the people he felt responsible for. She was the only woman in his life apart from his mother and sister and the cottagers, and even then she was there as a professional.

Neither he nor the cottagers had money to spare so like a lot more he gave her presents, game and fish and honey – there were several hives – in fact he was almost self-sufficient, with his hens and ducks. He made sure to afford a pig or two in every row of houses so that the pig could be fed on leftovers such as they were. He had sheep and a cow and he grew corn and took it to the local mill, so but for sugar and yeast and one or two other things which had to be bought, he kept everything going as best he could.

Catrin thought the amount of work his sister had to do was far too much but the girl never complained. She kept the house clean, she cooked and washed and made cakes and spent a lot of time baking for the older people on the estate. She was well loved so it seemed to Catrin.

It was not as if her education was neglected. John had taught her to read and write and basic maths when she was very small. Perhaps she was lonely since she had no friends of her own age as far as Catrin could see. She was too different to make friends of the girls in the cottages and although she and John went to church every Sunday she kept close to him and because he was so much older, boys and girls of her age did not come near.

Anne tended to her mother, doing everything for her while the older lady grew more and more weak as the days went on. Catrin called in as often as she could but there was nothing much she could add to what Anne was already doing. She kept the old lady out of pain which as far as Catrin could tell was in her head but that was just as bad and Anne made her comfortable and encouraged her to eat and drink and even take a little walk around the upper storey of the house. They would pause at each window while she took in the views but Catrin was convinced that what she saw was Hampshire where she had come from, thatched cottages and tree-lined lanes, girls on ponies and warm winds such as never ventured here.

It was May when she took her last breaths. Catrin had spent most of the day there, leaving Roddy to cope as best he could. She felt that she owed to John and Anne that they should have someone there to help them through those last few hours while their mother slipped away. She died in the cold dark dawn as so many people did and Anne went on to the landing and put her hands over her face..

It gave Catrin an excuse to take the child into her arms but she grieved not only for Lady Reed but for the girl's childhood which had been long since lost. Catrin could not help but spend as much time there as she could manage while she had an excuse. Anne was in her mind all the time but she and John were so independently minded that Catrin could do no more than her job and try not to swamp them with the feelings that she had.

She had already checked what records there were while

saying nothing. Not that the council cared and as Mr Ferguson said there was little to go on. Also she did not want to tell this man about her child. She went to the vicar and she did tell him about the circumstances and he helped her as much as he could but there was nothing. It was so disappointing in one way and so hard for her not knowing whether Anne was hers and she kept on hoping that something would happen, something good so that she would discover whether this girl was her child or not. If not where was there to go next?

The funeral was well attended as many people cared for this family who had been here for so long that nobody knew where they had been before. John was popular, though they rarely saw him except at church, because he looked after the cottagers in a paternal way that good landlords did and because he kept nothing for himself.

After the funeral Tony and Susan Bainbridge had provided a tea in the church hall with sandwiches and cakes, whisky and coffee. Catrin said to John,

'Have you thought about what will happen to Anne now?'

He looked at her in surprise.

'What do you mean?'

'Don't you think she will be very lonely?'

'She has me.'

'She needs other girls.'

'She's never said anything. Besides she has to do her work, I can't afford to pay somebody else.'

'You want her to stay up there in that great big house cooking and cleaning for you for the rest of her life? She's not much more than a child.'

John didn't say anything and then he frowned at her. She was not surprised he was angry. He had just lost his mother. He shouldered far too much and did not understand that he was letting a young girl manage too much as well.

'She's not going to say anything to you, John, she cares about you far too much for that but she has no life.'

'I have no life.'

'That is not the point. You are an adult and have to learn to deal with such things. Anne is not and she needs more than you can give her. She needs some fun and laughter in her life perhaps away from here. She needs people her own age,' Catrin said, wondering that he could be so selfish and she said it so loudly that several people stopped talking.

John left her and took his tea to the window where she followed him. 'Would you like some whisky?' she said meekly in hope that he would forgive her.

'Would you like to stop telling me what to do?'

They were both speaking softly now.

'I think you could do with a drink.'

He actually glared at her. She hadn't thought he was

capable of such things and wasn't sure she understood why he was being selfish and not thinking of Anne.

He slammed down the cup and saucer on the nearby small table and walked out of the room. Catrin could barely keep her countenance, she was cross with him for not thinking more about Anne than he did about himself. She found herself moving away into the big room where several people, including her brother, were eating sandwiches and pies and cakes and drinking whisky or sherry, or in Susan the vicar's wife's case, gin and tonic.

'What on earth were you saying to John Reed?' her brother asked. 'You could be heard clearly by several people. His mother has just died, you know.'

'That girl needs a life.'

'That girl is nothing to do with you.'

'I feel as if she is.'

'You haven't been able to discover anything that could prove she is. You have no right to interfere in her life. You'll only make matters worse.'

'She deserves more. Surely he doesn't expect her to stay with him forever. She could do anything she wanted with a decent education and friends.'

'If it hadn't been for him she could have been dead long since.'

'And is she meant to go on paying for that for the rest of her life? She's fourteen, Roddy.'

At that moment Anne, in her black gown which had

obviously been hastily but neatly altered, presumably something else she managed for herself, left the vicar and came across to them. She looked so fragile in the velvet dress, black to her throat, her wrists and her feet with not even a piece of white lace to soften it, her face pale and her eyes sore from crying as she had been trying not to do ever since her mother died.

'Where has Johnnie gone? I want to go home.'

'I'll find him,' Roddy said and put down his drink and left them.

'I want to go home and find my mother still alive,' Anne said with quivering lips and Catrin urged her into the little room where various groups gathered during the week and a brave fire burned so that she could weep in unrestrained fashion as Catrin thought she had not done before now, as though she must keep her feelings locked up.

'It feels so strange with just Johnnie and me, she's left this huge space. I didn't think she would, she had been in bed for so long but I saw her every day, spent hours reading to her and trying to get her to eat and she loved me.

'My father was never kind to her or any of us and he spent so much money that the estate can barely manage now. Johnnie has had a very hard life with him. He was a bad man.'

'He must have had some redeeming qualities.'

There was a long pause and then Anne said,

'He was the person who found me, that's what Johnnie says, though I'm not sure I believe him. Maybe Johnnie just said that so that I might have a happy memory of his father. It seems that I was wandering around on the fell and he picked me up and put me on his horse and took me home. He seemed to hate the sight of me after that. If I walked into a room he would walk out. I think I would have died then had he not found me so how could I help but love him however horrible he seemed to be.'

Catrin was dumbstruck, thinking of how close this child had come to dying and but for the disagreeable man would probably have perished. Her heart thumped so hard that she couldn't breathe for several moments.

'And nobody knew where you came from?'

'Johnnie tried to find out. His father had a woman he went to and John thought at first that it was something to do with her, but what woman would turn out her child into the winter night? Johnnie made a lot of enquiries at the time in case someone had lost a small child but it was no good. It was almost as though I had come from another planet. John teases me about that sometimes. We go outside and he points out the various planets we can see and then he tells me that I came from Mars, or that someone on Venus gave me to the earth because she could no longer keep me. That's my favourite explanation.'

Catrin said nothing for a long time, trying to absorb this information. Anne had already gone back to thinking about her brother. She always thought about him first, Catrin realized.

'Johnnie is so good,' Anne said sadly, 'he always thinks everything is up to him, everything he has to deal with and get right. He won't ever allow himself to fail.'

'He told me he wasn't a good rider.'

Anne smiled.

'He never says he's good at anything. He was deliberately bad I think at all the things his father wanted him to be good at. Johnnie can be very stubborn. He doesn't ride much because we can't afford horses. We only have one now for the work and John always says he has too much to do to ride for pleasure. He never went to school you know, Father wouldn't let him so he taught himself to read and write with mother's help and he is a good farm manager. It could all have gone wrong again. I'm so glad it didn't.'

'What will you do now?' Catrin asked gently.

'Go on as best we can, I suppose. Johnnie was terrified that she would die but then he didn't sleep. He knew that sometimes she walked the house. He had to make sure he bolted all the doors so that she didn't get lost on the wretched fell, she hated it so.'

'I don't think he is aware you knew this.'

'No.' Anne smiled almost secretly. 'It wouldn't have

helped if he had known that I worried about her too. She wanted to die, that was the awful thing. She felt as though she had nothing left to live for.'

'I don't think that's true, I think it's just her mind would not get used to the idea that your father was dead and she could not bear it, difficult as he was, he was still her husband and she had his child.'

There was a slight pause and then Anne said,

'Do you want to get married and have children, Doctor Morgan?'

'Not really.'

'You are getting old for an unmarried woman.'

Oh dear, Catrin thought, now I'm an old maid.

'I think it's more important for me to be a doctor.'

'Couldn't you be both?'

'I suppose I might some day. What do you want to be?'

'Nothing. Just to look after Johnnie. It isn't likely that he will marry even if he could. He has so little to offer and I think he has a secret dread that he will turn into his father and make any wife of his very unhappy so I will be there for him.'

'You're very young to take up such a role.'

'Who else would do it? Can you think how lonely he would be if I went away?'

'Don't you think that getting away might be good for you, to see other places and do other things?'

'Where is the money to come from? And I would be

miserable away from him and he would be from me. We are tied together for life.'

'That's a very hard way to look at the future.'

'What else can we do?' Anne said.

Just then John came in and collected his sister and after they had thanked the vicar they left. He did not speak another word to Catrin and that was when she realized that she had liked going to his house, that she was just as concerned for him and his sister as she had been for their mother and now she would have no excuse to go unless one of the cottagers was ill and she thought John would probably stay out of her way.

'I could have murdered another glass of whisky,' Roddy confided as they walked home.

'The doctor cannot be seen toping,' Catrin said.

'This doctor just wishes he could afford to tope a bit more often.'

Anne bothered her. She had no life just as Catrin had had no young life and sooner or later she would begin to feel tied down and neglected and maybe then she would rebel. Why didn't John Reed see that? It stopped Catrin from liking him.

Nine

There were a few warm weeks and then it rained hard and turned a lot of roads and byways to mud. Catrin spent most of her time on horseback though she hated to go out in case the mare slipped and broke a leg. Mr Benson would never forgive her so she only went out when she had to. The Hilda House was freezing and the rain tipped down all through July.

They did have a little more money now courtesy of various businesses in the town, and Mr Swan's and other folk's generosity, but Roddy and Catrin worried constantly about the coal bills and the work and fell into bed only to be awakened by people being ill during the night. Why did it happen more at night? Catrin had no idea.

During the first week in August the pit siren went off in the middle of the day. People knew that this meant an accident. Roddy was making house calls so Catrin hurried up to the pit along with a lot of anxious pit wives and the small children who were not yet at school. She could see Mr Dunstan's secretary, who was unmistakable in her neat coat and boots, her grey hair permed and set and the grim smile with which she greeted Catrin. Catrin found Jack Dunstan disagreeable but that wasn't fair. She had asked him for help and he had refused and he was obliged to do nothing, whereas she was obliged to turn up here and offer help.

'Miss Waskerly?'

'Oh, Doctor, I'm so glad you are here though there is nothing to be done until we find out what has happened. He's down there.'

The women and children stood about in the warm wind for a long time but nobody wanted to leave since no news was not good news, it made one anxious, Catrin thought.

Several of the women from the village, including Mrs Clements, brought flasks of tea, sandwiches and cake. The rescue workers said that there had been a fall and they needed more men down there to help clear it.

When Roddy came after doing his calls it was halfway through the afternoon and Catrin found John Reed near them, silent.

'Has it happened before?' she said.

He shook his head.

'Dunstan is known to be careful.'

The first of the injured men were brought to the surface and Catrin and Roddy were busy. She was glad to be able to offer something rather than just waiting but injuries such as these when there was a rockfall could be dangerous and many of the men had crushed limbs.

By the end of the day there were three dead. The fall had been cleared away. They were lucky there was nobody still behind it or that it had not been the kind of fall which could not be cleared quickly. Miners died in such ways. At least these deaths had been instant. Several men would never work again and a number would not work for some months as their injuries were severe.

Mr Dunstan did not even thank the doctors for being there. Neither did he stay around. He would be blamed whether he was responsible or not. Roofs should not fall down if there were enough timbers to hold them, John Reed said, but mining accidents were common and surely the owners were not always to blame. Somebody had to be to blame and there was a lot of muttering against Jack Dunstan.

When the work was finished Catrin and Roddy fell into bed, they were exhausted. The three men were buried that week and everybody went to the funerals including Miss Waskerly and Mr Dunstan.

By the end of the week there had been a huge delivery of coal at both the Hilda House and the surgery house and Mr Dunstan even came along to the surgery and thanked her.

Catrin was not expecting him and was embarrassed but he said roughly,

'You will have money from me put into your bank every month from now onwards for the men and their families and there will be coal for you to heat every room in both houses always.'

Foolishly the only thing Catrin could think of was to say,

'Miss Waskerly was horrified that you might have been killed.'

He smiled grimly.

'She would have been out of a job,' he said.

'Oh, I don't think so. Somebody as efficient would find a job easily,' she said and smiled.

He didn't smile back, he just left and she wished she hadn't said it. She could find no way to get to know him and she wanted to understand why he was so distant and cold. Was he unhappy?

She mentioned this to Mrs Clements who knew everything about everybody except that when Catrin asked her about Anne she only replied that some foolish lass had been stupid and the poor little mite had had no home.

'Oh, he's married but she never goes anywhere. Goodness only knows what he's like at home. He's a hard man is Jack Dunstan. Never gives anybody the time of day and he built a great big wall around his house and there aren't many people let inside. The tradesmen have to leave stuff beyond the gates. Normally the local bairns might steal from it but they wouldn't dare with him. He terrifies them if they get in his way when he walks around the streets.

'Mind you I did hear that there is to be a deputy manager. Coming from Sunderland. They have big pits up there you know. Horrible mucky place but it makes money. Not that any of it goes anywhere but into the owners' pockets.'

Catrin couldn't stop thinking about Anne and Anne was special to her. Roddy noticed.

'She's not your child, Cat. She has green eyes.'

'You know as well as I do that anybody can have any colour eyes. It's got nothing to do with it.'

'That's not quite true. Usually a child has the colour eyes of one of its parents and since you have told me that you are almost certain Joe had brown eyes it seems most unlikely that Anne is anything to do with you. And even if she was you couldn't say anything to her.'

Catrin didn't reply. He was right but she wanted to see the girl more and more, to be something to her, if just a good friend, but since she had spoken out of turn at his mother's funeral John ignored her and she didn't blame him. She knew how stupid she had been but also she knew why. She longed for a child, for her child, and it was not a feeling which went away. She kept telling herself that Anne was nothing to do with her but she couldn't convince herself.

She could not go there without a good reason and even if he asked her to see somebody at the cottages he was never present. She would send him a message afterwards telling him about the illness and what had been done but she also began sending him proper bills. Things were easing financially and everybody in the village was contributing especially since the pit disaster. What would they have done had she and Roddy not been there?

The practice could now afford to take on a chemist. They had been doing all this work themselves. Mrs Clements had given up her post at the Station Hotel and was now at the Hilda House full time which made a huge difference.

Roddy advertised in the local newspapers for professional help, the nearest being the *Auckland Chronicle* and *Durham County Advertiser.* Also the *Consett Guardian* so that the whole nearby area was covered.

Several letters came in but the applicants didn't seem to have real qualifications. In more than one case they were made up, Catrin thought. Nobody offered paperwork to prove their professional status and it seemed that the whole idea would come to grief because after six weeks of talking to everybody in the area, advertising as discreetly as possible, they had found no one.

A nurse was easier come by as a lot of women were

natural nurses and in any case Catrin was eager to find someone who would care as well as be competent. She found Mrs McNorton at her door telling her that her niece was a nurse. She had been working in Newcastle at the Royal Victoria Infirmary but had been away for a long time and was eager to find a place as near to home as she could be.

'I don't want you to feel obliged to take her on, Miss Morgan, but I think you will find her satisfactory if you once meet her.'

Mrs McNorton's niece was a woman of thirty. Her family, the Greens, still lived here and they were a close-knit bunch. She came home within a few days to be interviewed and Catrin took a liking to the woman as soon as they met. Her name was Eileen and she had been a nurse for ten years but was homesick and wanted to come back.

Jenny – this was Mrs McNorton – with the best will in the world was no good with people who were sick and in such big families often help was needed by various members. There were two other sisters to help though, so she would still have time to look after the patients at the practice. Catrin thought they needed two nurses but a nurse and a chemist would help a lot and though it meant that she and Roddy would have little time off she no longer cared. She wanted this practice to work as she had wanted nothing in her life but her child and now that seemed impossible.

Eileen Green made life easier for both doctors right from the start. She was not a pretty woman, being little, round and extremely homely looking with nondescript hair which she fought to keep out of her eyes, but she wore such a sweet smile on her face that none of this mattered. She could talk anybody into anything, that was what Roddy said.

Catrin's view after Eileen had been there for a week was that if Eileen had had education, opportunity and money she would have made a fine doctor. She had good instincts and could tell what was wrong with some people the moment they set foot in the door. She put everybody at ease because she was friendly without becoming inquisitive and everyone liked her. The people of the area were proud that one of their own had done so well in a difficult job. Her family had lived in and around Weardale for a very long time and it stood her in good stead.

A lot of the older men said they had known her since a little lass and by, hadn't she done well and she was such a canny body, she was that. They would let her examine them when they would not have let Catrin anywhere near and if Eileen was at Catrin's surgery they came to her just as they would have gone to Roddy and it was all because of Eileen.

She had the sweetest smile Catrin had known and her laughter was so infectious it eased many a day for many a patient. Children opened up to her, she would give each of them a sweet after their treatment. Old women remembered her grandmother who had been just like her, they said, always with a smile and a kind word for everybody. She was old Dora Green in person, who had had a farm at Satley, just a few miles away.

The young men flocked to her. At thirty she should have been an old maid and a plain old maid at that, but Catrin could see straight away that Eileen Green was single because she chose to be and that many a lad was upset because she would not go for a walk with him. Her parents had long since despaired of her and given in because they were so proud.

'Couldn't we find another nurse to help Eileen, somebody as good as she is?' Roddy said when she had been there for about six weeks. 'She is so popular that which either of us has her with them everybody goes to that surgery. It's like a tug of war.'

Eileen lived in a terraced house on the front street. Her dad was the signalman at the station. Her mam had brought up ten children and was now besieged by grandchildren and Eileen did everything she could for her sisters and brothers and their offspring and her parents when she was not at the surgery.

*

'You like Eileen, don't you?' Catrin said to Roddy one evening in September when yet another wind was howling across the fell and they were cosy by the fire, hoping that nobody was ill and needed them.

Roddy didn't meet her eyes but after a little while he said,

'I think she is very good at what she does. We should find other help so that Eileen can do more specialist work with us and she is a good administrator.'

'What do you mean?'

'I don't know exactly, just that the moment you think you are getting any nearer to her she is gone and you are left with a great big space. I have noticed that a lot of young men around here are interested in her, but she is not forthcoming about her personal circumstances. They come to the surgery when they know she is there but she is polite and a nurse and nothing else.'

After that Catrin watched Eileen more closely. Roddy was right, she was the most attractive woman in the area and she did not seem happy, but was nursing to be all there was in her life?

'Doctor Morgan, I want to talk to you,' Eileen said shortly afterwards, when the two women were alone in the surgery. It was early evening and the last patient had gone.

'Yes of course. Is everything all right?'

'I need to tell you something so that I'm sure I have you on my side.'

'Yes of course, always. Sit down,' and so they sat down together and Eileen said,

'I thought I must explain myself to you.'

'You don't need to tell me anything. Your life is your business and you are very good to be here for both of us. We wouldn't ask more of you.'

'I know but I wouldn't like you to think that I was deceiving you. People don't understand why I don't marry.' Here she stopped,

'Marriage isn't for everybody,' Catrin said.

'Is that how you feel?'

'I think your circumstances are different but maybe our aims are the same in a sense. I want to be a good doctor and do my best with my patients. Perhaps you feel the same and that you cannot be everything to everyone.'

'It's not exactly that but you see I am already married.'

Catrin stared at her. Eileen took a deep breath.

'Nobody knows but I was married in Newcastle because I was expecting and when I lost it they had to take everything away or I would have died. I live in fear that he may find me again. My husband, he wasn't a nice lad but I wanted him, I got him and I'm still married to him though he ran off when he found out I was pregnant. I think he was just scared but he was able to get away. I wasn't. So as far as I know there is no reason he should come back but he knows where my family lives and I'm scared.

'I want to stay and work here and my family is glad to have me but I know at the back of my mind that I should go somewhere else and tell no one where I am but I don't want to be so alone, I really don't.' At that moment Eileen broke down and cried and after that Catrin dreaded that Eileen should find another job somewhere no one knew her and she felt selfish wanting Eileen to stay but there were so few people able to do what she did and probably not half so well.

'Oh, Eileen, I'm so sorry.' Catrin was tempted to tell the other woman of her own circumstances but she didn't think it would help.

'Anyway, I did want you to know because I like and respect you and I am staying here even terrified he might come back and I would fall in love with him all over again because I have no more sense. I want to be close to my family, to the people who love me.' Eileen's voice broke once again and Catrin leaned forward and took both her hands.

'Roddy and I will help as much as we can. I swear I will never tell a soul and we are so grateful to have you with us.'

Eileen nodded and took a few deep breaths and then she looked at Catrin.

'I just want to go on nursing now and for my family never to know about the awful things I did.'

'You didn't want more than most women want and they will never know it from me,' Catrin said.

Eileen smiled just a little.

'My mother is so keen for me to marry. I don't think she cares about what I do but I must marry. She says there is no other way to live for somebody like me, like us. I will be nobody in spite of my achievements if I don't find a husband. I feel so caught. But I'm happy at work with you and Doctor Morgan. You're so very kind.'

'It's easy to be kind to you, Eileen, because you are so good to everybody you meet and Roddy always says that doctoring is partly how you treat the patient so that they are as easy as they can be about what is happening to them and that helps them to get better. You are here for all of us, Eileen, you're making our job so much easier.'

At that point Eileen hugged her. Catrin was pleased and taken aback at the same time as she had discovered that the people here were not given to affectionate gestures and she liked Eileen all the better for it. Eileen was like Lucy had been, a good friend to her and Catrin was so glad to have her there.

She also took on two women from the village who were not professional nurses but they were good at helping Eileen and they learned as they went along.

*

Catrin talked to the chemist in Stanhope, she'd heard that he had a daughter who had recently qualified. They ran his business together. Catrin thought that they might know somebody who would become the Hilda House chemist. Mr Melrose sold a lot of things which had nothing to do with people's medical needs and it was a very good business. It was, Catrin thought, a very clever and well-organized shop. There were baby products, skin cream and make-up for women, walking sticks and plasters and bandages and supports for weak limbs.

The glass cases were full of jewellery, earrings, necklaces and bracelets in red, blue, yellow, white and green in gold or silver, scarves with patterns of blue birds and grey doves, orange roses and pink daisies. There was a special part of the shop filled with soaps and scents and nail varnishes and matching lipsticks. He also sold cough drops and various minor remedies, like antiseptic ointment and salves.

Catrin wished he lived in her village. She knew that a great many people would have taken his advice before they went to a doctor. He was a loyal and well-trusted man she had learned from the people she talked to, with a smile for everyone and they could go into a little booth and have small matters seen to. He sold sanitary products but as discreetly as he could so that no embarrassed woman had to buy such things with other folk looking on. The shop was big enough to have two rooms, some parts of these broken up so that nobody need worry no matter what they needed because nobody else could see what they were doing.

Catrin went in for the first time when the shop was empty and although they had not met before he came to her with hand outstretched and a big smile on his rather handsome face. The chemist looked slightly foreign to her but he was actually Scottish and came from the far side of Dumfries. She thought he looked more like a Highlander with his dark eyes and black hair.

'Doctor Morgan,' he said, 'I've heard so much about you.'

'Mr Melrose. Please give it all up and come to us.'

That made him laugh. As they stood, a woman in a white coat came from the other room – Mr Melrose's daughter, Agatha. He introduced her and told Catrin that she would have applied for their vacancy but did not want to leave him just at the moment. It was well known in the area that Mr Melrose's wife had died only months since and Catrin could understand that he would want his daughter close and that she would support him. He was obviously very proud of her.

She was a tall, pretty woman with her father's looks and confidence, and despite having been born in north-east England she retained the Scottish accent of her parents and her voice was very sweet.

'Agatha is all I have left.' He glanced at his daughter

with such affection that she looked at him just the same way.

Agatha went off to sell a gaudy necklace to a girl whose mother was having her birthday that week, so as other people came in Catrin said her goodbyes. She lived in hope that Agatha Melrose would decide she could fit more into her life and might consider coming to work for the Doctors Morgan.

Ten

John Reed came to see Catrin. He was last as usual as though he didn't want other people to see him there. He brought her eggs and butter and cream, and vegetables. It was all in a basket and he held out a pound, then said hastily,

'I didn't want to see you. I wanted to be cowardly and go to your brother but last time we met I behaved very badly so I come in peace and hope that you will come and see Anne. She isn't well.'

'Sit down,' she told him, taking the gifts and glad of the pound. She had had a tiring day but seeing him so kind and repentant made her feel much better so they sat down and he told her about his concerns for his sister.

'I did try to get her to do something more adventurous. I have a cousin who has a very good school in Gosforth and would have been happy to take Anne and introduce her to other girls and could teach her things which would be all together new with the idea that she would become an assistant teacher. So I took your advice but she wouldn't go. I never could get her to do anything I wanted. I also offered to have more help but she wouldn't have that either. I'm at my wits' end. What do I do?'

'How do you know she is ill?'

'She has passed out twice in a week. One of these days she will hit her head on the floor, I'm so worried about it. She won't rest, she gets up too early and goes to bed too late and never sits down. She's all I've got.'

Catrin wanted to tell him to get married, that that would sort out the problem but of course it wouldn't. It would only make life more complicated. Anne had just lost her mother. To bring another woman into her life at this point would be a serious mistake but then it would be good for him to be married. Was he too not lonely and did he not want someone to comfort him and children so that the line would be carried on?

Not being able to say any of this she told him that she would come and see Anne the following morning. He looked slightly relieved.

Catrin could see what he meant straight away. Anne did not look pleased to see her, but she was white and skinny.

'I wish Johnnie hadn't come to you. There's nothing the matter with me. I'm just upset. I keep going upstairs and I half expect to find my mother there and the bed is empty. I know it's stupid of me but I can't help it. And I'm finding it difficult to eat and sleep.

'He keeps talking about sending me away. Why would I want to leave him? He's the only person in the whole world who cares about me. Why would I want to go away? He's completely alone. He has no friends. He goes nowhere but church. It isn't good for him.'

Anne sighed.

'Do you have headaches?' Catrin asked.

'No.'

'Do you sleep?'

'Not always.'

'And you don't eat?'

'I just wish Mama was here, I miss her so much. She didn't want to be here, you know. That was the hardest thing of all. She wanted to be with him and after the way that he had treated her. She was the only woman who was ever kind to me.'

Catrin felt badly for her. If she was her daughter then she was having as bad a time as Catrin had had but in a different way.

Catrin looked hard at the girl. Anne held her gaze for a second and then looked at the floor which was so clean that it shone.

'Now that Mama has gone I worry that he will go and then what will happen to me. If he died I would be on the street. I have no rights here.'

'Does he know you think of it like that?'

'The wretched place is entailed. It's the next man in line.'

'And who is that?'

'Oh, I don't know. Some man who lives in Berwick. We never see him. All Johnnie is interested in is this place. He can't know what it's like trying to see to everything in the house but I don't want some gossipy woman from the village here.'

At that moment – his timing was always exact, Catrin thought – John walked into the kitchen, his brow furrowed. Anne cast up her eyes once more.

'Must you do that?' she said. 'This is a private conversation. I am dying of something horrible and it's nothing to do with you.'

John sat down at the table opposite Catrin with Anne sitting at the head of the table.

'Tell your brother what you said to me,' Catrin urged her.

Anne did not look at her and did not reply.

'I think you two have things to discuss and it's nothing to do with me,' Catrin said. 'Having said that I think you may have anaemia, low iron in your blood. It's quite common in girls of your age. You must try to eat more meat and vegetables, fruit and nuts and take better care of yourself and go for a walk every day. Try to be more sociable. There must be other girls your age in the village. If you could make friends it would help a lot.'

John walked her outside and there he turned and smiled suddenly and his eyes lit, which Catrin thought suited him and made him look younger and more carefree. She was glad to have made him smile but his presence seemed to be getting heavier and heavier since his mother had died. No wonder Anne found it so hard.

'Anne is worried that something will happen to you. You're all she has and that isn't good either.' Then Catrin had an idea. 'If I asked you for Sunday dinner would you come?'

Eleven

'You said what?' Roddy demanded as they sat down together that evening.

'I couldn't think of what else to do. They are dying of loneliness, the pair of them and apparently if he dies she gets nothing.'

'What a dreadful idea.'

'Isn't it?'

'Who else would we invite? There's nobody on their level.'

'What about Mr and Mrs Reynolds? They are lovely people and they have children about Anne's age.'

'Both away at boarding school.'

'They'll be home for the October half-term though.'

Sam Reynolds was the local solicitor. His wife Cynthia was well liked though Catrin did not know her. She was the kind of woman who was on committees and helped to run the local branch of the Women's Institute, the Sewing Group, the women's church group and a great many other things which Catrin had opted out of thankfully because she was too busy.

'The Reynolds are great friends with Susan and Tony and nobody invites the vicar and his wife anywhere because they always seem to have to do everything. Let's outwit them before they start issuing invitations.'

'And where are we going to put everybody in a place this size?'

'We won't have it here. We'll have the meal up at the Hilda House. The rooms are drying out now that Mr Dunstan has come down off his high horse and provided all the coal that we need and we should invite him and his wife and Mr and Mrs Swan.'

'We haven't even got a dining table.'

'We will have. I'm going to make Sunday dinner a day when we invite people to a meal in the middle of the day. That will keep us in with the local people and will help all round.'

'Oh Lord,' Roddy said.

Catrin went to Mr Barron and he found a huge table with two big leaves and sixteen chairs second-hand for her. They were very cheap. The chairs were sturdy but the table was badly marked. He also found her a huge white cloth to cover it. She wasn't sure how ambitious she was being but she didn't care. When they asked the vicar and his wife she could see joy on Susan's face.

'Oh if only you knew,' Susan said confidentially after-wards. 'We never get invited anywhere. Tony thinks it's our duty to have people here all the time and it's hard going. Thank you, Doctor Morgan.'

'Please call me Catrin.'

'Have you sufficient cutlery, crockery and such?'

'I was hoping I could borrow from you. Just for once I'm going to have this my way and it will be a kind of opening day for the Hilda House. I'm determined that in time we will live there.'

Catrin was grateful now for having learned to cook and bake in her father's kitchen. John Reed offered her pheasants he had shot and that he would make them ready for the oven and advised her to pot roast them with vegetables and cider. Mrs Clements got very excited and offered to make apple and blackberry crumble and they could have local cheese and port to finish with coffee afterwards.

It had seemed like such a good idea but Catrin started to worry as the day drew nearer. What if nobody wanted to come? What if everybody was ill and she and Roddy had to turn out and were too exhausted to cope and people had to stay at home? What if it snowed so badly that nobody could leave their houses? Whoever had thought this was a good idea?

It would be so cold up there at the big house and she dreaded the idea that she could make it anything she wanted. It seemed to have a mind of its own and if it rejected her plans nothing would work out. She tried to tell Roddy this but he just laughed and in her better moments she could see that he was right, but she felt that so much depended on it. She could not afford to fail here for all sorts of reasons.

Almost as an afterthought she asked Lily Bell. She didn't think the poor woman got asked anywhere as a single woman and had no life. She didn't tell Roddy. She also asked Amy Snow, who had been widowed some months since and had no children but whose husband had been a sea captain. When he died at sea she had moved back to the dale to a married sister and no doubt she had a decent income. It did sound very mercenary but if John Reed would marry either of these women his life would be much different and hopefully improved.

To her joy everybody said that they would come. She was worried about it but felt that she needed to make a bit of a splash. In the meanwhile she began to pay a local builder to do the necessary repairs on the Hilda House. His charges were reasonable and she liked him. He was about her age and had started with his father when he was just a child so there were few things that Rich Carpenter couldn't turn his hand to.

She could tell also that he was interested in the old property and enjoyed having a project to go at. Luckily the roof and walls were sound but he sorted out the plumbing so that finally they had a bathroom and hot water in the kitchen. Catrin spent as much time as she could getting the sitting and dining rooms decorated. She also got him to put new windows and new doors into the original surgery as she could not bear that it should not go on doing its bit as well.

She bought second-hand furniture which Mr Barron found for her from a house sale in Stanhope. Lots of shabby chairs but with a rug or two and the fire on if the weather was bad she thought it would do.

'Lily Bell?' Roddy said in anguish when she told him on the eve of the party. 'Oh, Cat, you didn't.'

'And Mrs Snow. '

The weather was fine for which Catrin was grateful and Mrs Clements had offered to come in and see to the dinner while Catrin and Roddy were at church. She seemed almost gleeful.

'My husband spends his Sundays in the pub. He comes back for his tea and then goes back so I have nothing to stay at home for.'

The sun got out and Catrin was very pleased with herself. All her guests were church-goers and they met up after matins and so she was extra happy that day.

They trooped back to the Hilda House and the sun shone through the windows. It was still rather bare, Catrin thought, but she had done her best and it was the only way that she could have had people to a big Sunday dinner.

Mrs Snow seemed so grateful and Lily Bell had gazed

longingly at Roddy in church. Catrin just hoped she wouldn't do that all day or the poor man would find somebody ill to go to.

John Reed looked very uncomfortable in his smart suit and Anne all decked out in her black velvet funeral dress, probably the only smart frock she had, looked as though she would rather have stayed at home, Catrin thought.

The vicar and his wife, well versed socially, talked to everybody, the fire burned brightly and they all drank sherry before dinner. The two Reynolds children stood together as though attached. The boy, Albert, was younger than his sister, she being about the same age as Anne.

Anne ignored the Reynolds children. Catrin sat them one at one side of the table and one at the other facing Anne. She had put Amy Snow next to John Reed and broke up the couples so that everybody would have to make an effort to talk. She had the feeling they all knew one another vaguely from church but whether they had all sat round a table together before this she was unsure.

Anne didn't speak at all and the Reynolds children whispered together across the table. Albert ate hugely of everything though he didn't say he was enjoying it. Penelope ate very little and Catrin began to wish she had not invited them None of them had remembered their manners.

Mr Reynolds had brought wine with him including

two bottles of champagne which most folk had never tasted before. The meal got off to a good start when even the younger members of the party were allowed a little fizz. Anne was silent.

Mrs Snow was in her element with John Reed and chatted happily. Mr Dunstan, who had come without his wife, thawed somewhat and luckily he was sitting next to the vicar's wife which made life easier as she could get anybody to talk to her. It was a good mix of people, Catrin thought, and she had tried so hard that it had to be a success.

Roddy sat across the table from Lily Bell but for once Miss Bell seemed to remember that she was on show and made conversation with Mr Reynolds and Mr Dunstan. The Swans were both from local families and knew everybody which helped. There were compliments about the pheasants. Catrin was able to say that had come from John Reed who took the kind remarks with a smile. The younger people seemed to like the crumble and so did the men.

Catrin realized then that she had never met Jack Dunstan's wife, she had just assumed he was married. Mrs Clements said so and she knew everything. He didn't say he was coming by himself but just came and didn't explain himself. Did he ever explain himself? Catrin didn't think so.

Mrs Clements went home after she had washed the dishes and provided tea and coffee later in the afternoon.

There were a few flakes of snow and it was cold but Mr Dunstan's coal had sorted out the temperature in the house and Catrin was not backward in telling him so and how pleased she was that he could come. He managed a smile. He was a strange man but she thought he was glad to be there.

Catrin managed to get Cynthia Reynolds to herself and complimented her on her children only to have that woman say, softly and when they were beside the window, with nobody else near, 'That's very kind but I'm not sure we can take all the credit. My sister sadly died when they were quite young and we were obliged to take them on so it hasn't been easy. Their father died years ago so all they have is us.'

Anne stood by one of the windows while they all drank tea.

'Can I get you something else to drink?' Catrin asked.

'No, thank you. I would like to go home. I don't know what to say.'

'I just thought it might be a good idea to get people together.'

'It is good it is for my brother to have other people to talk to. He never goes anywhere.'

Susan Bainbridge confided to Catrin,

'I feel sorry for Amy being widowed and not even having a child. We do try to involve her in church activities but it isn't for everybody.'

Amy was ill at ease in one way but her gaze followed John Reed as he spoke to different people and she came to Anne and said,

'I didn't know you existed until now. You are a lot younger than John. I daresay he's almost old enough to be your father.'

Catrin knew that Amy was finding this difficult but Anne looked up at Amy in some surprise. Amy Snow had never seemed so tall but she was, she must be five foot nine.

'I heard that John's father found you on the fell outside in awful weather. My father was like that. He was always bringing stray kittens home. Do you remember it or were you too little at the time?'

Anne stared at her and then a great red flush appeared on her cheeks and John came over – Catrin thanked his timing which was always good – and he said to Anne,

'I think we must be off now. Thank you Doctor Morgan, for having us to your house. It's been a pleasure.'

'Yes for all of us,' Amy put in and she beamed up at John and she said to him, 'You won't forget my invitation now, will you?'

John's face also changed colour and he merely nodded and left.

'Fancy him being Sir John Reed,' Amy gushed. 'It's so very grand having somebody like that among us. I have invited him to dinner. He's very shy. Did you know his mother well? I understand that she was a society beauty. It must have been very odd for her to marry and come here but perhaps she was enthralled by the idea of being Lady Reed. I'm sure a good many women would.'

Amy almost ran from the Hilda House, she was so eager to get away and presumably enjoy the thrill of having John Reed as her new friend. Catrin saw her from the windows.

'I don't think I like that woman,' Roddy said and Catrin realized that he did not mean Lily Bell. 'I think she's a social climber.'

On the Monday of that week, to Catrin's delight, she had a visit from Agatha Melrose. It was fairly early in the day considering that Agatha would have had to catch a bus from Stanhope. Catrin could see the young woman's excitement.

'I want to come and be your chemist,' she said.

'And what does your father say?'

Agatha looked helplessly at her.

'He wants me to stay there but I would like a place of my own. At the moment I have to do everything he tells me and he always thinks he knows better than me and I'm sure it's true but how will I ever learn for myself when he treats me like a shop assistant?'

Catrin was therefore not very surprised when in the early afternoon Francis Melrose appeared and he seemed none too pleased.

'I feel that you have stolen my daughter,' was the first thing he said. 'You do know that my wife hasn't been dead long and that I rely on Agatha not just to help me in the shop but also to run the house. I can't do it all by myself.'

Eileen came into Catrin's room then and Mr Melrose stopped, stared at her and then he said,

'Eileen. I had no idea that you were back.'

'I missed my family so much,' she said. 'How are you, Mr Melrose?'

'I think you are old enough to call me Francis now,' he said with a smile. 'The gap narrows as people grow older.'

'I understand that your daughter is going to be our chemist,' Eileen said. 'We are so pleased to have her. We are in sore need as they say. You must be so proud of her – Francis. She is so very like you.'

'Yes, I – well, I—'

Mr Melrose, embarrassed and at a loss for words, went back to Stanhope and Catrin smiled at her nurse.

'Eileen,' she said, 'you chose just the right moment.'

'I thought so,' Eileen said, also smiling. 'He's a lovely man but he could have done with half a dozen children and then he wouldn't be so fixated on his one chick. My mother says he has got worse since his wife died and Agatha finished her training and came home.'

It was a huge relief for all of them to move to the Hilda House where there was so much more space. They now needed three bedrooms and Agatha needed proper provision for her pills and potions as she so lightly called them so she had a proper chemist's shop within the house itself which made life easier. It was just to one side of the front door so people could go there separately and get things they would not need a prescription for but also they had privacy if they needed it as Agatha had wisely curtained off a small space so that people could confide in her. The two doctors were grateful for this initiative. It made their work so much easier.

Agatha therefore moved into the Hilda House with them though she went back to see her father at least twice a week. They did not mention Mr Melrose again but Catrin could see how hard it was for the girl that her father disapproved.

The Hilda House therefore became their main place for surgeries though they kept on the Surgery House because some people seemed to find it easier or they didn't want to go elsewhere though it was but a short way. So they split up the surgeries and continued to do them at both houses as best they could.

To Catrin's satisfaction they could now keep people overnight if they were not well. They only had a few beds but it was sufficient to begin with and it made their lives simpler when they did not have to send people home and worry that they would be worse without a doctor or there might be too many calls during the night that they could no longer manage during the days.

It was difficult now because they were both on duty all the time though the house itself was a joy. Once they had got what they wanted there were sufficient rooms to make it a home, a surgery and a tiny hospital and it therefore became part of a dream for them. They even bought a sign and erected it at the front. The Hilda House Hospital. They were so very proud of it and Catrin was glad to be able to make good memories of somewhere she had hated when she was sixteen. It felt like a personal triumph for her but also she and Roddy and Eileen and Agatha were now a team and she was proud of all they were doing.

Eileen did not move into the Hilda House because her family lived in the village but it seemed to Catrin that winter that the four of them were always there. They ate their meals when they had time, they discussed the patients and treatment. They became a single unit and very efficient, at least that was what Roddy said and Catrin thought.

Eileen believed that cleanliness was the most important

thing of all and insisted on high standards but a lot of these women were or had been miners' wives, daughters and sisters and had always had to fight against the coal dust and the general dirt, trying to keep their children fit and well, their hands washed, their faces scrubbed and their clothes out there on the line no matter what cold wind blew.

Catrin had begun to believe in cold. It was the doctor's friend in so many ways so she did not begrudge it. There was a saying that up on the tops it was nine months of winter and three months of cold weather and it could be true but she thought it made her more appreciative of the days when the sun ruled the sky. People made the best of it and took their chairs outside and sat on the front step, chatting to their neighbours, admiring how wonderful the day had been and watching the sun set beyond the houses. The weather was not the same two days running so they never took it for granted.

Not everybody was pleased at Eileen's work or her swift promotion. It had not occurred to Catrin that Eileen's mother would object. Her aunt had been so eager for them to take on the young woman. When Mrs Green came for some remedy for her swollen ankles she told Catrin that work was all very well but she did wish their Eileen could find a nice man to marry.

'She's not the best of the bunch of course,' Mrs Green said, 'she was never a looker and always thought far too much of herself for any lad to like her. Lads don't like a lass who is full of her own ideas. It's not natural. I did try to tell her but she would move away. I worried about her that much. Living in a big place like Newcastle with nobbut a room in somebody's house and nobody to call her own. I was glad when she came back but I didn't realize you would want her here all day and all night and even at the weekends. If she did attract some lad he would never stand for that. I wish she had been more like me and less like her father's family. I was the bonniest of all us four girls, everybody said so. Eileen takes after her father's family and they were never anything to look at.'

One of John Reed's cottagers had an accident at the pit and word was sent for Doctor Morgan to go as soon as he could. Roddy had already gone out, it was the middle of the morning and so Catrin went off to discover that Mr Dunstan was not there. A tall fair-haired man was in the office and he had the cottager, Ron Peters, with his foot up on a chair while the rest of him was sitting at what was Mr Dunstan's desk.

'Dr Morgan how good of you,' the fair man said. 'I'm William Armstrong, the new deputy manager. Mr Peters has had a huge piece of coal dropped on his foot, I'm afraid.'

'It's not that bad,' Mr Peters said. He obviously came from that branch of the male sex who would never admit they were in pain but Catrin could see on his face the effort it took not to wince from time to time and he was very pale.

Catrin examined the foot and decided that Mr Peters had broken several of his toes. She gave him painkillers and advised him to go home. Mr Armstrong offered to take him in his car. Hardly anybody in the village had a car but when Mr Armstrong helped Mr Peters to limp out of the office Catrin saw that the car was very small and so old that it was rusting badly, but it was still the best form of transport for their problem.

Mr Armstrong treated Mr Peters almost as well as she or Roddy would have done, he was so very kind as though Mr Peters was his family. Catrin remembered she had been told about the new deputy manager. How different he was from Jack Dunstan. He sounded educated and had that sort of no accent that rich people usually had and his father owned huge pits apparently over on the coast. What then was he doing here with Jack Dustan's pit which while big for the area was very small compared to the pits by the sea? A lot of men had made fortunes from such ventures but Will Armstrong was a sort she had not met before. He was kinder than Jack and more gentle, but thin and his clothes though worn were good as though he had had them for a long time. She was interested in him and wished she could talk to him but there was no chance of that now as he went off with Mr Peters.

Catrin had promised to call in some days later to check on how Mr Peters was getting on and when she got there Jack Dunstan was in the house.

She hadn't seen him or spoken to him since the October Sunday dinner and didn't expect to see him there since he was not known for his benevolence.

'Doctor Morgan,' Jack Dunstan acknowledged her with a nod of his head but no smile.

Ron Peters was hobbling about with a stick while Mrs Peters was hovering about the pit owner and giving him tea and cake and she offered the same to Catrin who had had a heavy week and was grateful for the tea. The atmosphere was strained. Ron was very white-faced, his wife was not much better and Mr Dunstan ate his cake in silence. When he left she went with him.

'I met your deputy manager when I went to see Mr Peters at the pit.'

'Will is very useful to have around,' Jack Dunstan said. 'His father has pits near Sunderland but he wouldn't pay Will and then got rid of him. He's the youngest of four and is very disappointed about it. So I got him here and he's a big help. He's very good at what he does.

'I've given Ron Peters an office job until he stops limping. For such a clumsy man he has a decent brain. Let's hope he doesn't make a mess of things.' Catrin could not help but wish that Jack Dunstan would need her help on a personal basis and she would have the choice of whether to give him painkillers. She said as much to Roddy later and in the privacy of their own fireside Roddy laughed but said, softly,

'He's a nasty bugger.' The only time her brother swore was when nobody was there but she and even then he was usually restrained.

'He is providing our coal,' Catrin said.

'And three people had to die to get that,' Roddy said, which she knew was unfair and unjust, but neither of them were feeling particularly friendly towards the pit owner.

She got to thinking and asked Eileen if she had met Mr Dunstan's wife.

'I haven't. I don't know anything about her. I don't think they have any children and even though they live in the biggest house in the area they don't have any kind of help. Nobody is ever invited there and as far as I know he goes nowhere but the pit. I'm surprised he came to your dinner.'

'I invited them both but he didn't say anything about it. He has awful manners.'

Catrin couldn't stop thinking about what Jack Dustan's

wife would be like. She walked past the house and was there when the local grocer dropped off supplies. Usually there was conversation between grocer and home owner, but she could clearly see that the door did not open and that the food was left on the doorstep or beyond the gates if they were locked. Catrin wanted to stay and see what would happen but she thought that she would be noticed.

It was a very good-looking house, strong and sturdy, but if the gates were closed you could not see inside. Whether she had been noticed she had no idea but always after that when she came past the gates she could see nothing. There was a huge wall around the garden as though the man was obsessed with his privacy.

It was silent in a special sort of way.

'You're making this up,' Roddy accused her when she talked to him about it over the fire.

'What do you mean?'

'Just because he's rude to you and you don't think he treats his men well you think he's murdered his wife.'

'I don't think anything of the kind.'

'Then what do you think?'

'I don't know. What if he does treat her badly?'

'He won't be the first.'

'But somebody ought to find out.'

'I don't see how that can be done.'

'Why did he come to our dinner? He could have cried

off but he didn't. I hate mysteries,' Catrin said. 'There has to be a way round it.'

The more Catrin mentioned Mrs Dunstan the more worried she became. What if he kept his wife locked in the cellar or had so cowed her that she didn't want to go out? The tradesmen's bills went to Mr Dunstan's office and were paid that way she discovered but a lot of businessmen did the same.

She realized that her Sunday dinner had been not just unusual for Jack Dunstan but unique. Mrs Clements always knew everything about everybody and was eager to talk about them. He went to work and then he went home. He had gone to church that once then not again and his wife did not leave the house. He seemed to have no family and neither did she. Nobody knew where they had come from ten years ago and they had no friends and then she thought of Will Armstrong. The two men had known one another for a long while, she thought, so perhaps Mr Armstrong knew more about them but then she had barely met him and could not ask.

In the end Catrin went to Jack Dunstan's office, asked for a meeting and was told to come back by his secretary. When she went again he was not there so she made another appointment and in the end she got to him by waiting for him to go to the pit office and there she followed him inside. It was early and to her relief his secretary was not yet at work.

'I've been trying to get hold of you,' she said.

'I'm very busy.'

'So am I.'

He went through into his own office and would have closed the door but that Catrin made it impossible for him though she was rather scared. He was a lot bigger than she was and they were alone with the doors closed. He was a most unpleasant man. Perhaps he would turn upon her.

They stood facing one another like gladiators and his eyes were wary and hard.

'I want to ask you something, Mr Dunstan.'

When he saw that she wasn't going to go away he looked at her, quite steadily and said in a low voice,

'And what would that be?'

'I want to know why you came to my dinner party?'

He hesitated and his voice softened slightly as though it was a happy memory.

'Because you asked me.'

'But you came alone and didn't say why your wife was not there. Usually people are polite enough to say that their wife is ill or has some other reason for not responding to a social event.'

'I don't think my private life is any of your business, Doctor Morgan. Perhaps I was rude in not having said that my wife could not be there. If so you will have to forgive me.'

'Your wife is one of my patients. That makes her my business and since nobody ever sees her I would like to make sure that she has come to no harm.'

Catrin was shaking with fear now. Her hands trembled. To her surprise he answered her.

'My wife doesn't care to go out or to see people. She is entitled to her privacy, you know.'

'So you haven't murdered her?'

Catrin wasn't sure that she had meant to say such a thing. And even more amazed when he said in a very soft almost amused voice,

'I haven't thrown her body in the river, nor have I beaten her. Now, perhaps you could go away.'

She knew that but for her dinner party he would have been a lot more difficult to deal with. Even so she caught at her breath.

'I just want to make sure that she is all right. If she needs any help—'

He sat down abruptly and at that moment Miss Waskerly walked in and after that Catrin left, angry, frustrated and feeling so stupid that she could have hit herself.

'You didn't go and see him, Cat? You idiot,' her brother said. 'Just because you don't like the man does not mean he is abusing his wife and even if he were—'

'Even if he were what?'

'There isn't a great deal you could do about it.'

'I would think of something.'

'He told you he wasn't doing anything like that. Why should he be a liar?'

'There is something wrong, I just know it.'

'There are plenty of people who have things wrong with them and they come to us. You will have to give him the benefit of the doubt.'

'Why did he come to the dinner then and without her?'

'I don't know and neither do you so leave the man alone.'

That week Catrin went back to see how Mr Peters was getting along and he was much better. He was sitting on his front step in the sunshine.

'Doctor Morgan.' He smiled at her and urged her to sit down with him. 'Prudie has just gone in to make a pot of tea.'

Their door was open and his wife had heard Catrin and soon came out with cups of tea and big pieces of fruitcake she had made. It was moist and very good and Catrin enjoyed sitting in the sunshine there with them, pleased to know that he was getting better.

Catrin went inside with her to help taking in the crockery and quietly there Mrs Peters said,

'Was it you who paid the butcher's bill? I don't like to

ask but when I went in to tell him that I needed more time he told me that it had been paid.'

Catrin felt ashamed now but she couldn't pay everybody's bills.

'Do you think it was Mr Dunstan?'

Mrs Peters shook her head.

'That man has never given anybody anything.'

'Who else could it be?'

'Well it might be the new man but I can't see why. We barely know him but I am so glad of it. He's such a nice person and they do say he comes from wealth though you wouldn't know it but for his lovely voice.

'We grow what we can and the garden is still producing fruit and vegetables each year thank goodness but meat is dear and Ron needs it. Yesterday the butcher's boy came and there were lamb chops and steak – I never order such things, we can't afford them. We have a bit of mince and now and then I buy some stewing steak. I told him to take them back but he said the bill was paid and I must have them or Mr Cookson would be offended and nobody was to pay their bills twice over.'

This mystified the two doctors and only inspired Catrin more to find out what was going on.

Twelve

That winter Catrin was aware that Jack Dunstan was not at work on some days and that was new. That was probably why he had hired an under-manager. She half hoped that he would call her in and that his wife needed her help but the explanation was that because he had help he was taking a little time off which apparently he had never done before, according to Mrs Clements.

It was the Christmas carol service when Catrin and Roddy went to church and saw John Reed there with Amy Snow. It was their first appearance as a couple that Catrin knew of and she also knew that if they had been out and about before this Mrs Clements would have known of it.

Anne concentrated hard on her hymn book as the first carol began. Catrin had not forgotten that Anne had been worried about her brother and Amy from the day that they met formally at the Hilda House dinner. Catrin was pleased for them though John looked anything but happy and Amy barely glanced up except when the vicar addressed the congregation.

A pale sun shone and it was not long before the parishioners were outside, wishing one another a merry Christmas. Roddy and Catrin had been asked for dinner to the vicarage and she was glad to see that John and Amy and Anne were going too. They stood over the sitting room fire drinking sherry before the meal and she said hello and smiled at them but when Amy got caught up in conversation with somebody else she asked John how Anne's health was.

'You always ask me about her.'

'I am always aware that she finds her life difficult. It's very nice seeing you with Amy.'

He hesitated and then to her surprise looked at her and said frankly,

'Thanks. I have become very fond of her but then I need her money. Things are tighter than ever. If she didn't have money I wouldn't be able to marry her.'

'You are going to get married then?'

'She's thinking about it.'

Privately Catrin wondered about people who didn't know their own minds. Did Amy think that John wanted her only for her money? She was young and beautiful and she too must be lonely. When they had eaten she and Amy sat apart from the others and talked softly and Amy said,

'I don't know whether I can marry John. I would like to be Lady Reed, of course, what woman wouldn't but his sister doesn't like me.'

'I suppose that's inevitable. They've been on their own since their mother died and Anne has been running the house for years. Won't she learn to like you?'

It seemed strange to Catrin that she was talking to the woman who if things went well would be more of a mother to Anne than a sister-in-law.

'I'm not sure. I was an only one and my marriage was child free so I'm not sure how to go on with her.'

'Just be as kind as you can, I would think.'

'John says she likes Albert and Penny but since I have become close to John it's like she doesn't want to leave us by ourselves which makes it hard. It's easier for me when she isn't there but I think she is probably comparing me with John's mother and though I didn't know her I think I come out of it badly. His mother, so everybody tells me, was a real lady from the south with a posh accent and from a very high up family. My father was a grocer in Spennymoor and my mother cleaned other folks' houses. John is clever and well born and has been brought up so differently than me. He knows so much that I feel stupid and he reads all sort of very clever books. Also I don't think he would marry me if I was penniless and that upsets me.'

'He has a lot on his plate with all the farms and trying to keep everything together. I suppose he is obliged to be practical. I think he's always had financial problems but he hasn't asked anyone else to marry him as far as I know. And he knows Lily Bell.'

The attempt at humour made Amy smile.

'Lily has never had eyes for anyone other than your brother and even she has learned to accept that he isn't interested. The idea of marrying John still worries me. What if it turns to be a bad mistake? His father was a nasty man by all accounts.'

'People say John is nothing like him.'

'I think a man always takes things from his father, good or bad.'

After they had eaten, Catrin tried to talk to Anne when Amy was there but it was difficult because Amy was nervous and said all the wrong things.

'I keep telling Anne that it will be good for her to have another mother,' Amy gushed.

'I had a perfectly good mother,' Anne said. 'A sister-in-law is hardly the same thing.'

Amy said nothing for a few moments and then ventured,

'I want us to be close. We could go to Newcastle to shop for new clothes and perhaps stay over. You always seem to wear the same dress and if you don't mind me saying so you are far too young to wear black. It makes you look dowdy, like a little old woman.'

'I altered that dress for my mother's funeral.'

Amy tried again.

'But of course she wasn't your real mother, was she, so perhaps you will be ready to move on and will let me be there for you.'

Anne lifted pitiful eyes to Catrin and Catrin hesitated. She barely knew what to say. Yes, Amy was making a hash of this but she knew nothing of children and had lost her husband at sea so she was not at her best either. Amy looked helplessly at her and her eyes glistened with tears.

Just then John also came over and Amy clutched his arm and they moved away.

'I can't stand her,' Anne said. 'She's what people call "common" and I think John likes her money rather than her. She doesn't know how to use a knife and fork properly and she drops her aitches. She's embarrassing and always says the wrong thing. I don't know how John will put up with her and I feel like running away.'

'I think she is doing her best.'

'If that's her best what will we do after they get married? You do know they are getting married?'

'I had heard.'

'I think if John had wanted to marry somebody nice, maybe you, then I would have felt differently but she is just so awful.'

Catrin was pleased for the compliment and realised that she had been giving this problem a lot more thought than she had allowed herself to express. She would be a better support to Anne than Amy and she thought that the time had come for her to tell Anne what she suspected. It could make things better all round. On the other hand, it could always make things worse but she wanted a claim in this girl's life because she had grown up completely and was beyond the needing of it. She didn't want Anne to have to live with just this couple especially while she felt that Amy would fill John's life so completely that there was no place by his side and Anne would take a smaller role in his house where she had been virtual mistress for some time now.

She was reassured that this was the right time to say what she could and took Anne aside.

They went into the little sitting room, where nobody was at present, on their own and she sat Anne down and told her and the girl stared at her all the way through the speech and only when Catrin had finished talking to her did she say,

'You left me?'

'I wouldn't have done it. I would never have done such a thing. I would have given anything to have my child. I can't be sure of it because there don't seem to be any records but I would like to think it so. I was sixteen and had nowhere else to go and not a penny to my name.'

Anne was silent for so long that Catrin started to regret having said anything, too much or too little, and then the girl looked at her and her face shone.

'Even if you aren't sure I think it's wonderful that I might have had a real mother before Mama. I loved her so much and now there is nobody to hold on to.'

'You can hold on to me.'

'Oh, and do you think I might be clever like you?'

The moment the words were out they both started to smile.

'You don't need to be like anybody else. You are you and that's the best you could be.'

'And I will try to be nice to Mrs Snow. Do I have to tell them about us?'

'Not until I find out whether it's true.'

'I think I would rather not know, just in case you aren't my real mother and I would like it just to be a secret between us.'

And Catrin had the joy of having this girl who might have been hers throw her arms around Catrin and press her close. Long afterwards she shut her eyes and enjoyed that moment again and again and was so pleased for just for once something was working out.

John and Amy were to be married in April. Everybody was talking about it. Catrin soon found an excuse to go to Castle Hall. One of the cottagers' wives was having a baby and she had lost the one before so Catrin was keeping an eye on her. She was going along well but having miscarried once it was natural that she should worry up to the period of twelve weeks and Catrin was able to be reassuring. The baby was growing and she was eating and sleeping and looked very well.

Anne was inside and Amy was there too and John. Catrin was astonished. The house was being pulled to pieces, there were workmen in all the rooms.

'She handed over to him all her money,' Anne confided in a whisper in the hall, any noise they were making drowned out by the sawing and banging.

'The old place is looking better already,' John had said, obviously very happy that he was able to do necessary work.

Catrin didn't like to point out that many of the cottages were in a bad way and that he had said that his tenants must come first. Was all this really necessary? She had to tell herself that it was none of her business but she was obliged to curb her sharp tongue which she knew was one of her worst faults and go outside into the bitterly cold day. Anne followed her.

'I think John has lost his mind,' his sister confided. 'It is making them happy though. We are having a car delivered and the plans for them to go away after the wedding have been extended. Amy has ordered carpets and curtains and all kinds of furniture from a shop in London who sent her a catalogue. She is throwing out all the lovely furniture which was my mother's. I am trying to like her, I really am, because I know I must be as kind as I can but it's all so hard.'

Catrin assured her that it would get easier and once they had sorted out the house and the wedding and such like John would remember his plans.

'I don't think he really cares for her,' Anne said 'And I don't think she is sure either. She certainly doesn't like me. I think she's jealous of how close I am to Johnnie. She insisted on throwing out my oak desk which came from London when my mother married. She sold it for a good price, I know, and is now putting dreadful modern wooden furniture into my room, including a kidney-shaped dressing table with three mirrors and a lace cloth between the glass and the top. And all the furniture in my bedroom is now pink, like I was a little girl. I think that's what she wants me to be so that I might figure less in Johnnie's affections. As though she could ever push me out.'

Catrin wished that Anne was still a little girl, something she had never been as far as she knew and she was sorry. Every child needed a childhood and so many had no chance.

'I'm sure she means it for the best,' Catrin said.

'Yes, of course.' Anne had not forgotten her promise and they smiled a little at one another before Catrin went back to the Hilda House.

There was a huge party for new year and the first week

of January at Castle Hall, though where the friends had come from who gathered at the Hall Catrin had no idea. John had even bought several hunters and had hunted often that autumn so perhaps he had made friends among the hunting and shooting set. Amy didn't hunt, she said she was afraid of horses, but she liked her husband to hunt. Now he would be the man he was meant to be, she believed. The festivities at the hall went on for almost two weeks and after that the preparations for the honeymoon to most of Europe were set in motion and the days crept towards the wedding.

Only what were thought of as the best people in the village had been invited and a lot of people Catrin did not recognize but there was not one cottager or his family. John seemed blinded by his new wealth.

By then the hall had been made over, as it was called and gleamed, it was so clean. Maids in black and white uniform were everywhere. Expensive hothouse flowers bedecked every surface. The books in the study, the German ones presumably Catrin thought, had gone and the walls had been stripped of oak bookcases and papered with huge poppies. The furniture was light and a lot less severe than the dark oak which had been before, Amy told Catrin and Catrin was called upon to admire it when Amy as the bride-to-be invited her to see what had been done. She showed it all with pride, and Catrin pretended to like the thin flimsy curtains which would never keep out the howling gales. She saw the bedroom where Lady Reed had breathed her last and it was all new so that there seemed nothing left of the old lady. Perhaps it was for the best, that John and Amy would stand a better chance of happiness having everything fresh here, at least she hoped so.

Anne was a bridesmaid at the wedding and was wearing pink satin which did not suit her but she was doing her best and did not complain. Amy wore blue and John of course was in a morning suit as were the ushers and the best man, whom Catrin didn't recognize. She saw Mr and Mrs Swan and the vicar and his wife afterwards at the reception. Mr Armstrong was there too, representing Mr Dunstan.

'He needed a rest,' Mr Armstrong told Catrin and Roddy.

Roddy didn't make friends easily especially after having come unstuck with the Sutherland family but Will Armstrong was such a cheerful open person that Roddy rather liked him, Catrin could tell. She was glad that he joined in for once. After losing Fred in Edinburgh her brother had been reluctant to talk to anyone but Will was easy in manner and they started going to the local pubs when they had time.

She and Anne did not stick closely together on the day of the wedding but the bond between them assured Catrin that the girl cared for her and they sent smiles in one another's direction every so often and it did make life a lot easier.

Catrin tried to be careful when she talked to Will about the Dunstans and was rewarded by a slight shrug from him.

'I think Una is inclined to be reclusive. When they first married they were so happy but her parents didn't approve and that makes things difficult and Jack's family are all dead so they had nobody to lean on. I think I've made it easier coming here and I do like it. Everyone is so kind.'

Catrin thought this had a great deal to do with the way that Will Armstrong was so ready to like people.

'I have three brothers, all older. Herbert is a headmaster, Paul is a barrister and Lloyd is about to become a bishop. My brothers are all married and I have so many nieces and nephews that I can barely count them all.'

This was so obviously not true but Catrin liked him the better for his modesty. It sounded to her as though he felt left out and she remembered Jack saying that Will's father was disappointed in him. Surely things other than his achievements mattered though Jack had also said that Will was a good pit manager and she thought his father ought to have been aware of that.

'You have known Jack and Una quite a long time,' she said, hoping to gain more information. Will hesitated and then he said,

'I was very much in love with her but she wouldn't have me. I didn't intend to come here but he appealed to my better nature. I think they need to spend more time together and the pit is too much for one man. I wanted to say no to him but he's always been good to me and things weren't going well at home.'

Anne came across to them at that point and he told her how beautiful she looked in her pink gown whereas Anne looked quizzically at him and said boldly,

'Mr Armstrong, you are fibbing. It's a horrible dress and I shall give it away to the first girl I see, only I doubt anyone would wear it.'

Catrin was so pleased to find Anne happy though she would loved to have asked why Will's home life was so difficult that he had been relieved to be gone. It has obviously influenced his decision to come here. But loving another man's wife? It had not occurred to her that such things happened though it was obvious now that it did. Did Will love her still after all this time?

Catrin felt the blow and she had not realized until then that she was beginning to think this man was special not just to other people but also to her and now this mysterious woman had him. Not content with one man she had taken another. Catrin couldn't make it out.

Thirteen

By May the front of the Surgery House at one side had become a chemist's shop as well as the one within the Hilda Hospital and it was useful because it made money. It had seemed like an excellent idea at first with bigger windows to display goods and Mr Melrose made several journeys to help Agatha set up the second shop in the same way that he had done his, only Catrin could see that he liked his own ideas better than Agatha's and it was frustrating for her when she was trying to go forward on her own.

They did need another chemist but not Mr Melrose. He had put an assistant into his shop in Stanhope, he reassured Catrin when she felt he had outstayed his welcome. Catrin knew that he was lonely and did not manage well by himself. The few times he did venture back to Stanhope for a few days when he came back he was always unkempt now that he was living alone and talked too much.

Also Mr Melrose was making no secret of the fact that he liked Eileen very much.

'Eileen. How well you look,' he exclaimed with joy, his whole face lighting up when he came across her one day as he and Agatha had finished with the day's prescriptions..

'Mr Melrose,' Eileen said, smiling just a little.

'Eileen used to come and stay with her auntie when she was a small girl and I was getting ready to go to learn chemistry,' Mr Melrose said.

'You taught me a lot about medicine and such.'

'I don't think I did. I think you were a natural and now you have found your chosen profession. I'm so pleased for you and your auntie would have been delighted. You were her favourite and used to help her a lot in her shop.'

Proudly Mr Melrose talked about Agatha, and Agatha and Eileen became good friends. Catrin was glad of it, but Agatha needed him to go back to his own shop and if the people around her helped in whatever way it would make her life the richer.

Agatha began to stock useful items connected with health so that people could aid themselves when the matter was not important. There were bandages, salves, various mixtures which had been devised by the doctors and with her father so cough medicine, throat lozenges, soothing lotions and antiseptic balms were all available. She kept all kinds of baby equipment, bottles with teats, baby shampoo and talcum powder, baby oil to soothe nappy rash and various sore spots which babies tended to have and skin creams for adults, bath salts and loofahs, sponges and facecloths. Agatha's shop was an interesting place to visit. Catrin loved to go in to see what else Agatha had thought of. Also it made all their lives much easier when Agatha could give help and advice and people soon learned to trust her.

Catrin and Roddy by this time had more work than they could cope with since they were setting up different kinds of clinics. A mother and baby clinic was the first thing and a special children's surgery. All this meant extra work but they knew that in the long term it would keep the population of the village healthy, useful and prosperous.

The small hospital took up an increasing amount of time and they had a separate area for suffers of tuberculosis which had been called consumption because people who suffered from it tended to lose a lot of weight. Luckily the air up there on the tops was said to be like champagne and a great help in such cases.

Mr Benson's wife, Felicity, had begun growing herbs and medicinal plants and she taught Catrin and Roddy about these. She was writing a book, which she had illustrated simply, and the local publisher and printer Alan Barclay had promised to produce this for her. She thought that various ailments could be helped if not cured by what people ate and drank and what they put into their bodies and Catrin and Roddy were certain that she was right.

The various libraries round about had ordered copies, so had the doctors in a wide area and there would be copies on sale for general use. Also Mrs Benson had begun selling herbs and medicinal plants for people's gardens. She had a stall right beside the Hilda House Hospital just outside her big walled garden. Mr Benson had it repaired and put greenhouses into the sheltered corners. The greenhouses had stoves in them with pipes which ran around the walls so the seeds and plants were able to thrive during the months of frosts and snow and ice. Now that the bad weather was over they would begin to plant out the various remedies.

Catrin learned to love the way that Mrs Benson had created her garden, in diamond shapes, oblongs or squares, with raised beds or special hedges and with the weather so much improved they would thrive out in the warm air.

Catrin felt like celebrating warm weather and sunshine in a bigger way this year because they had achieved so much. Roddy took it personally when he could not cure a patient or when that patient had the same illness over and over again. He complained when people smoked pipes or cigarettes but it was still widely believed that smoking was good for the lungs and also it was believed to make people feel better in their nerves.

'It's a bad drug,' Roddy would argue and Catrin had to steer him away from his favourite subject when they were in company as he seemed to take the whole thing personally

'How can it be good for them swilling ale, hardly able to make it home to their beds and spending money which is badly needed for their families.' Since there were a good many public houses in the village Catrin begged him not to talk about this for fear of giving offence. Once started up on one of his hobbyhorses Roddy got heated and angry.

'It isn't good for your heart and you know it,' she told him. Sometimes he was ill himself and it was because he tried to do too much, he did not rest enough, sleep sufficiently or eat enough to please her.

'You are turning Methodist on me,' she said.

'There is nothing wrong with Methodism,' Roddy declared though he always went to the parish church on Sundays. 'It's other people's fitness I worry about.'

Sometimes he was so quiet and tired that she despaired of him.

'People also have to do things which are good for them in other ways and I don't think a few pints of beer on a Saturday night matters,' she told him. Roddy was having none of it.

He scowled at patients who wouldn't take his advice. Sometimes he seemed so old to Catrin in his views and ideas. She wished he would find some sort of a social life. They had been so busy that he had stopped going out. Will sometimes called on him to go to the pub but Roddy was becoming too aware of himself as the doctor in the village and the few times he went out they went to the local farmers' pub and there Will drank beer and Roddy, to everyone's horror, drank lemonade.

'He's letting the side down,' Will whispered to Catrin and made her giggle.

Amongst Roddy's new ideas was that he wanted women having babies to go to the hospital to be checked regularly and to come into the hospital to give birth. He didn't trust the way that some women used to go to others to be helped rather than coming to him or to Catrin or Eileen. He took everything to heart. A lot of them hated the little hospital and wouldn't discuss the matter.

Some didn't see Catrin or Eileen or Roddy at all during their pregnancies and Roddy would just have to live with that. He hated last-minute emergencies in such matters and thought that most things could be avoided if care was taken at the right time. Eileen privately thought that women who were perfectly healthy took up hospital beds when they didn't need them. Roddy was a man with several missions and wore himself out trying to fulfil these. No woman should have a difficult time at giving birth was his mantra.

'I won't let them die of neglect,' he said.

He had become such a good doctor, Catrin thought,

much better than his earlier untried views of such things but he kept nothing back for himself and it concerned her. He took no notice of anything she told him and sometimes his hands would shake in the evenings and his breathing became uneven. She had talked to him about it very often and had to be content to hold her peace.

Towards the end of May he went out on a cold, wet night and got back just before midnight soaked to the skin. Catrin tried to make him stay in bed the following day but he wouldn't.

Two days later he collapsed and had to be carried to a hospital bed. Catrin was horrified, it was the last thing that she would ever have thought of. Catrin and Eileen nursed him devotedly but pneumonia developed and he was feverish with a cough and hard-won breaths. Catrin wished and wished that the weather was better but the cold rain didn't stop and was followed by a searing wind from the fell. She and Roddy had put in place such a good system but within days of him having taken ill it became over-stretched and she hardly had chance to sleep. She tried to give time off to Eileen and Agatha and the other people who cleaned and nursed and worked for her. She also tried to keep them away from Roddy so that he should get better in quiet and comfort.

She was also worried that she could end up ill and useless herself and then where would they be? The idea haunted her so much that she found sleeping and eating and trying to keep regular habits and times more difficult than ever.

Catrin thought of how she would not be able to manage if her brother died, not just with the hospital but in her life. He was the most important person of all. She could spend very little time now looking after him because she was the only doctor in the place but it was a fight between her work for the area and her love for him, also trying to keep the others from him, especially Eileen who was obsessed with cleanliness, hand washing and wearing a mask when she went near anybody who was ill. This, she insisted, would keep her well and to be fair it did.

Catrin tried to reason with herself that she had Eileen and Agatha, Mrs Clements and Mr Melrose, good people all of them but none of them could fill Roddy's role and she was soon beyond tired. She slept fitfully face down on the bed, without even taking off her clothes.

Agatha and Eileen kindly took shifts to see to Roddy, and Eileen insisted that Catrin should go and lie down halfway through the afternoon.

'You look ready to drop,' she said. Ten minutes later Eileen had to come and disturb her. A farmer two miles away had badly cut his hand. It was his fingers. He was a very big man and had fainted with pain. His young son told Catrin that they were half cut off and although his mother had been able to staunch the blood, he needed attention as soon as possible. Catrin could not stay here now.

Mr Benson saddled the mare and she went off with the farmer's son alongside on his pony through a cold foggy afternoon. The little grey buildings were lit and the farmer's son took the horses into the stables while Catrin hurried into the house. The son was right, Mr Rippon had almost lost two fingers, a lot of blood, but she did what she could and it was well done. It could have been worse, the fingers were still attached by tendons and muscles so she was hopeful. She began to stitch them back, giving the man as much painkiller as she dared. She was not sure whether he would ever have use of that hand again and it was his right. He had been chopping wood.

She wished so much that Roddy had been able to do this. His stitching was neater than hers and she believed more effective. A farmer with a useless right hand was going to be in a bad way.

Luckily the farmer's wife and son were calm, sensible people and when Catrin declared that she could do no more and must get back Mrs Rippon looked gravely at her and showed her the way that the darkness had come down and the fog had become so thick that it would be dangerous to go through it. They had managed to get Mr Rippon as far as the farmhouse kitchen and now he was unconscious and lying there on an old sofa.

'I must get back to my brother,' Catrin said. 'He isn't well.'

'Doctor Morgan, you cannot go out in that. People get lost in weather like this up here and I would never forgive myself for letting you suffer because you had to come and aid us.'

Catrin knew that she was right but it was a dismal way to spend the night, worrying though she knew the others would do as much as she could. She sat by the fire, unable to eat any of the good food which was pressed on her. She drank tea and tried to talk , but even though they gave her a comfortable bed and a fire, she lay there waiting for the dawn and when it finally arrived the fog lifted.

Only the injured man slept, for Catrin had put him out of pain. His wife and son were too upset even to go to their beds. The mare had been well looked after. Catrin thanked them and made her way home as quickly as good sense would allow.

She was so relieved when she got there and Mr Benson settled the mare down for her and looked after the animal's needs and Catrin, almost frantic, calling herself names because she had left her brother, went into the Hilda House. Catrin hoped and prayed that Roddy was a little better, but she knew the moment she saw Eileen's face that Roddy had not survived. Eileen stood still at the bottom of the stairs.

'He knew nothing about it, Doctor Morgan. We did the best we could but he died so very softly.'

Catrin tried to believe her. The idea that her brother had died desperate for breath and in panic stayed in her mind for many a long day.

'I ought to have been here.'

'Even you can't be in two places at once,' Agatha said.

Roddy looked as though he was asleep but she was looking at him through her sister spectacles, not with her doctor's gaze. He was so young to die, far too young, she thought, so young and at what cost not only to her but to the whole village.

Her head told her that she had done all that she could. Her heart found her guilty and wanting and neglectful but still the following day she went back to High Hill Farm. Mr Rippon had actually opened his eyes. She thought he was beginning to get better.

Mrs Rippon didn't need to ask about Roddy. She could see the message in Catrin's eyes and understood.

The first thing that Catrin wanted was to run to Roddy for comfort, to tell him that her world had fallen apart but of course she couldn't. It was a feeling that she must try to get used to. Her world had ended because he was not there. The difference between someone ill and someone dead was the worst thing that had ever happened to her. The world was shattered and empty now. She looked for him everywhere. Disbelief filled her.

Every moment he was not there and every moment she had to remind herself that he was not in the surgery, not out on his rounds, not waiting for her in the evenings by the fire.

The world was a great big empty shell and there was nowhere to run and nobody to run to. Other people ate and slept and moved about. She did nothing and yet her life was filled with space.

Susan and Tony came to see her together. Everybody said how sorry they were. People left flowers on her doorstep. Somebody left a big ham. Dozens of notes were put through the door, falling in piles on the floor. Boxes of vegetables were brought. Mrs Clements took in several pots with cooked casseroles, bags of fresh bread, fruitcakes in tins and little boxes of freshly made biscuits and butterfly cakes in little coloured cases. John Reed sent her fish, pigeons and rabbits. It somehow did not matter that she could not eat. The food was eaten at the funeral tea and everybody in the village came to the service, afterwards flooding through the big rooms at the Hilda House Hospital. Catrin could not close her eyes at night to find any relief in sleep.

The first positive thing that happened was that Will came to see her.

She badly wanted to throw herself into his arms for comfort but she couldn't do it.

She let go in front of him to a certain extent.

'I will never forgive myself for not being here when he needed me,' she said.

Will shook his head.

'You had to do your duty and he would have wanted you to be there for your patient.'

She put both hands up to her face and Will came over and took her into his arms. He did it very gently so that she should not mistake his intention but she found herself clinging as she had always sworn she would not do to a man. She wanted never to let go of him.

'Call on me, I'll be there for you,' he promised her and she had to stop herself from crying.

She was never tired. She had to be reminded that she had surgeries, twice as many as before because she wandered about unsure of what she was trying to do. She had so much to deal with but Agatha and Eileen took as much of the strain as they could, dealing with the lesser medical problems, trying to lighten her load.

Mr Melrose came to help them but he fussed so much that they would have been better without him. Also he haunted Eileen's days to the point where she seemed always to leave a room when he came into it. He had a habit of telling everybody what to do as though now he was the only man with any medical knowledge he knew better than everyone else which Catrin found infuriating. To have to listen to his theories on everything they had to deal with exasperated her and this, along with her constant grief for Roddy, made her impatient and bad tempered. Must he explain himself in such a roundabout way? She knew that Agatha was embarrassed too as Mr Melrose thought he had become the most important person at the Hilda House Hospital.

Fourteen

Anne was living alone with servants all this time at the hall. Catrin would ask her to come and stay and especially now she thought it would have been lovely to have Anne around her but she felt that the girl didn't want to leave the house where she had known some happiness when Lady Reed was still alive. Perhaps Anne felt that she would not be happy anywhere else or that somehow she would be betraying the old lady. Also, hard as it was, Catrin wanted Anne to make her own decisions. To ask her to make such a big decision and for someone else's benefit at this stage would be damaging so she held back although she wished more and more that Anne would come and live with her, but she also told herself that she was lonely without her brother and that was not fair.

On the day of Roddy's funeral the rain never stopped as though the day was crying in sympathy. Many people cried also but Catrin stood there dry-eyed, thinking she would never know anything but sorrow again. Her whole body seemed to have dried out. Even her voice had gone hoarse and almost deserted her.

Time lost its meaning. She would wake up and not know what day it was, the days and nights blurred and yet she went on struggling without him.

Life continued as though nothing had happened. Catrin was astonished that it did. She felt as though she couldn't go on but was being made to go forward and had to struggle to keep up. It was so trying. Summer arrived but stupidly Catrin felt as though her life had become a winter without end. Hard frost and ice seemed to encase her stiffened hands and feet and fill her mind so that it numbed. She wondered what she was doing still alive when Roddy was dead. He had not even left a wife or a child so that there might be shared grief or comfort.

At night she envisioned a woman pregnant with his child so that all was not lost, but when the dawn arrived the image and the idea vanished and all she had was the day to go through, yet another day, she counted them one by one, without him.

After Roddy's funeral, despite Will offering to take her, Catrin did not go back to the church for several weeks. She told herself that she was too busy, too tired, too upset. She made all manner of excuses to herself but the truth was that she did not want to go because the funeral had been one of the worst days of her life. She knew that she would get there and see his coffin exactly how it had been and was unsure that she would be able to get through the morning service without breaking down.

She told herself that she would go to evensong but she didn't. As the days moved forward it became harder and harder.

Will would come to the hospital to visit but she didn't want to see him. She didn't want to see anybody. Her thoughts were now of nothing but her brother's death. Susan and Tony came to visit her twice and then left her alone which she thought was wise of them. She had to get used to Roddy's absence. Her days were overflowing with broken bones and childhood ailments and old people with rheumatism and arthritis. She took refuge in her work and hid there. When she did finally go to the Sunday morning service it was almost autumn.

Will had gone back to Sunderland. He called to see her and tell her.

'My father has been taken ill and my mother has sent for me,' he said and he didn't look at her.

'I've never got on with him. He wanted me to be something other than a pitman and I couldn't be the obedient son and give him what he wanted. It's one of the reasons I came here, not just because of Jack and – and Una.'

'I hope he recovers and that you are able to come back here soon,' she said and hugged him before he left. The Sunday after he had gone she made herself go to church. She had been thinking that she would go with him and now that he had left she gave herself a brisk talking-to and walked slowly to the church.

From the moment she stepped inside it was a shock. Nobody bothered with her except for a few general hellos. She shook hands with Tony at the church door when the service was over and all he did was wish her well so that by the time she got back to the Hilda House she was amazed to discover that the rest of the village had gone on without her. It was almost as though Roddy was forgotten or had never existed.

Nobody spoke of him. Nobody asked her anywhere. She had thought that Tony and Susan might have invited her to Sunday dinner but in some ways it was as though her partner and not her brother had died. Although he had not been her husband it was like she was no longer important because she was a woman by herself. She was to them the doctor's sister who just happened to help him, without him she did not earn the same kind of respect. She was astonished, aghast. Most importantly of all, men did not come to see her as patients. She was not a doctor who could help them, it appeared.

Mr Rippon got better though it took a long time. He gained the use of his fingers again and was grateful to her. He apologized for taking her away from her dying brother but she did notice that even here she was not left alone with him.

Her fireside was empty now as it had never been

before. Her life was so much poorer without her brother. Her world was all women and there was no way that she could suggest a man might be brought into it even professionally if any man had wanted to. It would look too bad. It was as though she missed Roddy and Will like they had gone off somewhere together and not come back.

With Will gone it somehow made things harder than ever so when Anne came to see her Catrin had to be careful not to be over effusive. She didn't want the girl to see that it would have helped so much if Anne had moved in.

Amy and John did not come back and she could see how lonely Anne was getting with nobody but the servants and the tenants around her. It seemed to her also that money was not being spent as John had originally intended it to be but so little was heard of that nothing more could be done and she didn't want to worry Anne perhaps unnecessarily at that time.

Mr Melrose was getting harder to deal with. Lately he had been doing more and more of the important prescriptions and sometimes as she went past she could hear him berating Agatha for not getting something right.

Catrin understood that they were all under pressure but Mr Melrose had a loud voice and if people were about they would hear the discord.

'He's always telling me what to do,' Agatha confided. 'He thinks I'm still a child. I can manage much better without him but he doesn't see it. '

'Then you must tell him.'

Agatha looked at her and then away.

'He misses my mother. I'm all he's got. I did think he might ask Eileen to marry him but somehow I don't think she would and he knows it which makes everything worse.'

Only in one way, Catrin thought, for there was no way she could manage without Eileen now and to have Eileen marry Mr Melrose and go back to Stanhope at this point was unthinkable. Catrin was selfish enough to be glad that Eileen couldn't marry Mr Melrose though she felt guilty about it.

'You're an adult. You need to move forward, surely.'

'I know but I can't be nasty to him. He's done everything for me. He worked hard so that I could become a chemist. It was all he wanted for me and all I wanted for myself.'

'And now?'

'I don't know. When you have what you had wanted all your life and your father tries to take it away from you where do you go from there?'

Eileen of course was married but only Catrin knew. Whatever was she to say to this poor man who was trying to get his life back on the tracks it had been on before his wife died or even better that he could go forward into a new relationship. She could see why he liked Eileen, everybody did and of course she could not tell him that while Eileen might want to marry him, he was clever and respected and not much above forty-five, she could not. What a mess, Catrin thought.

Catrin decided she must talk to Eileen since Frank Melrose seemed to be pursuing her and it was not right but she was unsure how to deter him. He could not be told that Eileen was already married but it was causing problems. Eileen wanted to be with her family even though she risked being found by her husband. For her own selfish reasons Catrin needed the support in their work and Eileen needed it possibly against her husband Tel Collings, her family and now Mr Melrose. They talked about what they might do but it seemed to have no solution other than being rude to Mr Melrose. In the end he butted in when they were together. He had been trying to get Eileen by herself for days but the two clung resolutely together so he finally came into Catrin's office and ignoring her he said to Eileen,

'I've been looking for you everywhere. I want to talk to you, preferably alone.'

Eileen didn't look at him but at the floor and she said,

'I can't do that, Francis. I like being here and I know

you have a preference for me but I enjoy my work at the hospital and the surgery. That's all there is to it. I'm just so worn out,' she said, slumping down into one of the three chairs that were provided.

Having got so far he appeared now not to know what to say. He gazed at the free chair but didn't move while he gathered his thoughts.

Catrin gazed down at the big pile of papers on her desk. It might have been polite to leave them to it, but just as she looked up Eileen threw her a glance of desperation so avoiding his eyes she went back to her paperwork even though it danced before her eyes.

'We get on so well,' he said.

'I like it here,' Eileen said, 'having more responsibility. It suits me somehow. I feel like Catrin – Doctor Morgan's right hand.'

This ought to have discouraged him, she thought, but it didn't.

'We've known one another a long time and I have always liked you. Of course when I was married it was different but now that we are both free—' He took a deep breath before he said any more of this so obviously rehearsed speech. 'I have a good business and a pretty house that goes with it. I'm in good health and although I'm older than you I feel that we would deal very well together. I want you to marry me.'

Catrin listened to the silence and heard Eileen hesitate

and she knew that Eileen was trying to do this without hurting him. He waited.

'Mr Melrose, I'm very flattered of course but—'

'Oh, don't turn me down. I know you are younger than me and have a very good job here but I think you would be a huge asset to the shop in Stanhope you are so very good with people and though I ought not to say it I do have a very respectable reputation. I could buy a new house if you feel the one I have now isn't good enough for you. A local builder is building some lovely new houses just at the edge of the village with a view to one side of the river and the other of the hills. It's so pretty, Eileen, say that you will.'

'I'm sorry but the answer will have to be no.' This time Eileen managed to put steel into her voice so that it was flat and forceful. Mr Melrose got up and left the room hastily and the two women let go of their breath and went back to work.

That was not quite the solution. Sometimes, Catrin thought, when you imagined the mire could not get any worse events improved things without you actually doing anything and this began the next day after Mr Melrose's refusal of his hand in marriage and Agatha was the person who set it in motion.

*

'My father told me what has happened,' she said when she had gone into Catrin's office at the end of the morning. 'I must say I did rather hope that Eileen would accept him but it was selfish of me. I just wanted him to go back to Stanhope and let me carry on with my work here. He was so much in my way. Now I feel awful that he'll be by himself and I know how lonely he is and how much he relies on me.' She stopped for a few moments and then looked despairingly at Catrin. 'I can't go back there. I know he is about to suggest it to me because Eileen has turned him down but I can't face it. I think my future is here. Tell me what you think. I need your advice so badly.'

Catrin took a deep breath and then plunged in.

'I think the last thing you should do now is go back to Stanhope. I have the feeling that if you did it would be difficult for you ever to get away again.'

Agatha also waited for a few moments and then she said bravely,

'There is another reason why I don't want to leave.' Here she hesitated and then looked at Catrin and said,

'I've had a letter from a man I met while I was studying. He's called Tim Blackwood. We were good friends and I even brought him home a couple of times but my father didn't like him. At the time my mother was ill so I didn't ask again but things have changed. He wants to come and see me. The thing is that his family is very poor and not very respectable and my father would be appalled if I had anything more to do with him but I liked him very much. He is about to start in Crook as an assistant chemist. He's done it so that we can spend time together. Now he wants to come and see me and I'm so excited and so nervous and—' Here she stopped and sat down, almost in tears with such a brave effort.

'He wants to come next weekend. Would that be all right?'

'Yes, of course. Why don't you ask him for Sunday dinner?'

'Do you think I should?' Agatha brightened immediately and then jumped to her feet. 'Then I will. Thank you so much, Doctor Morgan. Thank you.'

Tim Blackwood was a tall, slender young man, rather shy but he had perfect manners and Catrin and Eileen confided to one another that he would be an asset as long as he didn't run off with and marry Agatha so that they had to look for another chemist.

There was a train from Crook which took about three-quarters of an hour and Agatha went off nervously to the station and came back all rosy-cheeked and smiles with Tim slightly behind her like a man who isn't quite sure what he has got himself into.

He was easy on the eye and held on to Agatha's hand

like a man who is confident and yet needs her close. Both Eileen and Catrin took to him at once.

Catrin was pleased with her dinner. It was roast beef and Yorkshire puddings with horseradish sauce and half a dozen vegetables and cauliflower and cheese sauce. Catrin had come to pride herself on her dinners, especially her gravy which everybody agreed was the best they had ever tasted. She thought this had something to do with the way she put sherry into it but she didn't say so. After the meal Tim and Agatha went for a long walk and he stayed until the last possible train and Agatha came dreamily back to the hospital so that Eileen and Catrin were pleased at her joy.

'We could be bridesmaids,' Eileen said and they giggled like schoolgirls.

The following weekend on the Sunday Agatha went to Crook. Tim was lodging there in what she said was not a very nice place but it was clean and he was willing to put up with it. He took her out to a café for tea and they had lots of cake.

None of the women at the hospital had any male friends now so Tim was a step forward. Only Mrs Clements stood out, complaining about Mr Clements just as she had always done. It was about the only amusement they had left, that Mrs Clements' husband was 'a useless article' as she called him and there was a lightness about how she spoke such as there had not been before. It brought a little comfort to Catrin that Henry Clements was imperfect but vital to them, being still alive.

Will wrote short letters to Catrin telling her nothing. She longed for him to come back but sensed that things were not going well and although he didn't say it she got the impression that he could not come back at present. She wished and wished that his father would get better and that they would manage a closer relationship but all he talked about was stupid stuff like the weather and she couldn't press him so when she wrote it was about everyday doings at the hospital and not much more.

Catrin went to church two weeks running, making herself go in case she had overreacted in the first instance about how people remembered Roddy but it was just the same. Nobody spoke other than in greeting. She couldn't think now why she had expected or even hoped for any more.

After that she couldn't make herself go back. Susan came to see her though without Tony. Women's husbands all became very busy as though Catrin was going to fall on some man's neck through grief and loneliness.

She was coming back from a late-night visit one warm Wednesday evening – it was a birth and she had the satisfaction of knowing that another baby and his new mother were doing well though she did say she would call later in the week and if they needed her before then she would be straight there.

She saw a strange figure flitting in front of her in the street. It looked almost like a ghost. At first she thought she was seeing things and looked harder. The moon was bright and she saw quite clearly how the figure disappeared and the next thing she heard was Jack Dunstan's unmistakable Newcastle voice, thicker than usual and softer than she had ever heard before because he thought he was alone and could let go.

It was so distinctive here where he was considered almost a foreigner, with his sing-song tones of the Newcastle streets, but it sounded different than she knew. She listened hard, turned a corner and there he was with his wife in his arms, she with her thin white hands clutched up at his neck as though he was all that would keep her from falling, her face buried against him in fear.

'You're all right now,' he was saying ever so gently like she was a small child.

Then he espied Catrin and they both hesitated but they only stood still for a few moments and then he nodded briefly at her, clasped his wife ever nearer and carried her almost ethereal body down the empty pavement and in at the big gates of their home. For the first time in several months Catrin saw that the gates were slightly open.

She thought about this when she was back in her sitting

room. She only wished she could talk to Roddy about it. She was still avoiding the church and most especially the graveyard. It seemed appalling to her that Roddy was lying there instead of coming home, his body decaying under six feet of earth, as though he wasn't alive, as though he would never come back.

It was obvious to Catrin now that Una Dunstan had some kind of mental health problem. He hid her or she hid herself and when it all became too hard she fled to the streets in what undoubtedly was her nightgown. What the problem was Catrin did not know, only that Mrs Dunstan would be considered mad by other people and should probably be locked away.

Catrin could not rid herself of an impression of long, loose dark hair like a mane down the woman's back, the nightdress which almost resembled a shroud and the bare feet which looked so thin and somehow vulnerable. Catrin knew that she had wronged the man and what a difficult life he was leading with a woman he must love.

She understood now why they visited nobody and had no visitors or any help in the house and that even the doctor was not taken into his confidence because he doubted anyone could help in any real way. Perhaps neither of them could bear it. Perhaps he bore it all for her sake.

Catrin thought back to the dinner he had come to at her home. How different everything had been then.

It seemed strange and sad now that he had wanted so badly to be among other people that he had actually gone to church and to the Hilda House for a meal. He had dared to leave his wife and go somewhere. Maybe she was having a good day, maybe he could not help risking her because he was so desperate for company. It must have been a huge thing for him to do.

His wife must have been better then perhaps so that he could leave her alone for a few hours. Had it been the only time? Did she have good days and bad and he could never know which it would be? She must know when he was at work but other than that he would not leave her. Also with Will missing it meant that Jack would feel obliged to be there more often and perhaps that was also making things worse for them.

Catrin imagined Jack and Una meeting and falling in love. How hard he must have worked to earn such a splendid house for the love of his life or was she so bad by then that he took her to a remote spot and sank a pit and had the house built, set well behind walls and gates so that he could keep her with him. What was there left for either of them now?

Fifteen

Catrin had not understood how much she missed Will. She missed what company he had been and his good manners and his kindness. There didn't seem to be much of it about any more.

He was gone for several weeks so that she began to worry that he would not come back. It seemed silly but in a way Will might have made up just a little for the huge loss of her brother.

He did come back but she only found out through other people and she was slightly hurt because she didn't have many men in her life and he had been so good.

She didn't like to go and find him, it would have been rude and forward so she tried to pretend that he wasn't there or that he didn't matter. That lasted her quite well until the evening that he turned up and he looked anything but happy. Luckily she was by herself, it was well after surgery and she had been around the hospital making sure that everyone was as comfortable as they could be and that was when he came hesitantly to her.

'It's good to have you back. I missed you.'

She said it lightly and he nodded but she could see by the look on his face that things were very wrong.

He was obviously struggling to get words out so she encouraged him by offering a seat and tea. He took the seat, refused tea but still didn't help her.

'Is your father better?'

'He died.' Will could barely get such words past his lips she could see and his hands were trembling.

'I'm so sorry. How is your mother?'

'I think it was a huge shock to her. He was never ill, we thought he would live to be very old like my grandfather did. My father had cancer but it took a long time for him to tell anyone or to reconcile himself to the idea that he was ill and a long time after that before there were tests that were conclusive. He was so difficult and was in a lot of pain for so long that my mother despaired.'

Will said nothing more at that point but she understood how he felt. When Roddy died she could not believe it and it was the same now with Will and his father. You kept hoping and hoping that it would not be true but gradually you had to make yourself believe that it had actually happened.

'My mother didn't want my comfort. She didn't want me there. She said that I had made my father unhappy and that I was to blame for his dying. I went and stayed with my only sister, Pauline, who lives nearby and even then my brother-in-law made it obvious that I wasn't welcome but she insisted that I stayed, she said she needed me so I did but I wished I hadn't.

'It turned out that my father had left me nothing, that he – that he disliked or despised me so much that I was not to have any of his – his wealth. I didn't know that I was disliked. I know that he thought I was difficult because I wouldn't do what he wanted me to do but – it's not that I care about being rich, I don't. It's just being the only one left out that I can't manage. I thought he cared more about me than making such a huge point after he died.' Will hesitated there and tried to steady his voice and then he went on. 'The pits are to be sold and everything is to be divided between my brothers. My sister got nothing either but that was because she has married well and he assumed she didn't need it. It wasn't true. Her husband treats her badly and if she had had her own money she might have fared better. I always thought I would go back there and run the pits. It was all I wanted to do. I thought they would belong to me. I'm as good a pit manager as I believe any man is and I care about the men. I think that was my undoing. He used to say that I was far too soft to be a good manager. That I cared too much and that the men took advantage of me and so he made sure that they wouldn't do it again.' Will took a deep breath and then he said, almost smiling,

'I have nothing but my wage and being the idiot I am

I've always given most of it away to other people who needed it more than I did. Now I shall need it to live on.'

'Lots of people get by with much less,' Catrin said and then wished she hadn't, he looked stricken.

'I know. I'm sorry to sound so full of self-pity but I always imagined that I would go back there and run those pits. I can't think why I was so certain of it now. My brothers are embarrassed but don't understand. My sister's husband is my elder brother's best friend.'

'What does her husband say?'

'He's a fool,' Will said. 'He's stupid and acts like he's about fourteen. I don't know what she married him for. He doesn't care about anyone but himself and he told me to get out and that I was not welcome there any more. She couldn't do anything, she has six children and no money of her own.'

Catrin took him through into her own private sitting room and there she gave him whisky.

'This is what Roddy and I always did when times were tough,' she said.

'Good idea. It's hard for you.'

He was the only man who had said such a thing to her and she was grateful and thanked him.

Before he went he hesitated and then said,

'My landlady has moved away and I'm going to be staying at Jack's house. I must go. I've got my things to move. Luckily there isn't much.'

She could hear the bitterness in his voice and was sorry. It was then that Catrin realized that she liked him better and better. It was because he was such a mix, so intelligent and educated and yet now he had no one but the Dunstans, she could see, and he seemed grateful for that. And also she felt that Una Dunstan was in her way. Did he still love her? Did you go on loving someone when for years you had known that your sentiments were not returned?

When Eileen came running into the hospital one Wednesday morning in September she looked as though she was being pursued, she was red-faced and panting heavily. She stood there guarding the outside door with her back against it like all the devils in hell were after her.

Then, looking back at the door, she escaped into Catrin's office. Catrin followed her inside now that the round of the beds was done.

'It's him, my husband,' Eileen said when Catrin had gone inside and quietly closed the door. 'It's Tel.'

'Did he see you?'

'No but he knows that my parents live here and he will soon find them. What am I going to do? They don't know about him.' 'They' were her family. 'At least I hope they don't. I don't know how he got here. I thought he was hundreds of miles away. He was going to look for gold and I thought it was just a daft notion and that he said that just to be rid of me but he's wearing a good suit and looks rich and, oh my God, whatever will I do?

'I wish I'd never come home now,' Eileen said bitterly. 'What will my parents think of me? And my sisters and brothers will be horrified.'

'Maybe you should go out and bring him in here so that you can talk to him,' Catrin suggested. 'That would at least be discreet until you work out what he wants.'

'I don't know how to reason with him. I tried so often before. I ought to go and tell them before he does.'

'Go out the back way,' Catrin suggested.

'Will you come with me?' Eileen appealed to Catrin who hesitated and was about to say that she ought to go by herself and then the look that Eileen threw her made her change her mind.

'All right,' she said.

They were too late as Eileen had worried they would be. Tel Collings had found his way to her parents' house halfway up the main street. Eileen burst into the sitting room and there he was seated on the settee which was back against the far wall. Her father was on his feet, her mother sitting opposite the intruder, pale, though as far as Catrin was aware she was always ailing.

Catrin thought Tel Collings was the ugliest man that

she had ever seen. He had the appearance of a weasel. In fact that was doing the weasel a disservice. There was nothing wrong with weasels. He was skinny, short and slight, had the kind of complexion that made him look grubby. It was probably some kind of tan from warm weather so he had recently been in another part of the world. He was losing his hair which made him look a lot older than he probably was, he had various missing teeth with black gaps and his small dark eyes were too close together.

Strangely he was wearing what looked to Catrin like a very expensive suit, the kind of thing a gentleman would wear. He also wore a gold chain around his wrist and a gold stud in his right ear, not things that a real gentleman would sport.

Catrin wondered what he had looked like when Eileen had fallen in love with him. Surely he must have been much different a long time ago.

She did not know Eileen's family well. There were several grandchildren, all her brothers and sisters and their offspring lived close by. Catrin's contact with them was only medical – joint pain and palpitations in the worn-down mother, back pain in the overworked father, childish diseases with the little ones and births and deaths in the others. She did not know them individually, other than Mrs McNorton who ran the Station Hotel, only that she knew if the women had fewer babies and the men did not work so hard they would have fewer health problems.

Also Mr Green smoked and was fond of his beer, though how he managed such luxuries with a family of their size Catrin did not know. Perhaps they did not eat well. Mrs Green looked very old for her age and she also looked confused and unhappy and a lot of that was due to the man who sat on her best settee, a strange jumble of a gentleman, who looked to Catrin like some kind of seaman or adventurer.

From what she knew of Mr Green he had always seemed a fairly moderately tempered man but he stared when she followed Eileen into the room and he said looking squarely at her,

'I don't think we need bother Miss Morgan with our family matters.'

Since Roddy had died Catrin had gone down to being Miss Morgan to a lot of folk in the village but especially to all of the men. As far as she could tell it was as if his death had robbed her not only of status but also of her qualifications and ability in their eyes.

'I need her here.' Eileen spoke in a shaky voice.

'This man claims to be your husband,' her father said.

'We were married right enough in church in the toon,' Tel Collings said.

The town was Newcastle. Durham was the city,

Newcastle was fondly known as the toon by its inhabitants and lovers.

'You walked out and left me,' Eileen accused him.

'I was a young lad then. I've changed a lot and I want us to get back together.'

'You had a duty to me when you went and left me to have and bring up our child alone. I had nothing and nobody and you put me on the streets. I have not said so to my parents, but you beat me to the floor before you walked out and after that I lost the child I ought to have had and since it was yours I'm glad of it.' Catrin had never heard Eileen bitter before but she certainly was now, the words spat from her.

'I just said, I've had a lot of time since then, I've been a lot of places and I made my fortune and now I've come back for you, Eileen. I'm so ashamed of what I did. Let's try again.'

'We can never be together again,' Eileen said.

'I've prospered, look at me, can you not? I went to sea and found gold in America and here I am, come back to claim my wife. I can afford to keep us both now, Eileen, and we can afford bairns such as we never could before. I came back special for you.'

'You will drink and then you will do the same again. It wasn't once you hurt me, knocked me to the floor every time you got drunk. I was so ashamed I had married you but I managed to get myself back here and never told my family of what I had done and what you had done to me.'

'I don't drink any more. I'm a changed man,' Tel Collings said, getting to his feet.

Eileen took a step back. Bad memories flooded her mind now, Catrin thought.

'Can't we give it another try?' Tel said softly, looking at her in such a pleading way that Catrin was startled he could seem even remotely attractive.

'I don't want you,' Eileen said. 'Go away and leave me alone.'

'You must go with him, Eileen.' Her mother spoke for the first time. 'You hadn't even the sense to tell us you were married and to think that you had to marry him because you had sinned. There is nothing for you now but to go back to him. There is no other way. He is your husband.'

'I want us to try again,' Tel said. 'Please, Eileen, just try.'

'Never.'

'You can't stay here,' her father said to her. 'You must go. You won't be welcome in this house again if you don't live with your husband. Such things aren't respectable.'

Eileen left so abruptly that there was nothing for Catrin to do but follow her out. They didn't discuss it. Eileen went straight back to the hospital and continued with her day as though nothing had happened.

Before the day was over though they sat in front of the fire drinking tea and there Eileen confessed what she really felt.

'How can I stay at the hospital now? People will find out and they will talk about me. They will say horrible things as my parents have. Why should he have changed just because he has more money? I was trying to come back here and make a life for myself. What can I do?'

Tel Collings came to the hospital but Eileen refused to see him so he went away again and he looked disheartened.

Agatha saw her father very often. It seemed to Catrin that he could not bear to be away from Eileen even though he must know by now that Eileen was married and her husband had come back to her. Each time they met he would look longingly at her. Catrin wanted to ask him not to come to the Hilda House Hospital as much as he did and yet could think of no way to put it that wouldn't be considered offensive.

Catrin realised that because he could not marry Eileen he would concentrate on his child though Catrin thought that he was envious of his child's ability.

His shop in Stanhope was quite cast into the shade and word went around that Agatha was a better chemist than her father. It was unfortunate, Catrin knew when she heard it but there was nothing she could do. It became obvious to her also that Agatha wanted him there less and less because the tendency to tell her what to do and in front of other people grew worse and worse. He was a man and therefore must be in charge, at least Catrin thought that was it. It was probably the way that he had been brought up and nothing could unseat notions of that kind. Catrin tried therefore to include him in everything, hoping he would feel safe in his own position and not try to usurp hers but it didn't work. Everywhere she turned he was there.

Agatha seemed to do her work as well as ever and it was up to her to draw the line where she chose between her work and her life, but the trouble was that Mr Melrose could not accept that Agatha was an adult. He had more experience and presumably it was difficult to pass this on without interfering. He was not alone in it. A lot of men told their daughters what to do when they would not have said such things to their sons, and even then some of them thought none of their offspring had their ability.

'My father says that I should go to Stanhope and that he will be better here than I could be,' Agatha eventually confided unhappily. 'And I daren't ask Tim here when my father is around because I know my father would be upset and they would quarrel, but Tim keeps asking again and again and I feel so caught between the two of them.'

Tim put up with it until Christmas and Catrin was so glad that he determined to do something about it and that when he had a day off he came to the hospital. It was unfortunate that Mr Melrose was there but Tim stood his ground when Mr Melrose glared at him the moment he came into the dining room when they were about to have dinner. Catrin had told Agatha that Tim was always welcome at her table and she was not about to change that because of Mr Melrose's loneliness and his controlling manner with his daughter.

Mr Melrose hurried over his pre-dinner sherry and gaped at the young man.

'What are you doing here, lad?' he growled.

'I did say he was coming, Father,' Agatha said as softly as she could since Catrin and Eileen were there. 'Tim usually comes over here on Sundays and we are officially walking out together.'

'None of his family has ever been any good,' her father raged. 'I knew this would happen. That's why I've been keeping an eye on my Agatha. He has no right to be anywhere near her.'

'I have every right since she chooses to ask me,' said Tim, squaring up to him.

Had Eileen and Mr Melrose been able to marry Catrin had the impression that this would have been a much smaller problem. A newly married chemist in Stanhope was a less concerned father of his grown-up daughter wanting to get married herself even if he didn't particularly like the man she favoured. However fate was not acting kindly to any of them, Catrin thought cynically, and she could have done without more complications.

Mr Melrose glared at them, hoping, Catrin could see, that she would back him up in this matter. 'I've told her she can't. He's a bad lot. I want something better for my girl.'

'I took a job as assistant chemist in Crook so that I could be near Aggie,' Tim Blackwood said, plunging straight into his subject though how he could have led up to it Catrin was not sure.

Mr Melrose made thunder look pale. 'Agatha has a good home and a good life. She isn't giving it up for the likes of you and yours. I've told you before not to hang about. I knew you would come here. That's why I've stayed close. She's like putty in your hands and I know what's best for her.'

Nobody said anything.

'Well then,' Mr Melrose said. 'Since I'm getting no support I shall take my daughter with me back to Stanhope. Go and get your things, Aggie, we aren't staying here.'

Catrin held her breath. The relationship between the two young people was so brief and she knew how much Agatha cared for her father so this was to be a huge battle of wills and Catrin was unsure what would happen. Selfishly, she hoped Agatha would not desert her. She had fitted in well here and was good at her job.

Agatha didn't move but her cheeks told everybody how she felt. Had she coloured any further she would have been crimson and her head was down and although Catrin couldn't see she had the feeling that Agatha was about to cry.

'We are leaving,' Mr Melrose said and when she hesitated he closed the space between them as though he would get hold of her and propel her out of there but Tim was too quick for him. He got in front of her.

'This isn't your decision to make, Mr Melrose. If Aggie wants to be with you she will but in the meanwhile I think you must let her decide for herself.'

'She is my child and will do what I say.' Mr Melrose was all clenched teeth with a dark red brow and tight fists.

'I'm not your child,' Agatha said and she said it firmly as she looked him in the face. 'I'm a grown woman and capable of making my own decisions.'

He glared around the room, especially at Catrin.

'This is all your doing,' he said, 'with your wiles. You want everybody to give up everything for your wretched little hospital.'

Eileen was not looking at him. Catrin looked into his face.

'I think you had better go,' she told him, 'and when we

have all recovered from this I'm sure Agatha will come and see you and it can be sorted out.'

Mr Melrose was quivering now and he was quite a big man. Without another word he clashed his way out of the dining room. Nobody ate much dinner, they sat about pushing food around their plates and drinking their water with tiny sips in silence.

To Catrin's delight Tim gave up his job in Crook and came to the hospital. She did feel rather guilty about the whole thing but there was plenty of work and Tim turned out to be good at his job and the others liked him. Why wouldn't they, thought Catrin, he was good-looking, young, clever and softly spoken? Also he had proved that he could fight for the woman he wanted and she admired that.

Catrin had begun talking to Roddy's grave not just in her head but out loud when she visited him. She knew that it was stupid but she had to talk to somebody. Tim was too young to understand so she had Roddy for what use he was.

Unfortunately when she decided to take flowers to Roddy's grave for the second time in a week hoping for a little conversation she stopped short as she was about to step into the graveyard. Lily Bell stood by the grave. Catrin didn't know what to think at first. She knew that

Lily would have been the last person Roddy would want there. It was fortunate then that this was one matter in which he had no choice and if it brought any comfort to this woman he had not wanted who had loved him then Lily should have the best of it.

Lily was clad all in black and held a small handkerchief up to her face as she was crying. Kneeling down, she placed a big vase of flowers on his grave, very pretty, pink and blue and purple. Catrin was pleased somehow to think that she was not the only one who openly cared. If her actions brought comfort to Lily Bell why should she not use them?

Catrin crept away and put her blooms into a small vase in the hall of the Hilda House where everybody could see the blue and yellow flowers which brought a little joy into the patients' lives.

Sixteen

In the end Jack Dunstan came to Catrin. She had been half expecting him and then not, so it was something of a relief when he did so. She had been worrying the problem to death in her mind. It was similar to when John Reed had first gone to see her, at the end of surgery. Jack Dunstan would not want to be seen and thanked her when they got inside.

'Doctor Morgan?' he said.

As far as she could think he was the only man in the village who still referred to her that way. Yet how could he not when she knew so much of his private affairs?

He had come inside doubtlessly to make sure that she was alone. She managed a smile and beckoned to him.

'Do come into my surgery, Mr Dunstan,' she said as he hesitated. So he moved further in, closing the door quietly behind him as though he didn't know what to say. He stood with his hat in his hands, the fingers worked around the hat brim for something to do, she thought, before he looked at her.

'You have discovered my secret,' he said.

'Secrets are part of my job and I would never divulge any one's business. Would you like to sit down?'

He did after a few moments.

'You doubted me?' Catrin pressed him and that brought a twisted smile to his lips.

'I doubt everybody,' he said. 'I made myself not come here, for weeks and weeks I had this argument with myself but you see . . .' he hesitated '. . . Una is getting worse and I am at a loss to see what I can do. I'm only hoping that you might be able to help us.'

'I took an oath to do all I could to aid people. That's the whole point.'

There was a long silence. He went on turning the hat round and round in his hands.

'I enjoyed your dinner party,' he said.

It was the last thing she had expected.

'I realize now how high it appeared in your social calendar,' Catrin said.

The smile broadened just a fraction.

'It was a wonderful dinner. You can't think how often I bring it to mind. And when I had been so rude to you.'

'Rudeness can be a form of defence.'

'I'm not sure I remember what defence is. I feel as though I have none left. All I have now is my work. That's become hard too. That's why I got Will to come to the pit to make things easier but I miss it and I don't seem to be able to help her at all.'

'When you work how does your wife manage?'

He hesitated as though he might get up and walk out while his hands went on turning his hat and then he said, eyes lowered,

'She doesn't leave the house whether I'm there or not except that occasionally she runs out at night, as you saw. She is afraid of the light. She hates the summer. She feels safe only in the darkness, as though it is providing a cloak to hide her. She used to faint when she went outside. She's getting worse,' he said, 'sometimes she can't even leave the bedroom. She seemed perfectly usual when we met but since we married she has gone downhill. Her parents told me that they didn't want her to marry me and that they were afraid I couldn't look after her. They told me that she had problems but I didn't listen. I loved her so very much. I thought it would be all right, that she would be better with me and that I could cope.'

'What was she like when you met?'

His eyes grew dreamy and his look soft.

'She was the cream of Newcastle society and I was nobody. She was so bonny. I thought she was the most beautiful thing I had ever seen. She was very young. She was carefree and loved dancing. They were rich. They lived in a huge house in town and owned another house on the Northumberland coast and they had a house in London. They held wonderful parties.'

'You were invited to them?'

He laughed just a little and again his gaze was lost in memory. He shook his head.

'Only once. When her father found out who I was she was forbidden to see me. My father was a collier and he had many faults of the working man. He was a hard drinker and a hard worker. He cared nothing for his wife or children. He was disillusioned, I expect, and the work was awful, worse than it is now, believe it or not. He died.'

'How old were you then?

'Fifteen and I had been down the pit for years. I liked it. The only man who ever liked slaving for coal. I liked the men, I liked their sense of togetherness, how they were there for one another because there was no other way. We bonded. I became a union man and took on the bosses and I rose.

'God alone knows how, but I had instincts for mining. I thought everybody had them but it was almost like water divining. I knew where to look for coal, there were maps and such of course sometimes, but I seemed to know before other people did and without guidance. Very odd. The men followed me. I got to know Will and since Will has always cared about mining and he is so brilliant at it we became friends and as his family is so well known he managed to get me a loan to help me set this up.

'I won her. Will wanted to marry her but when he saw that she cared more for me he backed off. I tried to keep his friendship and mine on a business basis. His father was trying to make him into some kind of professional man, nothing to do with the pits, but he wanted to go off and do his own thing. He went into the army just to get away because his father wouldn't let him run the pits and he always had so much ability but his father never recognised it. Now that Will has come back it means that I can spend a lot more time with Una at home while he sees to the business. He's the only person I would trust with my business though I'm sorry that his father could not forgive him but then he wouldn't have been here. Strange how life treats us.

'Una's parents didn't like me. At the beginning they were hoping Will would ask her to marry him and she would accept because through his father he was wealthy and had good family at least on his mother's side. I didn't like Una's parents either because they looked down on me and thought it would be a bad marriage, but I won her. I was so amazed. She left her father's house and came to me and we were married without them. I built us a lovely house in Newcastle and for a while everything was fine, better than that, it seemed perfect.'

He stopped.

'And then?' Catrin prompted him.

'She began to find things more difficult than they

had seemed before. She started wanting to stay at home. We were very young and there was a wonderful social life for us to follow, dinner dances, parties, theatre. I was doing very well and even her parents had come to accept that we were married. The first time I worried was the night we went to the theatre and she ran out. I presumed she didn't feel well so we went home. It happened again until we stopped going to the theatre. If she was happy at home then so was I. I didn't understand her fear but the last thing she needed was for me to insist on her doing something which scared her so very badly.

'She began to make excuses to go nowhere at all. In the end I sank this pit and built this house and brought her here so that she didn't have to go anywhere or have people too near. I built big walls and fences around it for her. She loved the house but I think it has become something of a prison to her, she doesn't feel safe even there. She needs proper help and you are my last hope.'

After this there were several moments of silence but at least he was frank over his friend's kindness which Catrin was glad of and then he went on.

'She has only just begun going outside in the darkness. I daren't sleep or she creeps out. I'm so afraid she might put herself in the river.'

'Why?'

'Because she has nothing to live for, that's how she

sees it. I don't understand why but I think she wants to destroy herself.'

Catrin spent time taking all this in and while she did in those few moments he said,

'I don't know what to do.'

'I'm glad you came,' Catrin said.

He looked at her almost apologetically.

'I didn't mean to. If you hadn't seen us – I've argued ever since, back and forth with myself until I could have torn my hair out.'

'I'd like to try and help unless you think it would make things worse.'

'Things could hardly be any worse,' he said.

'I'm not sure I know anything about mental health. There are specialists—'

He waved away her words.

'I tried all that and they made her worse. Now she won't go anywhere or see any doctor.'

'Do you think she would let me see her?'

He looked so hopeful that she was almost ashamed. She had read about mental health but she knew nothing and as far as she was aware neither did anybody else very much, despite their claims.

Catrin spent a couple of days thinking about what she could do for Una Dunstan. She had never dealt with anything like this before. Yes, people had hard lives and many of them were scared and they got hurt and grieved but the trouble was that those who had family with mental health problems tended to hide them away. There was a shame about it because people did not understand. Did she understand it? She wasn't sure.

Was the only place Una felt safe her bed? Would she even want Catrin to see her when she had stopped seeing other people? Catrin sent a note to the pit to ask if he would talk to Una about whether they could meet even just for five minutes. There were to be no surprises.

He said that they would give it a try and that maybe Catrin would come mid-evening, the next day, well after surgery, he thought it might be best when the day was almost done so she finished the surgery, lingering there over her paperwork. Three days running he sent her notes saying that Una would not see her but on the fourth day no note came so she set off.

The gates were shut but when she tried them they were not locked so she walked slowly in. Nobody was about and she closed and bolted the gates behind her. She wasn't quite sure why, nobody would come in, nobody was used to being there and had no reason to. After that she went slowly to the front door and was unsure whether to knock and then he opened the door and let her in.

'I'll take you up to her,' was all he said.

Weak sunshine streamed into the house. The weather always made a difference and Catrin was glad of that. The house was warm after the sun and soft shadows fell across the big wide staircase. It was fully carpeted so that their footsteps were barely audible and then he took her along the landing and into a big bedroom at the back of the house where it would be most private.

'Here's Miss Morgan, Una,' he said, deliberately, she thought, calling her miss so that it seemed more informal. Catrin thought that it was a good idea.

Una wasn't in bed, she was sitting on a big sofa at the window, wrapped in a thin blanket. She must have been beautiful once but she was now very thin. The cheekbones of her face stood out almost like tiny jutting rocks, she was pale to white and did not smile. Her hair was long and free but had been brushed by someone – her husband, Catrin thought – and another chair had been pulled over. Jack sat down beside his wife and Catrin took the other chair. She didn't quite know what to say.

'Your garden is beautiful,' she said.

The garden went a long way back. She could see fruit trees, some of which were espaliered across the back wall and several of them here and there dotted like an informal orchard. There were seats and paths and a summerhouse and a big lawn. It was all very peaceful and surely must have helped Una to feel a little better.

'I don't sleep very well,' Una said and Catrin heard her fine tones, her voice was sweet and low.

'And you don't eat much,' her husband put in.

'I do try but very often I choke and vomit. I feel safe in this room.'

The curtains were almost closed and the room was stuffy. Catrin wished she could go around opening the windows and letting in the evening light but that wouldn't help Una.

'I long to go outside and see things. When I do I faint and can't breathe and have to come back inside until the panic subsides. It's easier not to go out.'

'Tell me about yourself, your childhood and how you grew up.'

Una's eyes grew misty.

'I had a very happy childhood,' she said. 'I had a governess.'

There was something here that wasn't being said, Catrin thought, hearing as Una spoke that there was hesitation, but she didn't like to interrupt as Una talked about the beautiful house where they lived in Jesmond. The big garden, where she and her friends played games and her parents' friends gathered at weekends in the summer to play tennis and croquet. The friends she played with in the nearby parks and the governess whom she loved very dearly.

She mentioned the governess more than her parents

which brought Catrin to the conclusion that her childhood had been run by servants. Catrin thought that this was common in upper-class children as far as she knew, which was mostly other people's experience. Una obviously had been very attached to her governess and perhaps before that her nurse and these people had left when she was grown and her parents did not feel her need for them anymore.

Catrin could see why Una's parents would have preferred Will. He was well-mannered and his mother belonged to a Northumbrian well-to-do family with small estates over near the coast. His father had not managed the pits, he had other people to do it for him, which made him respectable. Also she had the feeling that Will might have gone to public school and perhaps university after it. That was a far cry from Jack's childhood and his family. Catrin had the feeling that Will had stepped aside when it got him nowhere, it was the kind of thing he would do. He had therefore followed Jack here or Jack had asked him since their friendship had survived and perhaps because they both cared more for Una than they did for themselves. It would have been a good marriage, could Will have pulled it off, so her parents might have said and then she had met Jack and it all fell apart. No wonder her parents had been dismayed.

'Do you see them often now?'

Jack had said that her parents had become resigned to

her marriage but there was hesitation and it turned out that they had not seen her parents since they had moved here which was ten years ago.

'We have asked them to come,' Jack said and then there was silence. 'They refused and they won't let us go there.'

All this was very sad but Catrin didn't think it explained why Una Dunstan was so ill.

Una was now exhausted and Catrin left, promising to come back but she did not say when, she did not want to hold the young woman to any date or time.

When Catrin got back to the Hilda House she was worn out. So much had happened. She felt sorry for Una, for Jack, for Will and for herself, for how they had been treated, but was it the older people to blame, had they not too been brought up to be prisoners of their given ideas? If people did not get an enlightened education perhaps it would always be so.

Seventeen

Tel Collings moved into the prettiest house in the village which was not far along the street from the Hilda House Hospital.

The house was single storeyed. It stood in big gardens back and front. The garden had been given over to vegetables but Tel began to fill it with flowers. He was out there all the time so that people would see what good he was doing and so that they'd stop and speak and come to the conclusion that Eileen must be to blame for them not being together because beneath the ugly exterior the man had a heart of gold.

He dug a big bed and planted it with white roses that spring. He built patios in various places. He put in a pond and filled it with carp and invited passing children to come and see the fish. In the evenings he would sit outside and people began to drop in for tea and very often there was the hum of good conversation from the garden.

He came to the hospital and took blue and white and yellow flowers and presented them to Eileen so that

Eileen began trying to avoid him. It was difficult not to see the man differently. He did not make a nuisance of himself, he just called in, sometimes his pleading voice reached Catrin's ears as she went among the patients who were in bed or walking in the corridors. She saw him so obviously doing his best to let his wife know that all he wanted was to have her back again. Eileen would not agree no matter what the pressure from family and friends. It made her so unhappy that Catrin thought sooner or later she would give in because everything was against her though how anybody would fill Eileen's shoes she could not begin to imagine.

Catrin longed for rain. All through the spring there was dry weather. The river at the bottom of the village flowed slow and shallow over big, flat stones and the children made dams and paddled and there were picnics. People had taken to sitting outside their houses in the evenings and soon Tel Collings was welcomed everywhere.

Catrin became aware that the village was talking about Eileen and there came a day when Mrs McNorton and Eileen's mother came to the surgery and insisted on telling her that she must go back to Tel. He had turned over a new leaf and there was no reason why she shouldn't live with him now that he had become an altered man.

It had begun to affect the work at the hospital. Sometimes people would refuse to go to Eileen so that some days she had nothing to do whereas the others were all overworked. Catrin knew it was a situation that could not go on but she did not trust Tel Collings so when Eileen suggested that it was getting too much and she must go back to her husband Catrin didn't know what to say.

'People have lost faith in me and my nursing ability,' Eileen said. 'If I can't nurse then what can I do? When they come to the surgeries I'm standing here, my face red with humiliation, and when I go out people don't speak. This morning one of my mother's friends told me that I was a disgrace to my family. I'm going to have to go back to him, Catrin, I don't know what else to do. Things are getting worse here every day.'

It seemed to Catrin an impossible situation. Maybe she had been wrong, maybe Tel deserved another chance and Eileen felt obliged to go. It was a relief in some ways, as though things almost went back to normal but that they felt short-handed because she had always been so reliable. Catrin missed her. It had occurred to her that Tel might let Eileen come back to work or maybe Eileen needed to let the dust settle. Whatever, she heard nothing more for several days and Catrin tried not to worry.

Early that summer Anne turned up at the Hilda House and had tea with Catrin. It was obvious that she was not now enjoying being alone, which Catrin thought was a big step forward. Catrin waited for her to explain. She poured more tea, offered more cake until Anne accepted the tea, refused the cake and looked properly at her for the first time.

'I'm starting to think that John and Amy will never come back. There is a lot to be done to the cottages and on the estate itself and I just thought you might be able to help. I don't know what to do. I ran out of money ages ago and he kept promising to make more available but nothing has happened and it's starting to show in all kinds of ways.'

Catrin didn't know what to do either but she could hardly say so. She wondered whether Mr and Mrs Benson might help but it was very difficult to involve anyone in such a problem.

'I wish he had never married her,' Anne said and Catrin could understand this though it was not helpful. He had said he needed the money for the estate but to spend it on other things seemed careless. She had wondered at the lavish wedding, the new car, the way that they had spent so much on the house and on clothes and yet Anne so obviously had little. Her clothes were old and she was far too thin. Her face was white and her eyes had huge shadows under them. Catrin said the only thing she could think of.

'Why don't you stay here for a little while? You aren't

responsible for your brother's problems and you look as though you could do with some company.'

Anne's eyes filled with tears. She had obviously been worried far too long for somebody her age.

'I would feel like a traitor,' she said.

'Nothing of the sort,' Catrin said as briskly as she could. Secretly she couldn't help cursing John Reed. Yes, it was understandable that he had baulked at his responsibilities after so long but it was unfair on his sister, his tenants and the village itself if it had to put back together the pieces of his neglect.

She didn't know what to do but she wanted to reassure Anne that everything would be taken care of.

Catrin was happier after Anne moved in. They got on so well together and Anne started to look better. Catrin fed her up, as they said in that region, and she knew that Anne slept well because she would hover outside the bedroom door and was so pleased to hear the soft and dear to her sounds of deep sleep.

Una had had all kinds of treatment, Jack had said but nothing had helped and it was no good trying to encourage her to eat. The more notice you took the less she got down and as for going outside, she could not do it. What had happened to make her so scared of life beyond the house? She would not leave the bedroom though she did sometimes go as far as the window and would sit there on a small sofa. That was all. She wouldn't talk, she was always white-faced, always worn out and why wouldn't she be, Catrin thought, the effort involved in her illness must be exhausting.

Will was now living at the house, which Catrin thought must be difficult for him, to see them together, but there was some measure of relief for both Jack and Una because Will had just about taken over the pit and it meant that Jack could be with his wife so much more often. How kind Will was, how self-effacing.

Catrin was hoping that as the nights lengthened, the days shortened and an icy blast crept across the fell Una might feel better. Catrin wasn't sure she understood but in a way it also made her feel less sad about Roddy dying.

In good weather, when the evenings were filled with sunlight, it was as though every corner of her grief was seen, every hurtful image was drawn without mercy and so to her surprise she began to recover. She wished she could say the same for Una. She did a lot of reading and thinking and finally Catrin suggested to Jack that Una had what was called shell-shock in the Great War.

'I think something has happened to her which she couldn't control. Something so awful that it made her feel completely crushed and now she tries to control the small world that she has managed to create over however many years she has had this problem. She's never dealt with it and it has got bigger and bigger.'

Jack frowned over it. Una was asleep and Will was at the pit so they sat there over the fire in his sitting room. Fires brought comfort, Catrin thought.

It had become the norm for her to sit before a big fire, eat her meal at a small table with a tray, have a glass of whisky afterwards, watching the firelight until she was drowsy enough to make her way slowly to bed.

She could feel herself getting better but she was becoming more and more concerned about Una.

'But she has had a very good life,' Jack said, obviously completely lost off.

'Something somewhere has gone wrong and from what she says I can't make out what it is. Perhaps she has completely blotted it from her mind because it was too heavy to be borne.'

'And now it's trying to kill her,' he said in a flat horrified tone.

'She's fighting as best she can so that it doesn't overwhelm her and it hasn't, not yet.'

'It shifts and moves,' Jack said suddenly. He had obviously given it a great deal of thought which was hardly any surprise. 'Whenever she has seemed happier it's like some evil genie is waiting for that and makes her panic in a new and different way. Maybe also it's partly my fault. I think I have given her the chance to let it into her life because I'm there so she can face it and battle it and at the moment it's winning.'

'She's still fighting.'

'It's a horrible thing is bad mental health,' Jack said.

'I'll do everything I can and you are here so often now and the house and garden look so much better.'

Jack almost laughed at that.

'That's mostly down to Will. His spell in the army made him try for perfection. He doesn't talk about it much. His father had the impression he was going to be a general or whatever these things are but he insisted on being a common soldier as his father put it. I sometimes think he did it deliberately to upset his father because he was so badly treated.'

'Why would his father do that?'

Jack hesitated, smiled just a little and then he said, 'He got all the looks, all the class and most of the brains in the family. His brothers are awful people and I know it isn't fair to say so but they have all gone bald and boring and dull. I think Will's father wanted him to do better than the rest because he had so many gifts but Will didn't see it that way.'

Catrin's response was that she wanted to run to Will and take him into her arms. He shouldn't have to fight such battles alone. She wanted to be with him, to help and be involved in his life and it was the first time she had felt such a rush of emotion since Roddy had died. She was so grateful to feel like that that she closed her eyes for a few seconds in relief and joy.

Eighteen

That autumn Catrin had a typewritten letter in a thick cream envelope and when she opened it, it was from a Welsh solicitor telling her that her father had died. How had they found her, she wondered, and they must know that Roddy was no more because it was addressed solely to her.

She replied and another letter swiftly followed from Griffiths and Jones and with it the details of her father's will. He had left her everything he possessed. Catrin began to think that she would never receive any news or have anything happen to her when she didn't want to cry over it. She would never get wrinkles, her face was always soaking wet. Her father had only acknowledged her by despising and ignoring her. He must have known that his son was dead. He had shown scant evidence that he cared for Roddy.

They had met only once as far as she knew, after Roddy went away to school as a small boy and that was when he had finished school and spent the summer with his father and had got to know Catrin. But for that she would still be in North Wales and what would have befallen her in between then and now?

Yet the allowance he had given Roddy had been more than enough to put them both through medical school and keep them comfortably. Without that she would not have become a doctor and would not have this difficult yet to her important existence up here on the high fells. Stupidly she wanted to thank her father that he had enabled her to do so.

She did not know what to do. Should she sell their home? Did it mean anything to her other than a place where she had been unhappy? Her father was English, but it was not just that, she had so few good memories of Dolgellau.

It might be years before she could get away from here and Wales was a very long journey. She decided that she did not want the house which had belonged to her family and if she sold it she would never have to go back and the money that it brought would mean she could do more to the Hilda House and expand her practice and perhaps take on a partner so that she could have some free time though what on earth she would do with it she couldn't imagine.

So she urged the solicitor to sell the house and its contents. The money would come to her and she would have closed that chapter of her life and need not think about it any more. The idea made her feel free. She would throw the bad memories out of her mind.

The solicitor informed her that there were some private papers which had belonged to her father. Some of the envelopes were sealed. Would she like him to forward these to her? She couldn't imagine they would be of any interest but in the end her curiosity bettered her and she asked him to send them.

She had known her father so little that perhaps she might learn something about him from letters and documents and that would be a bonus. Did she really want to know? She decided that she did. Also she thought that they might contain photographs of her mother, perhaps a photograph of them all together. She longed for such a thing. It would give her a sense of family.

A large box arrived in the weeks that followed. She had still not got round to trying to find another doctor to help. It was ironic that she needed the help but hadn't time to sort it out and it wasn't the kind of thing you could ask anyone else to do. She was aware also that such partnerships did not always work out so it was a huge step and once done would be irrevocable.

There were no photographs which was a huge disappointment and when Catrin had chance to look through her father's papers most of the information was ordinary, like wedding certificates, birth certificates and receipts of sales he had made of antiques and paintings. To her surprise there was a letter from the Blessed St Hilda's Orphanage. They were able to inform him that his daughter, Catrin, had given birth to a girl. Taken by Mr T. Raine. That was all the information she had.

She told Anne all about it. It would have been unfair not to but Anne, while she was pleased being told about the house sale and the money which would come in and for Catrin to talk about the father she barely knew, wasn't sure how much she wanted to know.

Catrin went to the council offices and there she discovered that Theresa Raine had been a single woman who lived on a tiny farm not that far from Castle Hall so there was a possibility that there could be a connection.

On a fine Saturday afternoon Catrin and Anne set off to walk along the fell to find the house where this woman had lived and it was only about a quarter of a mile away. The house was ruined now and could not have been substantial when Anne had been a baby but Anne needed to see it and they wandered the ruins sorry that the woman had died.

They imagined the circumstances. Perhaps she had been lonely and had wanted a child to help or to be a comfort. This was what Anne said and then she had died and somehow the child had wandered the fell until she had been picked up and taken to the hall so her future could have been worse. She could have died out there in bad weather or because she was so small that nobody would see her and nobody might think to look for her.

There was no death certificate and no grave and Catrin

imagined that the poor woman had died somewhere out there and never been found. She didn't think it was a very satisfactory history, but it could have been a lot worse. She didn't say this to Anne who seemed glad that they had located where she had lived before she was found and taken to the hall. As far as Anne was concerned things were now getting better. She had lost one mother but found another. They walked back to the Hilda House feeling somewhat better. Even if it couldn't be proved that Anne was Catrin's child they had gone so far together and went on hoping that they could bridge the gaps in their lives. They had unravelled some of the mystery and it had brought them closer.

Nineteen

Eileen came back to the hospital three weeks after she and Tel got back together in the pretty house. Eileen looked happy, younger, and Catrin was so relieved, so pleased that Eileen and Tel had managed to start again, it was not something that was given to most people.

In the first week she had expected Eileen to come running into the hospital for escape but nothing had happened and in passing she had seen them coming out of the house together and they were smiling and chatting so she merely waved and was grateful.

It was so good when Eileen was able to take on a lot of work. She said people were beginning to respect her again and come to her and her mother and father and all her family were so glad at what had happened that they had started coming to her house to see them and on Sundays very often now she and Tel would go to the Green house where all the family gathered and have a big dinner all together.

And then about six weeks after they had moved in Eileen came to the hospital in tears. Her mother had told her that she was not to work any more. She didn't need to. All Tel asked of her was that she look after him and his house and he had so much money that there was no need for Eileen to work and it was shaming that she would choose to do so. Had Tel gone to her parents? Eileen didn't know and Catrin didn't ask.

So Eileen was no longer at the hospital and Catrin missed her right from the start. She didn't feel that they could be friends, her family and Tel wanted to own her, Catrin could tell right from the start. They were the kind of people who did not encourage friendships outside the family circle.

It felt to Catrin as if Eileen had died or at least had gone a very long way away, not just down the street. She never saw her. At first she held to a dream that Tel had changed and that he that he would want to let Eileen do the things that she wished now that she had given in and gone to live with him.

When that didn't happen she pictured them together in the garden when the weather was fine or sitting over a cosy fire as rain pitter-pattered on the village streets but although she looked everywhere for Eileen she was never about.

Perhaps she wanted to keep not just Tel but her family happy and it seemed to Catrin that families so often overreached themselves in order to assert their power and strength even if members of that family were made unhappy by their needs or demands and yet she had the feeling that none of that occurred to him. Where there was that kind of dominance in love you must give up your free will, your needs, yours wants.

She had seen it in the way that Mr Melrose had tried to call Agatha back to him. Catrin thought it was selfish but she knew that Mr Melrose would not see it like that and he would feel his grief and loneliness so badly that he entrapped his daughter for relief as he had no other outlet for his emotional needs.

There was no respect, no acknowledgement that you had the right to go and take up your existence as you chose. You must learn to bear it under the weight of that expectation. Catrin found that the members of Eileen's family, her mother, her sisters and Mrs McNorton would cross the street to get away so that Catrin could not even enquire about the woman she had come to like and enjoy working with so much.

Did they blame her? She thought they did. Eileen's and their respectability came before everything and made them righteous and unfeeling. And yet she felt impotent. There was nothing she could do.

Tel came and went but he didn't glance in Catrin's direction. She thought she saw a swagger about him as the days grew shorter, he had won, he had got back his wife and now he could do whatever he wanted. The odd time on Saturday nights he came back from the local pubs singing, not rowdy just drunk enough to be happy.

At that time of year when the nights drew in there was little else for men to do but go and carouse and since Tel had a lot of money and didn't work he must want to go out and see other men though it seemed to Catrin that Eileen went nowhere except among her family. Was she happy like that? Catrin didn't think so. If she had to make evening visits she noticed that there was never a light on in their house and she imagined Eileen sitting by herself in the darkness waiting for him to come home, forbidden as she was to do what she wanted.

Perhaps she was wrong. Maybe Eileen was content. There was no evidence she could see that he had treated her badly. She could go to her mother or other relatives in the evenings if she was lonely.

The weather was cold and wet and all the flowers in Tel's garden drooped their heads under the storm. Leaves were swept into the hedges and stuck fast before turning to slime. There was a storm which lasted for three days. The small stream that ran through the hospital grounds became a river, rising quickly and flooding the streets and all the way past the houses before it joined what had been a beck at the bottom of the village and had now become a raging torrent.

Some inhabitants, fearing they would be drowned, had retreated to friends and family further up the village away from the water. Many of them wore their night things with shawls or coats hastily flung on before they left. Some held cats or dogs, small children or precious items in case the houses should be flooded or swept away.

Catrin took as many as she could crowd into the hospital and provided food and tea and beds. She and Tim looked after the few who had been injured by stones flung up or had stumbled and cut and bruised their bodies in their haste to get away.

When the storm finally subsided there was a lot of damage. Many slates had blown down, windows were broken, gardens were flooded, trees had crashed into buildings.

Eileen's mother brought Eileen to the hospital. She was battered and bruised and she did not look at Catrin. Her mother seemed nervous but blamed the storm for such things. It looked to Catrin more like somebody had beaten her more than once because some of the bruising was days old but there was nothing to be done. She could not fight Tel, Eileen's whole family and the village who did not seemed inclined to think anything was the matter.

Eileen did not say a word, did not cry. There was resignation in her eyes as though there could be no assistance anywhere. Catrin wanted to go and see Eileen but she knew that the neighbours would notice and some of them would undoubtedly make sure that her husband found out and it would go badly with her. She wished that there was more she could have done but it was something she had not met before and didn't know how to make it better. She hated that Eileen suffered and nobody seemed to be there for her but what to do about it?

Twenty

There was still no sign of John and Amy coming home. If she waited until the deepest of winter Catrin knew that the tenants would suffer and she could not sit around doing nothing. She did think of asking Mr Benson and his wife whether they could help but in the end she went to see Will at the office. He was there most of the time and she didn't want to burden Jack with problems when he was trying to concentrate on Una but she doubted Will would be there now.

She was seeing Una twice a week and was trying various ways to help her such as new techniques she had read about in various medical journals, like imagining better scenarios for the things that had happened in her life and trying to put a positive slant on it. She encouraged Una to talk on any subject she liked but it was hard because all Una could think of was how lucky she had been with her family and her circumstances and was ashamed that she had failed so badly. She had married a man her father despised and let him take her out of their reach. Was that how she really saw it? Catrin was half convinced that Una had what was becoming known as a fear of open spaces. Una could not bear the idea of leaving the room where she felt safe. The twice that Catrin had managed to get her as far as the door she had passed out from fear.

The stairs were cavernous to her, the house huge and terrifying. Catrin could not work out where these fears came from. She obviously felt so guilty about her parents and she spoke of them warmly even though the love she thought she had offered them was rejected in her choice of husband. And she adored Jack. She watched the door for when he would come to her. She was so needy. She drank in the sight of him and cried when he was away for any length of time.

She would rarely see Will. It was almost as though he was a ghost and he came back to the house less and less and was almost always to be found at the pit office until very late at night and then from very early in the morning. It was a very hard way to live for all of them.

The surgery had finished late, it was a Friday and she wanted to see Will by himself, not make it a doctor's visit, but to her relief there he was in his office quite alone and doing paperwork.

His presence was one of the few things in her life that Catrin now valued and held on to and she could not but help take to him the problems which she could not conquer alone so when she didn't know what to do about Anne and her family she went to him for advice.

As he heard her, however, he looked up, at first glad and then concerned. Will knew most of what went on and so she didn't have to explain much but she did have to tell him about Anne's problems on the estate though she didn't want him to know that Anne was her child. It was nothing to do with the current situation.

'Why do you think he hasn't come back? Can he be so enamoured of his new wife that he prefers Rome?'

'Who wouldn't,' Will said. 'But I think it's possibly something else. You know the saying, there are only two tragedies in life, one is getting what you want and the other is not getting it. John Reed has had both and it may very well have unnerved him. He had to marry because of the poverty of his estate.'

'And is regretting it?'

'Letting yourself be bought cannot be pleasurable.'

'Amy is beautiful.'

'I think she's rather like the impression I have of John's mother, meek and not very strong-minded, and the one thing his mother needed for some reason was his father.'

'What an awful idea.'

'Isn't it?' he said. 'There she is leaning all over him and so instead of investing his money in his estate he can't cope and he squanders it.'

'Anne is staying with me but she is very anxious.'

'She's a lovely girl,' Will said to her surprise. 'If anything should happen to him does she get the estate?' Catrin had not realized that Will was interested in the family and was grateful for his understanding.

'No.'

'A difficult situation,' he said.

'I have some money coming. Not yet, but soon.' She told him about her father dying and said that she could pay workmen to help.

'There's no real reason why you should.'

'I think somebody ought to and to me it would be a kind of investment. People who live in bad conditions end up in my surgery or worse still the hospital and if they cannot work and do not get better the situation becomes intolerable. If we do something about it as soon as we can it will help.'

After the storm, when a lot of damage had been done to so many buildings, the men of the village got together and began repairing roofs and putting in windows and clearing gardens and streets. John Reed's estate was included in all this and the women did a lot of work in one another's gardens. Catrin wanted to get the rest of the work done before the winter set in and since Jack provided money for tools and materials and she said she would pay him back when her father's house had been sold they got along fairly well and Will seemed always to be there and she was so glad, he was such a reassuring presence. The winter was not usually bad until after new year and since the storm it had cleared and been better so it was easier to work, nobody going home frozen or drenched.

A lot of apples and pears had been blown on to the ground. Those which had not turned to mush were put away for the winter. The same with root vegetables.

Mrs Clements and an army of other women made meals up at the hospital and there was always soup and sandwiches for those who needed it. The smell of freshly made bread was one hospital smell that everybody enjoyed and it helped having a cheerful attitude to those who were ill or in pain or just plain hungry.

Mr Benson provided stabling for sick animals and was very good with them and so was Mrs Benson. Catrin made various excuses to go and see Eileen but she gave up when Eileen looked unhappy to see her and the house was dark and gloomy. The garden was wrecked and had Tel been a nicer man maybe other people would have been more help but he did not want help and was no longer showing his better side.

Catrin was afraid of him. She had not understood but this was the other reason she did not like to go anywhere near, she was nervous should he come home and find her there, the worse it would be for Eileen and possibly even herself if she lingered and would people think she had been overstepping the mark since nobody was apparently ill at the once pretty cottage.

The cottage itself reflected Eileen's situation. The fire was often out, there were no cooking smells, Eileen wore drab old clothes and was pale, having no energy, waiting for him to come home. Did he ever give her any money? Catrin was convinced that he did not. She did not see it for herself but nothing got past Mrs Clements and thankfully she was on Catrin's side and was horrified about what was happening.

Catrin even invited Tel and Eileen to spend Christmas Day at the hospital but they did not come, presumably they went to Eileen's family. Catrin liked to make the hospital as festive as she could and there were plenty of helpful people about. Even Mr Clements came and strung streamers over the ceilings in criss-cross style. Catrin rewarded him with beer and Christmas cake and a chicken dinner.

The weather was mild after Christmas and by new year it had not snowed which was most unusual. Catrin thanked God for the weather and continued to ride Cymbeline out to the various farms and hamlets when there were messages that illness had broken out or accidents had happened.

In the middle of January as she came back she saw a very big woman walking up the street with two boys in tow. Neither of them had reached maturity, they were just at the gangly stage, sullen-faced and saying nothing.

The woman hailed Catrin and enquired if she knew the house of Tel Collings.

Catrin didn't know what to say. The woman wore poor clothes almost in rags and the boys were the same and yet the rags were mended and clean. While she hesitated the woman pushed back unwieldly dark hair from her face and pulled her hat further down over her head.

'Well do you or don't you?' she said.

'Yes, I, yes, I do.'

'Would you be the squire's wife and thinking I'm to be curtsying to you?' the woman said, glaring red faced at her.

'No. I'm – I'm the local doctor.' Afterwards Catrin was amused that the woman had so easily intimidated her. At the time she found herself wanting to ask why this woman was enquiring after Tel. She thought it could not be for any good reason.

'Are you a friend?' she timidly enquired.

The woman glared even more and her tiny black eyes seemed as small and hard as raisins.

'In a manner of speaking you could say so. I'm his wife. I've been looking all over for him for years and a little bird told me he was back here and shacking up with God only knows who. Aye, you may well stare, my lass. Walked out and left us he did and I was told he'd gone overseas and now he was back and had made money so I see no reason why he shouldn't share his ill-gotten gains with his lawful wife and two sons.'

Catrin was starting to enjoy herself, she really was. She gave the woman directions but she took Cymbeline back to the stables and bypassing Mr Benson who was always ready for a chat she went to Tel's house and was just in time to see Eileen being ushered from the front door, shouted at as she emerged into the garden. The older woman was pushing her out and throwing after her the odd comment as to Eileen's 'whoring'. Eileen was not crying. She was however hurrying as best she could to put some distance between the woman and herself. As Catrin reached the gate she was just in time to open it for Eileen. Eileen looked around her in some confusion.

'What am I to do? I can't go home. My mother will just tell me that it was all my fault.'

'You know very well I can't wait to have you back at the hospital,' Catrin said.

Catrin gave her food and drink and clean clothes and made sure there was plenty of hot water and within a couple of hours Eileen looked a lot better than she probably felt. At least it was a start.

Twenty-One

Bad weather set in at the end of January and went on in February keeping them busy. By March, the weather was as cold as ever and they were all desperate for a sign that the nights might be even a little shorter but the rain was succeeded by sleet so there was not even the brighter touch which snow gave. The winter dripped its way forward and the cutting wind off the fell nipped at people's throats, ankles, fingers and toes.

Having Eileen back at the hospital was not easy and both women knew it. People here were unhappy with change and Eileen was not a respectable woman any more so it was difficult every day. They talked about how awful her life had been with Tel but both knew that she could not stay here for long. The feeling in the village was against it.

'I can't think how I ever wanted him or cared for him, looking at him now,' Eileen confided.

'I think when we are young we see people as being better than they are,' Catrin said, remembering how mistaken she had been in Joe. It had affected the way that she regarded men since and even now. She felt as though she had been so badly hurt that she would never get past it but she had been so concerned with Roddy's death that having lost the only man in her life who had mattered to her she was now a mixture of hanging back and wanting to move forward. She was starting to like Jack and she liked Will very much though their talk was mostly of something about work.

Eileen was therefore reluctant to see anybody who needed nursing and since Catrin was convinced that they did not want to see her either she made Eileen's duties bigger, almost on a level with herself and Tim and under this regime Eileen began to look a little better, a little happier. Catrin could afford to take on more nurses because the bank had advanced her money as she would soon be in possession of her inheritance.

She was glad of Eileen, promoted her to matron and paid her more money so that she would have what freedom the people around her gave. Eileen therefore became important in a big way, in that they made all the financial decisions together, and Catrin relied on Eileen more and more in a hundred different ways. Eileen ran the hospital, saw to the rooms, kept the cleaners in order, counted the linen, got in the food supplies so that all Tim and Agatha had to do was order the medicines and make them up and distribute them to the patients and the nurses and read and study and urge the other two to move forward. Catrin was inclined to be cautious, Eileen had been hurt badly so Tim was the one providing the way to better medicine and new methods.

When her father's house was sold and she had the money Catrin got the builders in so that a part of the hospital would soon be just for its staff. On the first floor she had built a kitchen, a sitting room and a bathroom. Also she gave Eileen another room beside her bedroom so that she had her own private quarters. Eileen began to blossom with the responsibility but was very quiet the rest of the time. Catrin wished better for her but thought she had done all she could at least for now.

Catrin did not tell herself that she would go and see Eileen's mother, she got a note saying that Mrs Green had been taken ill so she just went and found that grim-faced woman leaning hard on the kitchen table with her head down. She was white-faced and in pain and rather than being sent about her business as they called it here Catrin found herself allowed inside. Mrs Green almost fell into a chair and it soon became obvious that she was losing a baby. Catrin was appalled that the woman was even able to be pregnant at her age but managed to get her on to a sofa, put her out of pain and when the miscarriage was complete she wrapped up the sodden bundle, washed the woman in warm water and made sure she was comfortable.

Thankfully one of her daughters called and Catrin was

able to give her the responsibility and made her promise that she would call at the hospital later when Tim would give her more pain-killing medicine for her mother.

There was no mention of Eileen and Catrin did not even tell Eileen she had been there. She felt guilty and yet the woman had needed her so it was just as well that she had gone.

In April slightly better weather arrived and there were flowers on the wayside. In Tel Collings' garden where all the flowers would have been about to do their work, Thora Collings, Ted's wife as she was now accepted to be, went outside with a huge spade and dug up the whole of the space so that people watched in awe. Half-grown flowers were flung out behind her. The heaps of discarded foliage grew into a mound and those whose gardens lacked flowers came in the darkness and took what they could carry. It was said in the village that Thora came from farming stock and was proving it now.

Her house, so the rumour went, was spotless. She never stopped, she was always washing her windows, hanging out sheets, blankets and clothes, good smells came from the open windows and the vegetables began to grow. She planted potatoes, carrots, parsnips, turnips, cabbages, cauliflowers, Brussel sprouts back and front and to both sides of the house. The whole plot apart from the trees was put under cultivation.

There was a huge leek trench. It was said in the village

that she fed her leeks tea but nobody knew for certain except that they grew much more quickly and were bigger than everybody else's. She fashioned a couple of large cloches in the part of the garden where the sun was warmest and here she put in tomatoes, cucumbers, radishes, spring onions and half-a-dozen kinds of lettuce. She put in the sunnier side of the garden lines of red, black and white currants, gooseberry bushes and she planted rhubarb under pails to bring it on.

Her two boys she found jobs for, one went to help in the Co-op grocery store, the other did odd jobs at the hospital and was handy to have about as he could fix anything. At the end of each week they took their pay packets home and tipped them up to their mother, being given back a few shillings in case they should want to buy something for themselves. They needed little. Their mother made all their clothes, she would have been at home in a tailor's establishment. Tel also had good clothes and he was like a different man, quiet, sober and even he had been found employment. He worked behind the bar at the Station Hotel. There was some justice in it, Catrin thought, working for Eileen's aunt and never letting a drop of beer past his lips for fear of his wife's temper.

Thora built a big run and henhouse for the back garden and then in the small building which might at one time have been some kind of barn she kept pigs. Tel Collings was no longer seen at the various pubs in the village except the one where he worked. It was rumoured that if he did not behave as Thora wished she would clout his lugs. Catrin took a great deal of pleasure from all this even though Eileen said not a word.

Catrin went back to see how Mrs Green did and the woman was obviously feeling better because she did nothing but complain about Eileen.

'Soft as clarts, she was and now look how it is. She should have known that he was no good right from the beginning.'

Catrin hated how being sensitive in places like this was seen as weakness so that in a way the more intelligent you were was the same thing as being held to be pathetic. Eileen was clever and to many people a clever woman was the worst thing she could be, unnatural and a threat to their way of living.

'You didn't see it. You and your husband wanted her to go back to him and when she did he was cruel to her.'

'Cruel? Huh, I'll give you cruel. Having ten bairns in this world, going through all that for yet another mouth and having to slave after them so that you have hardly enough to eat. That's cruelty. Our Eileen was given a man who had money and put her into a lovely house and she couldn't even hang on to him then. No wonder he got fed up with her. That Thora Mickleton is as rough as they come, she's from Rookhope where they're still eating their own bairns, but she held on to him and now she's reaping the benefits.' 'Eating their own bairns' was a nasty local saying about Rookhope because it was said to be the furthest back of anywhere, it was so isolated and the folk from there tended to be even more uneducated than anywhere else in the dale. 'She lacks for nowt she's got. Our Eileen's not coming back here no more, she disgraced us running after him in the first place and getting herself wed to a man who was already somebody else's. She was always gormless.'

Catrin was just thankful that Eileen had decided against going to see her mother. There was no point in her listening to such a rant.

Twenty-Two

John and Amy arrived home that spring. Shortly afterwards John came to see Catrin. She was horrified at how altered he was but tried not to stare. He was huge. His jacket was strained over his belly, he had a beard, not a neat beard, it was neglected and did not enhance the appearance of his three chins and the red hue of his cheeks. A large straw hat, very battered and worn, was on his head and the suit that had once been expensive and cream was now a dirty grey.

'Doctor Morgan,' he said and his voice was hoarse.

Catrin got to her feet, trying to act as though nothing was wrong.

'I heard that you were back. How is Amy?'

'She's increasing,' he said flatly and sat down heavily in a chair at the far side of her desk. 'I know I ought not to just turn up like this but things are such a mess.'

John's way of speaking of Amy's having a baby seemed to Catrin full of disrespect as though somehow he had had nothing to do with the conception, as though somehow Amy had done this on purpose and he wanted nothing to do with it. It was very upsetting for Amy, Catrin thought, and since John had changed so much and neglected everything he owned, Catrin wanted to say all manner of stinging utterances at him but she didn't. It wouldn't help.

Catrin didn't say anything and he didn't look at her from his dull and watery eyes.

'I understand that my sister is living with you and would like to know what right you have to move her from her home.'

Catrin couldn't contain herself. For him to pick on her like this was unacceptable.

'Anne was unhappy and alone and your tenants needed help. We had a bad storm here which made things worse and if it hadn't been for Jack Dunstan and Will Armstrong and all the rest of the village in fact you would have had very little to come home to.'

John said nothing, it was as though she hadn't spoken or he just chose not to hear. What man would admit that he had made such a mess of things when he had watched his father doing the same thing? Had it made no impression on him?

He put his hand over his face for a few moments as though he could bear no more and then he said shakily,

'She is terrified about having the baby. And right from the beginning I saw that we were not meant to be together. It seemed like the right thing to do but I couldn't do the things I should have done. I hate her and she hates me. We can't even be in the same room together. It's not physical. I don't hit her, I don't shout at her or throw things and neither does she, it's just so awful. She complains about everything and I just never wanted to come back. I didn't think going away would mean that I wanted to stay clear of this place for the rest of my days. I didn't know that I hated it so much. I don't know what to do. She cries all the time and she is so big. I don't think I have ever seen any woman in pregnancy that size.'

'When is the baby due?'

'Isn't that your job?' he said and it was the nearest thing he got to a smile but at least he looked at her.

'I'll come and see her.'

He looked so grateful that Catrin's heart softened for him. She wanted to ask what had happened to the money but it seemed such a stupid thing to say. If he had known that he should have been able to stop it trickling away.

And of course he blamed Amy.

'Nothing was enough. She had to refurnish the house just as she wanted and nothing I could say or do would stop her,' he said. 'She had to have a car and go abroad and everywhere we went she bragged to people that she was Lady Reed. You have no idea how embarrassing it was. She doesn't even use a knife and fork properly and she can barely read. Everywhere we went people laughed at how stupid she is.'

Not stupid enough for you not to get her with child, Catrin wanted to say but of course she couldn't.

'She is a fool,' he said. 'She is no use to me whatsoever. I need Anne back to see to everything.'

Catrin was horrified but not very surprised at his attitude. She spoke to Anne who looked scarily at her and said she didn't want to see John behaving like that and she thought it was awful that Amy was having a baby.

'I'm not going back there. It would be worse than before,' Anne said.

After evening surgery Catrin walked across to the hall. There was no answer. In the end she went into the house, calling out as she did so. She didn't want anybody to be shocked. Amy got up very slowly and carefully from the chair she had been sitting in and John had been right. She was huge. Either she was seriously ill or she was having twins, Catrin thought. She had been such a pretty woman. Now her body was bloated, her eyes were dull and she looked helplessly at Catrin.

'Amy, I'm so glad to see you,' Catrin said.

'I've turned into a whale,' Amy said with tears in her eyes and Catrin was grateful that she too was trying to keep her sense of humour. 'I hate it here and I hate John. He treats me like muck. I never thought I'd come to this. He gambled and drank the money away. We have very little left and look at me,' and she began to cry softly as though it was all she could manage.

Catrin asked her how she felt and it was obvious that she had been sick every day since she knew she was pregnant and perhaps even before that. She was nothing but huge bump and a skinny face and body. Her hair was wispy and thin and her skin was sallow. She had given all she could to this encumbrance. Catrin had never been able to work out why it was called morning sickness since a lot of women endured months and months of the horrible feelings which made them throw up. She could see also that Amy was too big to be comfortable anywhere.

'I think you need complete rest. I have a bed at the hospital for you and I'd like to take you there straight away.'

'Am I going to die?' Amy asked pitifully. 'I feel like I do want to die. Things are so awful.' She was obviously exhausted. Catrin wanted to blame John for not bringing her home sooner so that she might be looked after but then he didn't seem capable of managing anything at present.

'Certainly not. You are worn out and frightened. You can come to me and I can keep an eye on you and you will feel better very soon.'

'I think John will be pleased to be rid of me,' Amy said.

'Nonsense,' Catrin said briskly. 'He's worried about

you. He knows nothing about such things. Lots of men are scared of their wives giving birth but it's completely natural.' You lying toad, she told herself.

In the end John drove his wife and Catrin back to the hospital. He had volunteered to get the car so readily that Catrin had seen how very eager he was to give the responsibility to someone else and within a very few minutes Amy was in bed and looking, even though not feeling, better. She certainly looked relieved and grateful to be where she could be helped in the right way. She barely spoke to John and he did not look at her. He looked ashamed of himself. He left as soon as he could and went back to the hall though Catrin could see that he was reluctant. Other men had taken care of what was meant to be his and the evidence of it was all around him. Mended fences, sound houses, healthy animals. The house had been kept clean for their return. The coalhouse was full, the larder was stocked with food, everything was as it should be and none of it was his doing.

Catrin thought that Anne would want to see her brother but when Amy was brought to hospital Anne was nowhere to be seen. When he had gone and Catrin went into her surgery Anne appeared, as Catrin had thought she might, looking anxiously at her.

'I barely recognized him,' Anne said, 'he is falling apart and according to what I hear she is huge.'

'They are finding everything hard. Do you feel now that you'd like to go back and help?'

Anne shook her head.

'I want to stay with you. I feel that I shall always want to be with you,' and she flung herself into Catrin's arms. It was a sweet moment.

Anne was eager to learn from the people around her and she spent a lot of time in the kitchens helping Mrs Clements and learning about which foods were best for which patients. She spent time with Mrs Benson in the herb gardens and in the vegetable garden which the hospital now had helping to grow what would best sustain the patients.

When Amy had been at the hospital for two weeks Catrin found Anne at Amy's bedside quietly talking to her and she was so pleased to see them together and she thought that it did them both good.

Twenty-Three

Catrin kept going to see Una but it seemed to her that Una was there a little less each time they met like she was a photograph that was fading. Catrin couldn't say this to Una so she went to Jack's office and talked to him. She wasn't telling him anything he didn't know, she could see by his face, and she didn't get the impression that he blamed her, he didn't.

'I don't know what to do,' she admitted, 'I don't seem to be doing any good.'

'It was always a long shot but it was kind of you to try. She's getting worse, don't you think?'

Catrin admitted that Una was getting worse and she felt so helpless and no doubt he felt exactly the same way.

'Can you think of anything that might have caused this problem? She can't have been like this when you met or it would never have got this far.'

He frowned, trying to think.

'I don't know. I suppose it was just different. I wasn't looking for problems but around here most of the time unless it's unusually good weather people don't spend a lot of time outside and when we were together it was dancing and parties. We didn't go walking or stuff like that. I don't think people do in towns. What would be the point?'

'Would you mind if I went to Newcastle and tried to talk to her parents?'

He looked surprised.

'Of course not but I'm not sure it would do any good. They are called Watkins,' and he wrote down the address.

It was always difficult for Catrin to get any time to herself but as soon as she could on a good day – at least thus far – she finished her morning surgery very early for once and set off for Newcastle on the train with instructions from Jack as to the direction to take.

Newcastle was very busy but she managed to board a bus which took her down to the river and almost out of the town. There stood the house where Una's parents lived. If you cared for living in big houses and for status and such like it really was magnificent. She saw a glimpse of it from just further away on the rise. There was a lodge but when she banged on the locked gates and shouted and called several times there was no response so she went around the outside and she found toe holes in the stones where she was hopefully unobserved and she climbed in and over the top, landing better than she had expected to in long grass on the other side. The ground was hard but she was unhurt and rather pleased with herself though convinced that she had torn some clothing. She had heard a rip, brief but acute. However there would be time to worry about trivialities later.

The house was not far and she could see no impediment, no dogs running loose, no sound from the house that any dog had heard her or been alerted in some sense. There was no gardener to ask her what on earth she thought she was doing. She therefore made her way around the building until she found the front door.

She knocked on the huge oak door with what she hoped was the right kind of force and stood back on the top step for a couple of minutes. She could hear a noise inside the house. The door was opened by a servant, at least she presumed the woman in a plain black dress was some kind of maid.

'I am Doctor Catrin Morgan. I wondered whether Mr and Mrs Watkins are at home. I would like a short audience.'

She wasn't sure this was the right thing to say, she had rarely spent time with such people but the maid said in polite Newcastle tones that she would enquire. The hall was large and nothing was as Catrin had expected. Halls in the old houses where she had spent time were usually dark and held foreboding with gloomy staircases leading away into the darkness both upstairs and down, but this one was full of sunshine. It had been designed by a specialist. The rooms at either side had windows from the hall which looked straight into them and they had been housed so that all the light from outside got into everywhere and she thought it looked so cheerful and upbeat.

Did they not care for privacy? She could see books and sofas, huge rugs and curtains which were pulled so far back that no amount of light was stifled in them. The designer had wanted to show off the elegance of the decorations on the walls and ceilings and the fireplaces. Catrin was mesmerised at being allowed such glimpses into the way that these people lived.

Shortly afterwards she was motioned into a library as she had perceived with leather-bound books on every wall. It also had desks and armchairs and reading lamps and a big sofa before the fire where sat a man and woman who were undoubtedly Una's parents. She looked like both of them.

The man, Robert Watkins, got to his feet and he was a big, slender man, good-looking, his face red with anger just at present. He was glaring at her.

'Who are you and how did you get in?'

'My name as I said is Doctor Catrin Morgan and since your gates were locked and I couldn't rouse anybody from the gatehouse, though I shouted several times, I climbed over the wall.'

He seemed astonished, but how else could she have got in, Catrin thought.

'And this seemed suitable behaviour for a woman and a doctor?'

'I wanted to meet you and could see no other way to gain admittance.'

'We do not like strangers. Please leave.'

'I want to talk to you about your daughter.'

'Get out!' he said.

'Una is ill. I don't know what to do. I thought you might be able to help. If I knew something of her medical history it could be useful.'

The woman got up from the sofa and came over, face pale.

'Ill?'

'Nancy, we said what we had to say—'

'But if she's seriously ill? What are the symptoms?'

'If it hadn't been serious I wouldn't be here. You are my last hope,' Catrin said.

'We decided to have nothing else to do with them after she married that – that pitman.'

'Please, Rob,' his wife implored and he looked at her pale set face and then he said,

'Sit down, Doctor Morgan.'

She told them about Una's symptoms and their faces were grave.

'She was always a difficult child,' Robert said but without resentment.

'We were very sociable people,' Nancy said, 'We have

a place by the sea near Alnwick. She wanted to stay in and read when we went there. She wouldn't learn to ride, she wouldn't go into the water, she didn't even like the beach, the waves seemed to terrify her.'

'She didn't even want to build sandcastles,' he put in, looking down at his fingers as though he couldn't bear the memories.

'Did you make her go outside?'

'We tried to but she would scream and fling herself around,' he said. 'Even here she went nowhere and saw no one. She ought to have been a nun, one of those like the Carmelites who shut themselves away from the world.'

'Did she want to become a nun?'

He laughed and that was when he sounded bitter.

'Not she! She met that – that man and he turned her against us. He seemed to think he had all the answers. We could never speak to her after that. She ignored everything we said, everything we did. I wouldn't care but she met him here in our house. I would have given anything for it not to happen. From the first he determined to have her. Even though we were against it he kept coming here. We tried talking to him to tell him that she was unwell but he didn't listen. He wanted her so much. I don't call that love, it's more like obsession. He ran off with her in the night. That was the worst of it somehow, that she left us and went with him. I knew it wouldn't be any use.

'He's a nasty piece of work, lied and cheated to get what he wanted, grubbing his way to the top as though he thought he stood a chance, as though he was a gentleman.'

All Catrin could think at this point was how sad it all was. She was no further forward. Whatever had made her think that the answer to her questions was here, that there were any answers? Mental health was so complicated. Physical health was bad enough but at least sometimes you got an answer. Often there were several possibilities, there could be solutions, but she had the feeling that this was one of those problems that would keep her awake at night. She didn't know what to think.

She felt sorry for them all but especially for Jack who had thought the magic of love would help his wife. Catrin's instincts told her that there was something more here, something she was missing but she could not think of it and then she took a look around the room and realized what it was. There were no photographs of anyone as though the past had been so bad that they had erased it from their minds and yet Una must have been a lovely child and she was all they had. Everybody had photographs. Had they put all the photographs in a cupboard somewhere because they could not bear to think of her after she had left? Catrin didn't understand it at all. Was this their way of erasing the past as though it had been unbearable? She hated mysteries and yet didn't know what to do or say. She felt lost.

There was silence.

'Una talks about her governess but little about you,' she ventured.

Robert Watkins left his wife to come to the rescue but she was the one who said,

'We – we spent a lot of time with friends as Una got older. She had nurses to start with and . . . and . . . We had a lot of friends in London and places like that are not suitable for a child so we tended to leave her here.'

Nancy didn't look at Catrin and her hands worked twisting in her lap as though she couldn't bear the memories. Why? Why had they tried to cut this child from their hearts? Had she been mentally ill when she was small and they couldn't bear it and so pretended that she didn't matter. And it wasn't just that they thought she had married the wrong man, surely it must have started before that to have such an impact. What could she possibly have done as a child that made them not want to see her or have her as part of their family? Catrin didn't understand how that could happen. She would have given anything to have had Anne there with her right from the beginning. Her life would have been so much easier in so many ways even if people had despised them both for what she had done and brought upon her child. There was nothing more important than a child, surely?

Catrin looked around the room again.

'Have you always lived here?'

'No,' he put in. 'When Una was a small child we lived elsewhere in the town.'

'But you moved here.'

'Yes, we – we decided that as she got bigger—'

Here he stopped.

It was a limp explanation and none of what they were saying was true, Catrin was certain but she couldn't make it out.

'It must have been very hard for you to have only one child,' she said finally. She knew what it was like now to have one child and lose her but she also knew the joy of having regained that child. Yet somehow and for some reason these people did not feel like that about their only child. They had left her with other people as though even the sight of her, even her presence would dismay them. Catrin knew that it was fashionable for well-off folk to treat their children in such a way, though she deplored it, but she was also aware that as the silence went on something was very much amiss.

'If there is anything at all which you think would help Una now, please tell me. I think she will die if I don't find out something which would help her and Jack – I know you don't like him but he is devoted to her, he loves her so very much. Please try and think of a way to help him, something perhaps in her childhood that went wrong, some difficult thing that happened or—'

Here Nancy burst out sobbing. Her husband looked despairingly at her.

'Stop it, Nancy, stop it, please. There's nothing we can do.'

His wife managed to curtail her sobs as though she had had to take control of her emotions a hundred times before. Within seconds she was not crying and not shuddering and to Catrin it was like neither of them could bear anything in their lives and that the only way they could manage it was to deny what had happened.

'Did you dislike your only child?' she threw at them in a last-ditch attempt to find the truth.

He caught hold of his wife's hands and looked into her eyes in case she might say something. His steel gaze held her there and neither of them spoke.

Catrin wished for the thousandth time that Roddy was still alive. At least she would have somebody to talk to about what, if anything, she could do. She must go and tell Jack what she had found out. Was she right in what she thought? She didn't know. If she got this wrong she could make things worse.

Sitting in Jack's office that afternoon there was a long silence after she told him what she thought she had discovered.

'I could be wrong of course, it could be something she

was born with but I have the feeling that these things are produced or made worse by experience. Also it worries me that in making her think she remembers what happened I could make the problem so much harder.'

'It could be harder?' he said.

'Well—'

'She might kill herself. Catrin, she has no life.'

'What if she blames herself for something in her childhood.'

Jack looked blankly at her.

'Like what?' he said.

Catrin didn't know.

It was the end of the shift. Miners streamed down the path and out into the road. Catrin could hear the noise of Miss Waskerley's typewriter next door. And it started to rain so loudly that it stotted off the roof and cascaded on to the roads like a pale grey curtain, becoming impenetrable for several minutes and then gradually it ceased and after a short period of silence the sun began to shine.

Twenty-Four

Frank Melrose came to see Catrin. He looked sheepishly at her.

'I think you know why I am here,' he said. 'I have heard talk that Eileen's husband is a bigamist and that therefore she is not married to him. And that his wife and two sons are now living with him.'

It occurred to Catrin that if Eileen did want to marry Frank Melrose now she would fare much better in Stanhope than she would here where all her family and former friends lived, where she had been known as a child and was now seen as a disgrace.

'I'm also concerned that such an experience would put her off trying again,' he said.

'Eileen finds her life here almost impossible,' Catrin said.

Even then he hesitated and she reflected that it was not easy for him to try again either.

Mr Melrose seemed to spend a long time with Eileen in her own rooms that afternoon but Catrin was much too busy to pay attention. That evening she went to an outlying farm to see a dying man. His wife had especially requested that if Catrin was not busy she would come and be at his bedside. She had done so much for him over the previous months that they were almost friends so although Catrin could do nothing to prevent his death having already made sure he was in no pain, it seemed the right thing to do if it brought him and his family some comfort.

It was a dark rainy night but it was only a couple of miles away and Catrin was so busy at the hospital at the moment that it was a relief to ride away and breathe in the soft rain as evening fell. Although there was nothing more she could do she wanted to say goodbye to Mr Fellowes, who was a musician of some repute. He performed at concerts, in schools, in village halls all over the area. He had brought a lot of pleasure to a great many people over the years. Catrin had heard him play his beloved cello several times and had been more than happy to help while she could. He would be a great miss in the dale to everyone.

Catrin could not help thinking of Roddy dying as she rode Cymbeline through the rain. He had gone out in bad weather but her health was good whereas Roddy had always had problems.

The farm where the Fellowes family lived was not run as a farm anymore. It was just the house and gardens that he loved. The fields had all been rented to other farmers round about. It was a most comfortable place and when Catrin got there a ready stable lad came out to take her horse. The house was cream with light seemingly in every room and as she entered there was a maid to take her wet things and to show her through into where the Fellowes family and their friends were having a party for the dying man.

There was something so inspiring about this that Catrin felt happy. Musicians played, there was food and tea and whisky and the rooms were full of talk and laughter. Mr Fellowes was sitting up in his bed and although he knew his time had come he was strong enough to enjoy the talk and laughter and the music made him happy. Catrin sat down with him and took his hands and he and his wife said that they were so glad she had come.

As the night grew late people went home in a sky that had cleared and when it was quiet Catrin and Mrs Fellowes sat there with him while they talked softly and held his hands and Mrs Fellowes thanked Catrin so much. After he died his son and daughter went out to the stable with her and she rode away into the cool wind and back to her hospital with renewed vigour.

She thought about Tim and Agatha and how they had spent a long time working out the drugs that would help Mr Fellowes best as he became less and less able and she was so grateful that they had sat down and thought so hard about this and that they had got it right. She couldn't wait to get back to Tim and Agatha and tell them.

When she got back to the hospital Tim and Agatha were waiting for her and she told them of their success but she could also see that Agatha had seen her father and her face was grave. It seemed to Catrin that Mr Melrose must have been turned down by Eileen and how disappointed Agatha would be. She was such an unselfish person and felt guilty for leaving her father and Catrin was sorry too because she did feel that if Eileen could get away life would be much easier for her. However Eileen was waiting for her when she went into their sitting room and she was heavy-eyed and pale-faced.

'Mr Melrose asked me to marry him, Catrin but I couldn't,' she said.

'Too soon?' said Catrin, wishing she had had time to make tea before she had to endure anyone else's problems. 'Will you have some tea with me? I've been over to see Mr Fellowes and his family. They were all there for him and it was a peaceful death. I wish we could give everyone the same.'

'So do I,' Eileen said and then she stopped because she obviously had more to say but didn't want to but she went on anyway.

'I need to get way from here and a lot further than Stanhope,' she said.

Catrin had been dreading this. She knew that Eileen

was too sensitive to put up with the situation as it was but she didn't know what to suggest. Also she wasn't sure she could manage without Eileen but then she hadn't thought she could manage without Roddy. When you had no options you just got on with it and did the best that you could.

'You have your own life to think about, Eileen. Maybe this is your chance to turn things around and whether you do that here or somewhere else you know that I will always be pleased for you.'

Twenty-Five

It was Will who helped to move on Catrin's problem with Una. It wasn't easy for her to meet or talk to him. At Jack and Una's home she felt awkward and then she didn't know whether Jack and Will were at the house together or at the pit together so it was difficult to get Will by himself and she found more and more that she wanted to see him, to spend time with him.

In the end he sent a note to her at the hospital and she met him in the pit office which he had timed so that they should have it to themselves. He greeted her with a smile and sat her down and then he told her where the Watkins family had lived in another house in a different part of Newcastle.

'My father knew Una's father quite well at one time. They belonged to the same club and knew the same crowd. My mother didn't like Mrs Watkins so I don't think it ever became a social thing but they did have parties at their old house which my mother felt obliged to go to and I remember her complaining about it though never in front of my father.

'I could take you there if you think it might help. Jack isn't saying much but I did gather something of the kind. He doesn't believe things can improve. He's so afraid he will lose her and because he can't bear the thought he just can't go forward somehow.'

Catrin knew that there was probably nothing to be gained but she was at a loss as to get Una any further than they had now. Una was putting on a little weight but she kept losing it every time she was upset and she still could never bear to venture downstairs or out into the garden where Will was making such a difference.

He was doing the things Jack had not the patience or time to do and they had a good cook to tempt Una's appetite and women from the village to make sure that the house was in good order so that everything was as clean and neat as it could be.

On the first day that they had free Catrin and Will went into Newcastle. Will drove his little rusty car to the far side of the city and out almost into the country where the houses petered out and those that were still there had huge gardens around them.

The house was empty. She hadn't thought about that. She had imagined it would look like any other house. She even felt sorry for it, like the story where the princess had gone to sleep for a hundred years and her prince had had to hack through the trees to get to her except that it was nothing like that. It stood quite alone as though its history had condemned it to remain in solitary confinement for the rest of its life. The gates were padlocked but Will made short work of this, saying only that it was one of the useful things he had learned in the army.

The gates were rotten and creaked open and then she saw the house and yes, she thought, it had been punished, neglected because of what had happened. There was something about the place which she did not like and she was so glad that she had not come by herself or she might have run away.

Will led the way as they went through the trees and the thick undergrowth. The house was in a sad way. Its roof was half off, slates were scattered around it, the windows were broken, the wooden panes had lost their paint and were rotten. She and Will made their way around the side of the house and there were coach houses and inside them were stalls where horses would have been kept and above them haylofts with stairs up to them. The stairs were rotten and there were gaps.

Outside again and around to the left were huge back gardens and then fields, no doubt for the horses to graze. Beside them and just further along was a tiny house with a pitched roof and there was a well. The house had been painted red many years ago and the paint had peeled, leaving rotten bare wood beneath. The door had been bolted but it was easily got past and then inside was the well and it was boarded over.

Catrin could hardly breathe by then. Her throat ached. He got hold of her hand and looked into her face and said,

'Has this helped at all?'

'Not that I can see. I feel that there is something here that matters, which would alter how things are but I can't find it. Do you understand?'

'I think so. Your instincts are telling you that Una was unhappy here for some reason and that sounds good to me. You didn't feel that about the house where her parents live now, did you?'

'No, but strangely I preferred that. It's a very open place, as though there were no secrets.'

'Perhaps they left all their secrets here,' Will said and Catrin thought yes, he is right, I just wish we could find the connection.

'There were no photographs on the walls,' she told him, remembering. 'Isn't that strange?'

'Almost unique I would think. Even though I have fallen out with my brothers there is still history, there are a lot of photographs of us when we were children and growing up. It would take a lot to dislodge those things. Do you think there was some kind of tragedy here which affected the family very much?'

'I do.'

She was so grateful for Will's understanding. It was like having Roddy with her but different and she was so grateful for his insight that she could have kissed him.

'You're so very kind,' she told him.

'I hate to see Jack and Una unhappy. I didn't give her up so that he could move in and for them to be unhappy.'

'Do you still feel the same way about her?'

'I couldn't. I like them both too much and also I think now that I was too young to have made a decent husband to Una or anyone else. I think I need a different kind of person now.'

He didn't say any more and she didn't like to prompt him, but her heart began to sing just a little and she thought this house has already given something to us.

Before they left he said,

'I think it might make a difference if we could per-suade Una to come here.'

'You do?' she looked hopefully at him.

'Absolutely.'

'She won't leave the house.'

'From what you've said she is going to have to if she's to go on living and when she dies Jack essentially dies with her. We'll talk to him about it and maybe even talk to her and try to make them understand.'

Catrin went back to see Una. It was not that she was unwelcome there, it was that she had told herself she was being of no use and to see Una up there in that room a prisoner to her memories, to her past life and to the inability of medicine to get so far as to understand her suffering. Never had Catrin wished to be two hundred years ahead where hopefully understanding would be better, or would it? Did things really go forward or were they like the world, spinning around and getting nowhere?

Una was getting thinner and thinner. If anything happened to this woman Catrin would blame herself, stupidly she knew, but it was her job to make things better, to ease pain of whatever kind, for people to live to be old and have joy as well as sorrow in their lives.

She asked if she might sit down. All Una did was nod and look in front of her. Catrin didn't question her, she talked stupidly she thought, but perhaps slightly amusingly of stories of what was going on in the village, and gradually Una stopped looking vacantly around her and began to pay attention.

Jack brought up tea and toast since it was Sunday morning.

Catrin's Sundays had recently changed and she had been rather glad of this. She had fallen into a routine and was beginning to enjoy her Sundays, this being an exception because she constantly worried about Una.

Catrin had taken to going to Roddy's grave, to the church and then to take part in the service. She was deriving some comfort from it and it made Sundays that little bit special. Sometimes too she saw Lily Bell there, dressed in black as befits a widow and Catrin had gone to her and offered her Sunday dinner at the hospital.

The first time Lily refused but after that she went back and it happened that everybody else was busy so they sat down just the two of them and it was as though a miracle happened. They talked about Roddy. Lily looked happy for the first time since Roddy had died. Her eyes shone and she listened and then she asked questions and Catrin found herself telling this woman about her early life and therefore Roddy's childhood and everything that had happened since. It was so good to talk about her brother. She loved the sound of his name on her lips.

Lily had imagined a future with Roddy, a home with children and perhaps even grandchildren. It was sad but at least she could talk about it, about what she had hoped for and even though it had not come to fruition it was another way of looking at the young man who had had such a short life. Lily had known so little of him but she confided to Catrin that she had fallen in love with him the very moment she saw him.

The following week she sent a note to Catrin asking if Catrin would like to come and have Sunday dinner with her. Nobody that Catrin knew was ever asked to Lily's house, which was huge and somehow secretive though Lily had lots of servants and they gossiped about her and her house and her loneliness.

Her house was so luxurious that Catrin was amazed at

the thick carpets, the damask curtains, the walls which had no paintings or photographs, the bookcases which were filled with what Catrin privately thought were ghastly ornaments but she admired them. Plates hanging on the walls featured puppies and kittens. The ornaments glistened pink and purple and yellow and were unlikely looking dolphins leaping out of an imaginary sea. There were shelves filled with shells as though Lily had gone to the beach especially for these perhaps on a particular seaside holiday.

The meal was served in the biggest dining room that Catrin had ever come across. Lily confided that she had never been asked anywhere in years,

'But I knew that you and Doctor Morgan were different. You were so kind. People did try to look after me when my parents died but somehow I couldn't bear it. I thought they resented how well off I was. I imagined they were after my money. Every bit of kindness seemed like an insult. After a while they stopped asking me anywhere. I never went out, I was even afraid to go to church that somebody might speak to me and say the wrong thing, as though every word wasn't wrong to me then.'

Catrin had never seen so many servants for one person. The meal was sumptuous and had been so well cooked that Catrin enjoyed it very much. Trout from the river in some kind of sauce which tasted like lemon and perhaps wine. There were potatoes baked to make what looked like a large wave. There was fillet steak, which Catrin had not often had before, cooked so gently and softly that it was like a sigh in the mouth. They had a chocolate mousse with light almond biscuits and blue cheese and chutney and there was even wine, white wine and then red wine, just small glasses but they were very welcome. After that they sat by the windows listening to the light rain and drank coffee and later tea and Catrin thought she had never seen Lily look so happy.

Sunday mornings then had changed. Often she had dinner with Lily, having met before at church but sometimes she went to see Una, half afraid that she would make things worse but one thing was certain. She could not leave things as they were or Una would die. One Sunday about a month after her and Will's visit to the old house she called in and Jack greeted her and made tea and ushered her upstairs.

Jack put down the tray and asked Una if she would like him to stay. His voice was filled with despair. Una shook her head very slightly and then he went out and closed the door gently.

'He worries so about me.'

'He cares very much. Tell me about you. I know so little.'

'I did tell you about meeting Jack and how we found one another. I feel so sorry for him now and it's all my fault.'

'What makes you say that?'

'I thought I could make him happy. I don't know why I thought I could when I couldn't make myself happy. If you can't be happy yourself how could you ever help anyone else? I hate myself so much. I should never have agreed to marry him.'

'You love him. Isn't that how it's supposed to work?'

'My love has been nothing. I can't bear to be touched. I can't bear to touch other people. I knew that when I met him. I thought those feelings would go away but they haven't and gradually the world has got less and less until very often there is nothing but this room except that occasionally I make myself be very brave and go outside into the night. The night hugs me and I don't mind. For a little while and then I'm so afraid that I can't move and Jack has to come and get me and bring me back here so that I can recover in this room.'

There was a long silence after that. Catrin didn't know what to say or do, she felt stifled by her lack of knowledge and it was so frustrating.

'Did you always prefer the night?'

Una thought hard.

'I think I did. There is nothing to fear somehow.'

'A lot of folk fear the darkness rather than the light.'

'I find the light intrusive. It gets into my head and shows up dark corners and won't go away. It's like it's nibbling at me, into my flesh, causing wounds that never heal. Full summer light is so harsh and unforgiving. I feel as if I wilt under it.'

'Did you feel like that as a child?'

'I liked being inside so much. It was safer. Outside there were so many other people that I didn't know and perhaps they knew things about me that they didn't like.'

'Why wouldn't they like you?'

'I'm not good enough.'

She said nothing more but Catrin knew that she was on thin ice here. A wrong sentence and Una would trust her no further and perhaps refuse to see her again.

'Did you always live in Newcastle as a child?' The Watkins had said so but she wanted to hear what Una thought and said,

'Not all the time. We had a house on the coast.'

'Did you like it?

'No.'

'Why not?'

'The sea came right up to the door. I thought it would come inside. Sometimes when the weather was very rough the waves seemed to scream at the windows, hurl themselves at the walls. We needed sandbags to protect us. The wind would scream around the house and make such awful noises. And it was always icy. The coal came from the beach and smelled of seaweed. I hated the smell of seaweed and how if you slipped on it you fell and hurt yourself on the big rocks.

'We had a nurse who would take me out every day and I grew to hate her. She made me wear a bathing suit that was horrible and itchy and kept falling down. Sometimes she would take me into water that I knew would go over my head and she would lower me into it until I screamed and flailed my arms around. I think it was a way of teaching me to swim. How wrong. I didn't understand why people have to go out when they don't want to. After all if you want fresh air you can open the windows. I had to go for long walks and they made my legs ache and my head and the sand was always so heavy, heavier with each step. I had nasty things to eat. She used to bake orange cheese in vinegar and mushrooms that she found in the fields in milk with salt and pepper. Sometimes the mushrooms had maggots in them.'

Catrin thought she would never eat a mushroom again even though she was aware that this could have been a childhood exaggeration and that it had probably happened only once. At least she told herself that.

'The cheese was like rubber and the vinegar made my tongue sore.'

'Did you have any family your age on either of your parents' side or any close friends when you were small?"

'I never had anybody close. Never anybody there. Until Jack came.'

And even that, Catrin thought, had seemed impossible. She had tried various things with Una which she thought might help. She tried to take her into her childhood in depth but Una had seemingly either had nothing bad there or had pushed it from her mind so forcefully that she could not tell Catrin anything. She tried different kinds of breathing but Una would either throw up or her breath would close her body down and she would faint. Not being able to breathe, Catrin knew, was the hardest thing of all.

There was, that she could see, no fault in her relationship with Jack unless it was so well hidden she was unaware of it and besides Catrin thought that Una had only given way to these problems when he had made her feel safe.

Twenty-Six

Catrin and Will talked to Jack downstairs without Una about what little progress they had made and about whether to try and persuade Una out of the house and back to Newcastle and the house where she had been born. Catrin was convinced that they had moved for a reason as both houses were of the same type, large and detached with big gardens, but neither of them was convinced it would do any good and Catrin was half sure that it would make things worse. It would not be accomplished soon or easily. Indeed, it might never be done.

Una began to go downhill rapidly, which was a shock to Catrin and Jack. He stopped going to work. He tried not to because he wasn't sure it helped, he told Catrin, but what else could he do? It was just as well that Will was so capable that somehow Will's presence had worked out because nothing else had. Catrin understood Jack's self-pity. It was aimed not at himself but at his beautiful wife who now slept little and what she ate came back. When she did get out of bed he carried her everywhere.

She weighed as little as a lapdog, he told Catrin when they were alone.

Catrin tried not to go every day. She was not helping herself or them, but she was so aware of her failure. In spite of telling herself that she had no idea what she was doing in this area and reading every book she could get her hands on and writing to various other doctors who might know anything which could help, she was no further forward and it had to be acknowledged that Una was dying.

Jack looked awful. She remembered the man she had met, how he was confident and seemed to her uncaring. She could see now that all the care he could manage had been swallowed up by his wife's illness. They talked a lot. It was the only comfort they had. Catrin was also aware that she must not neglect her other patients. She couldn't afford to fail anywhere else. She was grateful for Eileen and Agatha and Tim and the others who kept her practice and her hospital going. It was as though they were standing beneath her as she fell and she was falling now.

If they didn't get this right Una would die and Jack would be left like a man who had lost his balance at the top of a waterfall and was quickly tumbling into the depths with no hope left. She had the feeling that without Una Jack would not last. He had had a tough life and sometimes there was only so much people could bear. She thought that when Una died Jack might kill himself. In the middle of the night she called herself pathetic and stupid and that that was not true but then some people loved only once.

It was Will who suggested again they should go back to the house in Newcastle. Jack couldn't see the point and Catrin was worried that since Una couldn't even leave the house except at night, it might make things worse, but Will was adamant. Catrin didn't trust people who were so set on a certain way forward but she didn't know what else to do.

'We could go early in the morning while it's still dark,' Will said, 'and we'll cover her up and Jack can carry her into the car and hold her close so that she can shut her eyes and hide against him.'

So Will drove and Catrin sat beside him while Jack held his wife, wrapped in a huge blanket so that she did not have to look. Catrin was not convinced this would make any difference but she didn't know how to go forward any other way.

Morning was just beginning to lighten the sky. It had rained all night and over Newcastle there was a thick fog coming off the river.

This made it all more strange, Catrin thought. The fog was thick and almost pink from the many chimneys which made up the city and it moved and swirled. Sometimes she thought she could see and moments later she could not see the others or anywhere in front of her.

Una hid her face against Jack, eyes tight shut so that she could not glimpse the daylight which she had learned to be so afraid of.

They made slow progress. Will pushed open the gates and Jack saw for the first time the punished house. That was how Catrin thought of it for she had the feeling that something had happened here which had made the difference to Una's life. It was a grasping at straws she knew but she had no other idea which she imagined would help. Neglect produced such awful results, broken windows, scarred doors, shattered paving stones and, worst of all, the dreadful silence which means that someone has given up on this house as though it were to blame for what happened here. People cursed places. Perhaps they could curse nothing more tangible, maybe it was all they had.

Slowly they walked through the mess. The greenhouses on either side of the garden wall were great mountains of glass and rotted wood. Plants inside had been left and had reached up, strangled and desperate towards the light, with yellowed leaves and parched soil.

Catrin, Jack, Una and Will made their way all round the garden until they reached the back where there was a big space where no doubt in the old days carriages had turned. There were carriage houses and beyond the big stable yard where the horses would have lived there were several fields, and before you walked into the fields there was the well Catrin remembered from when she and Will had been there. Una was crying noiselessly by then, her clawed fingers thrust into the cotton of Jack's coat and her knees bent inward in defeat and yet he urged her very gently into the light. She kept her eyes tightly shut and then he talked so quietly to her that Catrin could barely hear what he was saying.

And then she opened her eyes.

'Where is this?'

'This is the house where you lived when you were a very small child,' Catrin said.

'I never lived here.' At first she denied it and didn't even peep out from Jack's coat but after a little while when all four of them just stood still she managed to look around and shake her head which Catrin counted as progress.

'You were born here and you lived here when you were a very little girl.'

'No I wasn't. I don't remember any of this. I think you've made a mistake. I would have remembered, I'm sure. I want to go home.' She began to cry helplessly. 'I want to go home, Jack. I want to go home to my own room and my bed where I feel safe.'

They waited until she stopped talking and crying and this time Una deliberately made herself look, she tried to take in the various buildings, the paths, the way that there were differently defined gardens which had walls and gates and hedges and the weather was with them. It did not grow light as the fog only lifted a little as it began to drizzle.

Finally she shut her eyes and begged to go home again and Jack was all for giving up. He shook his head. Catrin had the feeling that if they went further into the back and Una might look out over the fields and where the land began to go down to the bottom of the hill her memory might have been jogged and Una opened her eyes and gazed as best she could where, at the back of the house and beyond the buildings which belonged to it, there were fields.

'The horses would have been out here in fine weather,' Will said. 'And a lot of families kept the odd cow and when the weather was dry in the summer one of the stable lads would have come out here and worked the pump and primed the well with the idea that if you feed it it starts to give water and then the horses and cattle all come round to drink there. Don't you think it's such a lovely idea?'

Una stared in front of her at the well.

'It's a tiny house,' she said.

'It's meant to look like that because it does such an important job,' Catrin said trying just to keep the conversation going, it didn't matter what she said. 'I have the feeling that is what houses look like in places like Austria where they get lots of snow. The roof extends far out from the rest of the building so that the snow when it melts will slide off the roof. In some places the men climb up from the back somehow and shovel the snow if it gets too heavy so that it does not soak through the roof and into the rooms below.'

She knew that she was talking too much but her talking seemed to slow down the day as if there might be no other day, no forward, no backward. Nothing but the slide of her words into the stillness because it was a perfectly still day, only now the sound of rain gently pitter-pattering on the roof of the little well house and as it did so the fog began to lift and she could see the tops of the houses far below at the bottom of the hill.

Jack would have moved but Catrin squeezed his arm. She knew that he felt they had failed, that he didn't know how to do any more and he just wanted to go home and she didn't blame him, but she held him there as the day changed and as they stood a little brightness came over the day and from nowhere suddenly the grey and white clouds lifted and you could see clearly all around.

Una gave a shrill cry into the morning and hid her face and began to sob. She cried for a long time and when she had stopped she wriggled and struggled, breaking free of Jack's embrace, as though she did not see that it was light or as though she saw beyond it to some other time and she stood still and looked at the well. She gazed at it and then she said, in a very unsteady voice, barely above a whisper and yet it contained a sureness in its tone which Catrin had not heard from Una before,

'I was very small. We had been playing in the field, we had a nursemaid with us and we were gathering long-stemmed buttercups. You held one under your chin and if it glowed then you loved butter.

'We had been learning a nursery rhyme and Sebastian was singing it and singing it. There was a nursemaid who was called Betty. She shouted. She ran across the lawn and she shouted. I was running, I was running across the grass here and I was being left behind because my legs were so short. I was left and she ran on and I could hear his voice, he was singing one of the songs which she had taught him. 'Ding dong dell, pussy's in the well, who put her in, Little John Green, Who pulled her out, Little Tommy Stout. What a naughty boy was that to try and drown poor pussy cat, who never did him any harm but killed the mice in the farmer's barn,' and he ran on so that he would get pussy out and Betty was running after him and I was running too, not to get there but so that I could stop the rhyme that was playing on and on in my head and Sebastian was shouting,

'"I'll get her out. I'll get her out," and then he fell and he screamed and Betty screamed and so did I.'

In the silence that followed it began to rain harder as Una started walking over to the well, to the place where her brother had died.

Twenty-Seven

Amy gave birth to a boy and a girl. Catrin was half convinced that she wouldn't make it, her body was much too small but Tim, who had become essential to difficult births, was there the whole time. He fed Amy drugs so that she could manage the birth almost without pain and Catrin thought she had never been more grateful to anyone than she was to him that day. They spent the whole day and night until Amy was finally relieved of her burdens and they kept a close eye on her. Tim was worried about childbed fever or that she would die of sheer exhaustion.

Anne sat by the bed almost all the time for two weeks after delivery when Amy finally began to get better. Anne fell in love with the babies immediately and they affected her happiness such as nothing had done before. While Catrin was glad of this she realized that she was jealous of Amy. It was not Amy who was fascinating to Anne but somehow that didn't help. Catrin no longer came first with Anne and it made her feel lost and yet guilty. They did not know for certain that Anne was hers and she needed to try to step back and let Anne be the person she wanted to be. That was a lot more important than the relationship between them. Anne needed to stop thinking about what she was and begin to be who she was about to be as a grown woman so Catrin quenched the loneliness she felt as Anne declared with joy,

'I'm their auntie,' and her eyes shone.

She wanted to be there with Amy all the time and Catrin watched the relationship between the young girl and the young woman who was trying so hard to be a mother to all three and finding it very heavy-going. Anne would make a huge difference here. It would be good for all the family and now the two babies were the future and they had a mother and a father and an auntie. How lucky they were.

Feeding both babies proved too much and so Amy gave up trying to breastfeed them and after that Anne could do such a lot with bottles and nappies and shushing them to sleep since one would wake and then awaken the other. It was horrible Catrin told herself but she could not be part of this and therefore had no place in their little family.

It was three weeks before John came to the hospital, shamefaced but sober and he had lost weight and looked much better. Also he was very proud to have an heir so that his acres would not go to whoever the cousin in

Northumberland was and now he had a purpose. He would make things right for his boy, he said.

The twins were christened with a lot of fuss at the parish church and the boy was called John as were all the family boys and the little girl was very tactfully, thought Catrin, called Anne. She thought Anne would burst with pride.

John took his little family home and Anne went off with them without a word to Catrin who had to stop herself from crying.

Agatha and Tim now had defined roles. She would deal with the general drugs and with the public but he was now into measuring the drugs which were given when there were severe problems. They worked like one person in that way, Catrin thought and she was grateful for it.

Catrin was now paying so many wages to make all her schemes work that she wished there was more money coming in. Her father's money had gone to all kinds of practical uses but people were making such good use of the hospital that she began to worry about money all over again.

It was the only hospital for miles around so that a great many people turned up whom she could not accommodate and she could not turn them away. It irked her to send out bills to people but Eileen who was a lot more practical kept this up and some money did come in but it was not enough.

'We aren't a charity here, Catrin,' she said in the end.

'What can I do?'

'Why don't you talk to Jack Dunstan?'

Catrin had told Eileen about the visit to Newcastle and how it had affected Una and how she hoped that Una would get better.

'It's a long shot,' Eileen said, 'but you have done a great deal for them both, though I am starting to suspect that your visits are not entirely altruistic.'

Catrin tried to look away and not to blush but it was impossible.

Eileen laughed.

'I think it would be fitting that you should ask Mr Armstrong to dinner.'

'I don't feel as if I can.'

'Why not? He can hardly ask you, he has very little money and lives with his boss. Give the man a chance.'

It had been three weeks since they had gone to Newcastle. Then, Jack had taken Una home and Catrin wanted to leave them in peace for a few days, hoping that Una would start to get better. So far she had heard nothing and was reluctant to go. She did not want any more bad news. She felt that she had done everything she could for Una but she did also want to see Will but she had no idea how to approach him.

Jack came to her as he had done before right at the end of surgery. She was glad to see him but Jack's face was unreadable so when he sat down across the desk from her and smiled the relief was huge.

'She's improving?'

'Just a little. She has begun dressing and coming downstairs in the evenings for a little while when it's dark. '

'That's real progress. I think it will take a very long time for her to come to terms in her conscious mind with what happened.'

'As soon as she is well enough to travel I want to take her somewhere else, somewhere warm so that she recovers more quickly. The winters here are so cold and if I can persuade her to leave the house we are going away. Will is perfectly capable of managing everything for me.'

'Where will you go?'

'Spain, I think, when Una is fit enough to travel that far. The winters there are so much warmer and I feel as though we need a fresh start. We can take it slowly if need be and travel by night if she can stand it and stay for as long as she takes to recover before we go on. I don't care how long it takes.'

He looked down at his hands in slight hesitation and then he said,

'I want to donate some money to your hospital. Without you my wife would have died. Don't go saying no, I am aware that you appear to be keeping the entire village and also when I think how I was when you got here. I had almost given up in despair. This place has cost you a great deal. I think that had you lived in a warmer climate your brother might still be alive.'

'You have to live your life in the way you think best,' Catrin said. 'When are you leaving?'

'As soon as you think Una is able to travel, even just for an hour or two. You will come and see her?'

So Catrin went. Una did look a little better, her eyes were less troubled. How she would cope with the new knowledge Catrin was unsure but she wasn't going to say that to them. They had hope. She mustn't squash it now and maybe warmer weather would help. A change of place, to be far away from her unhappy childhood, might make a huge difference.

Una was still pale, still thin, but within another month she was up and dressed and smiling. Jack sat on sofa with her as though he couldn't bear to let her out of his sight.

'I can sleep now because I know he's there,' she said, casting a loving glance at her husband.

'I was there before,' he pointed out.

Una clasped his hand.

'But I wasn't,' she said. 'Going somewhere new I think would be good for me. And in time – in time I want to see my parents. Jack has written to them.' Una stretched out and took Catrin's hands. 'Whatever would we have done without you, and he has told me about how badly he behaved when you first got here.'

'He didn't trust me.'

'He didn't trust anybody,' Una said.

As he saw Catrin downstairs and to the door he said to her,

'I've talked to my bank manager and he will make sure you have funding for whatever you need. Will is to live in this house but I'm sure if you need any more help he is the right man to ask and he is quite happy with the idea that I have suggested to him that you can use the place as an extension to the hospital.'

'You aren't planning on coming back, are you?' Catrin said, gazing around the neat lawns and orderly flower-beds. Something else Will would take care of.

'No,' he said. 'Thank you for all you've done for us.'

Twenty-Eight

That summer Catrin finally felt that she had got things more or less the way that she wanted them. It was as if her hard work was helping the village in a bigger way than she had ever envisaged. Though she still mourned her brother she knew that she was doing good work and that people were happier and healthier because she and her staff were hard-working all the time and it gave for a more cheerful attitude.

It couldn't last of course. She began to feel the restlessness in Eileen, and she knew that things would not get better after that. She had still been hoping that Eileen would change her mind and marry Mr Melrose because although she had her work she was unhappy and Tim and Agatha were the same. None of them was now moving forward and it was important that everyone moved on.

Eileen waited until deep summer. Catrin was tired so she did not pretend to herself that Eileen was coming to her to say that she had decided enough time had passed and she was going to marry Frank Melrose. Catrin did not deceive herself. She was loath to lose Eileen but there was no gladness in Eileen's gaze and she thought there would have been slight regret but an excitement that she was about to move on in such a way.

'I've been offered another post,' Eileen said, rushing into her subject as though she could do no better and wanted to get it over with. She was pale with emotion and effort.

Catrin gave herself a few seconds to understand that this was not what she wanted but it might be good for Eileen to get away so she made herself smile.

'That's wonderful for you. Where is it?'

'Middlesbrough general hospital. They have offered me an administrative job with a lot of responsibility. I think I will be able to do it. It needs a few skills which I'm fairly new at but it will be a big step forward and I want to get away from here properly, not just as far as Stanhope. I have a distant cousin who works there. My mother did me a service by telling her what I was doing here and she said that they would be able to offer me this post. I will be her assistant.'

'Oh, Eileen, that's marvellous. I'm so pleased for you.'

Eileen nodded but said nothing and took an interest in the floor since her eyes were tearing up.

'I won't forget how kind you've been to me.'

'It isn't kindness. I could see your potential straight away,' Catrin said. 'I hope you have a very happy experience there and your parents must be very pleased.'

'They are glad to get rid of me,' Eileen said hoarsely.

Catrin didn't know what to say. It was true that Eileen's family shunned her but in the end her mother had come through by helping her to get away and for that Catrin could forgive her a great deal.

'Nothing that happened is your fault,' she said. 'You married Tel in all good faith.'

'I need to move forward in a new way,' Eileen said, 'I am going to make a life in another place though I wish I didn't have to.'

'I wish you didn't have to go but I understand what you mean. I just know that I will find it hard to replace you here at the hospital and impossible to find another friend such as you have been to me.'

They looked at one another with a mixture of sadness that they would lose their friendship but joy that Eileen could make another life for herself and that Middlesbrough was not that far away so that when Catrin did have a day to herself she could go and see Eileen settled into her new post with a house that was hers and a future that looked brighter than it had for a long time.

Eileen whisked herself from the room before either of them cried.

The hospital was overflowing and Catrin went to talk to Will about moving patients into the house which she was beginning to think of as his. She was shy about asking, it seemed somehow not right.

He had not come to her to back up Jack's idea that the house would be available for some patients. It could be something of a rest home, a place between hospital and being completely well enough to go back to their real lives. Will had enough on his plate because Jack and Una had gone to Newcastle to visit her parents and they would then go on to Spain while the good weather lasted so it was a blow all round.

In the end she went to see Will at the pit and it was very awkward. He was so quiet that she didn't know what to say and but for necessity she wouldn't have gone. She didn't want to go to the house where as far as she knew he was alone but she felt bad here now and she wasn't quite sure why.

Will hesitated and then he said,

'Jack's house is available for your patients. He did say that.'

'Yes, he told me but I don't want to intrude on your peace. You seem to have little of that since you came here.'

'I like it here,' he said.

'But you must miss your family?'

'I hear nothing from any of them and I can't go back. This is the only home I have now.'

'That's why.'

He got to his feet as she spoke, wandered about the little office and then he said,

'Look, I only need a bedroom. You can move as many people in as works for you.'

That made her smile which made him smile.

'Are you sure?'

'I'm certain. It's so quiet it's driving me mad. I was never used to being on my own.'

'Couldn't you go and talk to your brothers?'

Will shook his head.

'I've had a formal letter from their joint solicitor, telling me they want nothing more to do with me.'

'That seems a hard thing for you to accept without trying to put up a fight.'

He looked at her.

'You do like a good scrap, don't you?' he said but he smiled and she smiled with him.

'Think about it. You have a big family to lose and you could all be a lot happier and better off if you made peace.'

'All right, I'll think about it.'

Catrin began moving people to Jack's house and with carers and cleaners. She didn't want Will to feel totally invaded. It wasn't far but it did cause problems. Some people wanted to stay at the hospital even though she said she would visit every day. They were afraid to be at any distance while they were still vulnerable. Also Eileen was going very soon and Catrin had not found anybody who could take over her onerous duties and so she put in a matron and an office worker and she felt she could do no more just at present.

Without Jack and Una the place changed at once. Will was more and more at the pit office, no doubt he was feeling that Jack's loss was greater than he had imagined and a dozen people went to live in what Catrin, feeling guilty, had come to think of as Will's House. She felt the man had had his nose pushed out but when she did see him he didn't act like that at all. He seemed to have grown used to the idea sooner than she had imagined and was cheerful.

She found her life changed too now. Agatha and Tim were to be married in the autumn and she had no one of her own. In the end she made herself go to the pit office in the early evening several weeks after her collection of people had gone to live in Will's house. He was there as she had known he would be.

It was just after eight and the lights were on in the office as she had known they would be. He heard her and then when he saw her he smiled just a little as though it was rather an effort but she persevered, talking some rot, she wasn't sure what she said, just rabbiting on about the hospital generally until he put up both hands and said,

'What can I do to help?'

She sat down in the rickety chair which had always been on that side of the desk and she spent a moment irritated that Jack had never bought any decent furniture. Of course he had intended nobody to be comfortable in the office and he had certainly made a good job of that.

'Come and have dinner with me on Sunday.'

She hadn't known she was going to blurt that out. It fell into the stillness of the room with nothing to catch it.

He stared at her.

'Me?'

'Yes, you.'

He said nothing to that for so long that she wanted to run out of the office.

'Or are you having the day off and spending it at your house?'

'I usually come into the office,' he admitted.

'You don't feel like it's your house any more?'

'It was never my house. I've never had a house of my own. Jack always wanted to help you as much as he could because he says you did so much for them and he was very hostile when you first arrived here.'

'That's true. He certainly was,' and she managed a smile but he didn't. 'So you won't come?'

'I can't, can I?'

'Why?'

'Because it would look bad.'

'Why would it look bad?'

'Well, because everybody knows my circumstances and they would say that I was on the make.'

'The what?'

'You know. That's what they say around here, that I would be trying to make up to you when you're who you are and I'm who I am.'

Catrin stared at him.

'Has anybody ever told you that you have very strange ideas? What do you care what people think? You're clever and educated and talk like posh folk from London talk.'

'I do not.'

'Yes, you do. All those long vowels.'

'Says the girl from the valleys.'

'Dolgellau is in one of the most beautiful valleys in the world. Perhaps you would like me to take you there some time? One o'clock and don't be late,' she said.

When it was dark on Saturday evening Catrin could hear loud voices outside. There was a pub nearby, The Golden Lion, and occasionally on Saturday nights there were fights, small ones most of them but tonight as she sat up in bed and listened she was aware that it was a bigger fight than usual and she would have sworn that she could hear Tel Collings' voice amidst the clamour. This was most unusual. She could also hear Thora and her voice was lifted and clear.

'Come on, Tel, let's go home before you cause any more trouble.' Thora cared for Tel, that was the surprise of it all. She really did love him but of late he had been a man that any woman could love. When he was sober he was friendly and was apt to give to those who needed it money in their hands or fruit and vegetables from the garden or Thora's recently added greenhouse which she managed to heat all year round and sometimes on a fine day Thora would invite the church-goers in for tea and coffee and biscuits so they had settled into the village as well as anyone.

Catrin got out of bed and dressed, as she had the feeling somebody would try to break somebody's head as those round about began to argue. When she got downstairs, accompanied by Tim, Agatha and Eileen, as was usual in such cases there were several scuffles going on and bodies trying, somewhat ineptly after drinking ten or eleven pints, to knock out their opponents or at least hold them against the nearest wall while they applied fists and in some case knees and even booted feet, to get the other down so that he would stay down.

Tel saw Eileen. He stopped what he was doing and broke free from Thora and then he came across to Eileen just as it began to rain. It was the first time Catrin had seen him drunk in some time and it was not a pretty sight.

'There's the love of my life. That's the woman I love. I always loved her, I always did. Come back to me, Eileen.'

As he moved towards her, Eileen moved back and Tim got between them and said,

'Now, Tel, that's enough. Go easy, man, go home and sleep it off.'

Tel glared at him and tried to go round and when Tim got hold of him to try and stop him his face went red with temper and drink.

'We is thoo to tell us what to di?' He glared up into Tim's face and tried even harder to reach the object of his desire and since he could make no progress he began to try to push Tim aside. 'Ye canna gan and leave us, Eileen, yer canna. Yer all I've got, all I ever wanted was thoo. Howay me hinny, come to us.'

Eileen backed further as he reached out and said,

'No, Tel. You go back to Thora, she's your wife, not me. You know it.'

'Is that so?' Tel said, swaying just a little. 'Is that right? And has your Ma told the village that you's ganning away? Is that right too? You would gan and leave me, forsake me, when I loves thoo better than me life.'

He lurched forward and Tim pushed at him just a little.

'No, man, don't. She isn't your wife.'

Tel stared at him for a few seconds and then launched himself at Tim. Thora would have run to him and plenty of hands would have taken him away but the men were too drunk to aid anybody and Thora had been pushed back by the crowd.

Tim fell back against the pub wall and as he did so Tel came at him, got hold of his head and banged it hard again and again so that the stone behind Tim began to bleed. Even though Tim tried ineffectually to get away Tel kept clenched fists into his face, screaming and yelling and applying more and more pressure. He got hold of Tim's hair and thrust him back as though Tim was trying to take Eileen away, that he was to blame for everything that had happened and he had been the ruin of Tel's life. He must get to Eileen, he loved her as he had never cared for another woman and he must have her, he must have her now.

Will was somehow there too and Catrin was now as afraid for him as she was for Tim and even for Tel Collings. She hated men fighting. Will came and he got hold of Tel and pulled him away and even though Tel fought hard he was drunk and Will was sober and it was no contest. Will fought differently somehow, it was studied and yet instant as though he knew exactly what he was doing and Catrin felt nothing but relief. As Tel went down and didn't get up Will waited to see what he was going to do and then he started to pull Tel to his feet. Tel's face was bleeding and his face looked groggy.

Thora had reached her husband.

'Howay, man, yer daft bugger. You have no place here doing such.'

'Take them both into the hospital,' Catrin said and so they did.

Eileen and Catrin looked after them and Tel was full of apologies once he had begun to sober up. Tim had lost consciousness and Eileen and Catrin were worried about him but he woke up some time later in pain but cheerful. Somehow, amidst all the fuss, Will had left as unobtrusively as he had appeared.

Twenty-Nine

Catrin had thought that Will might not come for Sunday dinner the following day though she knew that the main meal of the week was a hard thing for any man to resist and anyway she wanted to thank him for rescuing Tim the previous evening. She was convinced that he would make an excuse and was therefore very happy when he arrived. They talked about the night before.

'I was in the Blacksmith's Arms and heard the noise,' he said.

'Did you learn to fight like that in the army?'

'I went in because my father didn't want me to except as an officer which I didn't care for but it was useful in a lot of ways that I didn't envisage. I'm just glad they are both all right and that Eileen can get away. She hasn't had much of a good time up to now.'

'I will miss her very much but she needs to get out of here in case Tel gets drunk again.'

'I think Thora manages him very well most of the time,' Will said.

They had walked back from church together. Catrin

had tried not to observe the looks they got from various people. Will took his duties as the pit manager very seriously and considered going to church and other social events in the village as part of his job. She knew also that he was very careful with his friendships but as far as she knew since Roddy had died he went out only to get away from the fact that Jack and Una's house had been turned into a care home and she felt sure that the patients were difficult and she doubted he would want to get involved.

Also as pit manager he seemed to think it better if he had nothing to do socially with the pitmen in case something went wrong and he had to sort it out as he had sorted out the fight the evening before which was why he didn't drink in the same pubs. She was just grateful that he had heard the fight and stopped it.

He looked as if he thought he should leave but reluctantly when the meal was over but she gave him tea and sat him over the fire and when she came back with the tea on a tray he had fallen asleep on the sofa. By the time he woke up it was dark and early evening. He sat up, embarrassed and apologised. Catrin didn't know what to say. She didn't want him to think she was pursuing him but also she felt the loss of Eileen who was off to Middlesbrough this week. Tim and Agatha would be married soon and she seemed to have no one to herself but how to encourage Will discreetly she didn't know and also she had brought to the front of her mind that she had been a very young mother and she had no idea how he would react if she told him such a thing. He would probably run miles, most men would.

Eileen was trying to make peace with her family and had spent the last two nights at home but Catrin saw her to the station the very next morning and it was hard not to cry. Eileen obviously felt the same but they both knew that it was the right thing to do and she could see the relief on Eileen's face. Once she got away from here she would have a much better life and would be rid of Tel Collings for good.

Agatha's father was not coming to the wedding as far as they knew. She had gone to Stanhope to speak to him but he ignored her and together Tim and Agatha had written a begging letter.

'I really want him to give me away,' Agatha said, almost in tears.

This was a distraction from Eileen leaving that Catrin could have done without. She could hardly appeal to Mr Melrose directly. It would do no good and she knew that he blamed her for the two young chemists meeting though the truth was that they had met while they were studying and it had nothing to do with Catrin.

She hated the idea of being given away as though one man was taking over from another because women were not capable of thinking for themselves but that was how the church saw it and she liked the vicar and his wife.

There were a dozen men she could have asked to take Agatha up the aisle to her future husband but none of them was special to Agatha and her falling out with her father had cost her very dearly.

Catrin wished that Mr Melrose could understand people wanting to get married. He had been married himself and although she gathered it had not been a good marriage presumably he had not forgotten falling in love. In the end she had to go and see him and to do him credit she could see by his pursed lips that he had been expecting her.

'Miss Morgan, who else?' he greeted her. Luckily the shop was empty.

'I'm sorry,' she said, though why she should be sorry was anybody's guess. She had taken on Agatha to be the chemist and had not regretted it for a second.

'I suppose you think I'm hard on my girl,' Mr Melrose said.

'It's not up to me.'

'If you thought it wasn't up to you what are you doing here?'

'I couldn't think what else to do,' Catrin admitted and she sat in a chair which was one of two Mr Melrose kept for those older more infirm customers while they waited for their prescriptions. Catrin was tired. She was tired of things going wrong one after another as somehow they appeared to do. Also Stanhope was nothing to do with her medically. It had its own doctor but he had of late sent a few patients to her small hospital but still that had nothing to do with Agatha wanting to marry and Mr Melrose not wanting her to.

'You were married,' was all she could think to say though she had said it to him in her head a dozen times.

'Worst thing I ever did,' he said, closing his lips tightly as though he wanted to be rude and wouldn't let himself. Perhaps he recalled how rude he had been to her the last time they met.

'You got Agatha from it,' she said.

'And now look what she's doing to me. Betraying me for a lad like that.'

'Isn't she entitled to be happy?'

'He won't make her happy. A year or so down the line when he's fathered a child on her, he'll take off, just like his father did. I knew the Blackwoods well and they were never respectable. Tim's mother kept taking his father back and he kept going off with other people. She ended up on her own with half a dozen bairns. Do you think that is what I want for Agatha after I moved heaven and earth to send her to the right schools, to pay for her to become a chemist and make me proud of her and now look? She needn't think she can come running back to me when he leaves her because she isn't darkening my door again,' and with that he went into the back of the shop and slammed the door.

When Catrin got back to the Hilda House Tim went into her office.

'You tried to talk to Aggie's father?' he guessed looking sympathetically at her.

'I did,' she admitted, sighing and sitting down.

'It's not that we want anything from him, only that he would come and do what fathers usually do.'

'Only some of them,' Catrin said remembering what kind of a father she had had. Tim sat down too no doubt thinking of his own.

'My father died,' he said.

'I'm sorry.'

'Oh, don't be. I was glad. Isn't that awful? No wonder Mr Melrose doesn't want me to marry his daughter. My family has never been any use.'

'You are very useful and in all kinds of ways and you know it. You are talented and dedicated and there is no reason why you and Agatha shouldn't have a happy marriage.'

'Have you seen any?' Tim said with old man wisdom which she regretted in him.

Catrin tried to think but everybody had problems, it just depended how you looked at it or dealt with them.

'If you care for one another surely it's worth a shot.'

Tim shook his head.

'I keep telling myself that but I have nothing to go

on. What if I do turn out to be like him? John Reed has turned into his father so folk say?'

'He is better.'

Tim looked hard at her.

'So far,' he said.

Catrin was trying not to think too much about Anne who appeared to be happy without seeing her but it hurt. She didn't seem to be able to have any kind of a relationship with her daughter at all and she longed for some kind of normality.

She did not know how John would treat his wife and children but he had always cared very much for Anne so perhaps things would be better than she thought.

In the end she went to see them and was very surprised and then not so much because far from waiting for her to ask him Will turned up shortly afterwards and it was obvious that the two men knew one another quite well. She saw now that John's getting back together with his family was partly because Will went there and helped. He spoke gently to them all and asked how everybody was.

He and John went to see the tenants at the various cottages. This was a double good for Will because several of them worked at the pit and would appreciate seeing their boss with the man who owned their houses.

Before he left Will said to her in confidence,

'I hope I haven't overstepped the mark here but it seemed like a good idea.'

'I'm very grateful for the help. It makes things easier for me.'

Will hesitated and then he said,

'I do think Anne could do with another life than playing nanny to their children. I know it's none of my business but if she is ever to get away from here and make a life for herself she needs more than playing nursemaid to John's family.'

This hurt Catrin but she could hardly tell him that Anne was her child and then she felt guilty all over again that Anne had not had decent schooling and that she had not been there for her.

It was funny how men viewed women, Catrin allowed. Anne had never been able to be a little girl and was unlikely to be one now but he was right in several ways. She had almost stopped thinking that Anne needed companions her own age or that she would have benefited from school. She was always so mature in her outlook. Catrin didn't how she could have done any more.

'She has lived at Castle Hall since she was a very small child,' she said.

'I can't imagine how that happens,' he said.

Catrin didn't think it was the moment for revelations so only managed,

'Children do get lost and treated badly and Anne has never known a normal childhood.'

'She won't get it playing nursemaid to two tiny beings. It seems very unfair,' he said.

That stung even more though she was sure he had not meant it to. He had no idea she might be Anne's mother and what would he think of her if she should admit it? She didn't like to wonder. She also wished that it could be sorted out so that she and Anne both knew whether they were so closely related though she knew that her position in Anne's life was nowhere near as important as it had been. Anne didn't need her nearly as much and although that hurt, Anne had her own life to lead even though Will seemed to think differently. She wasn't sure why he cared and then he looked straight at her and said,

'She matters to you. I see it in your face.'

So she sat down and sat him down and explained the situation to him. She didn't want him to think badly of her but there was no way she could keep the information from him as he also had become very important to her.

He let her talk and didn't say anything until she told him about how far they had got and no further. He was by then rather white-faced and she dreaded hearing him condemn her as a lot of other men would have and had up to now and her heart sank because she didn't want to see him angry and disappointed with her. To her surprise he said,

'And here was me mouthing off about something I knew nothing of. I'm sorry.'

She stared at him.

'You understand.'

'I feel much better now that you've told me. What a horrible thing to have happen and you so very young. I can see now why she is so important to you. I did kind of get it and that was why I wanted to try and help. There must be some way of finding out. It would make you feel much happier, I know it would.'

After that Catrin felt so light as never before, she felt as though she could float away on the feeling.

'Would you like to take me to see The Raine's cottage?' She explained where it was situated beyond the Hall and over the fell top.

'It's nothing but a ruin and there's nothing there.'

'Even so I would like to go again. I don't know this area at all except the village itself and would like to take another look.'

So the next fine day that they had free they walked over the fell.

Will stopped, gazing at the sky and the sheep, the long grey barns and the walls. 'I would like to build a house here, right away from everywhere.'

'Says the town boy,' she said, laughing. 'Not very practical.'

'Look at the views and to be here with just the sheep and the wind and the fell itself. I think it's wonderful.'

'I wonder if Missus Raine thought that, or Miss Raine

or whoever she was. All I could discover was where she lived and from the letter my father got that she took my child but of course we don't know whether Anne was that child. It seems likely but I would like some proof that she was.'

'I'm sure it would make you feel better and if Anne knew it then it might free her to be a different kind of person, somebody who might branch out more for herself, instead of always being there for other people which she seems to have spent all her life doing so far, don't you think?'

Catrin nodded enthusiastically and when they came in sight of the ruin it seemed to speak to her. She could imagine a woman in the garden that had been, the space front and back where she would have grown her vegetables and had a garden path and a line so that she could hang out her clothes. Catrin imagined Anne there as a happy tiny child and wondered what had happened. Had Miss Raine gone out with the little girl perhaps to walk to the village for groceries and there had been some kind of a storm and they had been lost.

And then the squire finding Anne? Strange that such a difficult man could have done such a generous thing even if, as John had thought, he afterwards wished he had not. It showed something human in him and perhaps that was what Lady Reed had seen when she met him and remembered it and afterwards even though he had regretted his action she had been strong enough to hold on to the child and that meant a great deal to Catrin now. The woman had been strong in one particular way and it meant that Anne had a future.

The house had not been small, a house with a few acres, she thought, which was what most people had here, perhaps twelve or fifteen acres and it had had a small kitchen and then a big dining room which was where you climbed the stairs and next to it was a sitting room with a window which faced the garden.

The roof was off and it had become home to wildlife. Some pear and apple trees still flourished but weeds had taken over both inside and out.

'It seems a shame that nobody lived in it after that and kept it right,' Will said.

'I expect that if she was lost and not heard of again people would feel suspicious about it, as though the house had done something itself.'

'Like the house where Una lost her brother. Something to do with atmosphere.'

'I think ignorance is to blame for most things,' Catrin said. 'This place must have been beautiful once.'

'You and Roddy brought the Hilda House back to life. Perhaps in time you might do the same with this.'

'It's too far away from the hospital and I love that building. I've wiped out the bad time I had there and have found happiness inside its walls.'

The sun was glinting in the garden and they wandered around trying to make out which plants had been where and whether Anne and Miss Raine would have sat on a wooden seat against the back wall when the late afternoon was fine and how much they might have enjoyed it.

In among the grass something glinted just a little as the rays of the sun caught at it. Catrin bent down to see what it was and it was a very fine silver chain with a silver cross, very small as well, like something a child might have been given for its christening present.

She kept it in her hand and carried it back as far as the Hall and there she found Anne sitting with one of the babies in her arms. The child was almost asleep. The other was really asleep.

'They haven't been as settled as this in days,' Amy said with a slight and comic shudder, so they talked quietly and then Catrin held up the little cross in her fingers as sunlight glinted into the room. Anne stared at it. She looked and looked and her face which had been pale with fatigue before began to brighten and Catrin could see her mind working and happiness began to glow in her eyes and she smiled.

'Oh,' she said, 'I've seen that before. Where have I seen it?'

There was what felt to Catrin like a long time and then Amy took the sleeping baby and carried it and put it very gently into its cot so that it did not awaken. Anne stared at the thin silver chain.

'It was mine. It was given to me. She was so kind. That's all I remember, that and the sound of her voice,' and at that point she lifted up her sweet young voice and sang,

> 'Oh where is the boatman, my bonny hinny,
> Oh where is the boatman? Bring him to me,
> Ferry me over the Tyne to my honey
> And I will remember the boatman and thee.'

'I can't believe it survived,' she said. 'Where did you find it?'

'In the garden at the house and that was where you lived. I'm sure of it now.'

'She loved me,' was all that Anne could say after that for her voice broke.

She stared misty-eyed at Catrin and then went to her and was clasped into her mother's arms.

'And in time you can go forward and be whoever you want to be,' Catrin said and hugged her daughter.

Catrin kept going every three days or so just to make sure that Amy and John were getting by and was almost satisfied. He was trying to stay sober and do what work he could. There wasn't much money left, Amy told her, though it looked to Catrin as though they avoided one another and that John stayed away from the house because their marriage was so toxic. Amy had enough on her hands with the children but as the days slipped past Anne became very quiet.

'You can come back to the Hilda House any time you choose,' Catrin told her.

'I can't leave them alone together. They barely speak and very often he shouts and swears in front of the babies. I feel I have to be here to stop things from getting worse.'

'That is not your problem.'

'I know. I just want to see the children grow a little and for me to feel my feet on the ground before I go any further. Besides, after my life who would want little ones not to have a real home? Mr Armstrong is always coming over. I know he thinks it helps John but he's always telling us what to do, me in particular. He goes on and on about things that aren't his business,' Anne said. 'It's time he got married and had his own children.'

Oh dear, Catrin thought, if only life wasn't so complicated.

'I don't think he's that old,' she offered.

Anne looked scathingly at her.

'He must be nearly as old as you,' she said. 'He's always

interfering.' She stopped there and then she looked hard at Catrin and her look softened.

'He comes because he hopes you will be here,' she said.

Catrin tried to deny it but Anne wouldn't be silenced.

'He does,' Anne insisted. 'If you aren't here he only stays to go round the cottages with Johnnie. I think if he had money and position he would ask you to marry him.'

Catrin stared. She had had no idea Anne thought of anything except the children.

'You think you shouldn't marry him because of me,' Anne said, 'but he knows all about it and so obviously doesn't mind. You cannot go on living in the past. I'm not any more.'

There was a short silence which Catrin thought she would fall into if it lasted any longer.

'You must marry him,' Anne said, 'or you are both going to lose the only opportunity either of you might have. You aren't getting any younger, you know, and surely you want more than one child. If you don't get a move on it'll be too late. And he's not going to ask you to marry him unless you push him because he's so humiliated about having no home and no money to give you. Men are stupid that way.'

Catrin felt more than happy about what was happening now and it was mostly because of the influence which Will had and how he would help those who were worse off than himself.

'I wish that you would go back and try to make things up with your family,' she told Will the next time they were together.

'I don't feel like trying.'

'I know you don't but I also think that you feel guilty about what happened whether you are responsible or not. I'm sure your parents did the best they could and, let's face it, we all make a mess of almost everything we try to do.'

That made him smile and Catrin thought that in time she might persuade him to take her to meet his family in Sunderland and that bridges might be built but she left it for now. One step at a time.

Tim and Agatha were to be married in October. She had opted for a white wedding dress and had tactfully asked Catrin, Amy and Anne to be there when she went for her last two fittings. For a bride she did not seem very happy but it was the wrench from her father that hurt. She thought she was marrying the right man and even if her father didn't like him it wouldn't stop her, but Catrin did hope even until the last minute that Mr Melrose would walk her up the aisle.

The wedding was to be at half past eleven. Anne was to be the only bridesmaid. After the wedding they were to live in their own little house which they had just rented and which was in the same street as the original surgery so close but still independent. This was what all their friends wanted for them. If only Agatha's father would turn up her day would be complete.

In the end Will walked her to the altar. He seemed to be the obvious person since he was involved in the running of the practice and now had a dozen patients and staff living with him. Catrin knew that he wasn't happy about this but could do nothing about it other than move into a house on his own and she was aware that he thought he owed her his loyalty so he endured it as best he could.

It was a fine day for the wedding and the reception was to be at the Station Hotel where Mrs Clements had insisted on being involved with the refreshments. It took Catrin back to when she and Roddy had arrived there and stayed at the hotel. She missed him most especially on days such as other folks' weddings and she remembered how he had fallen in love in Edinburgh and had expected to marry. But for her early mistakes they might still have been there and perhaps he might still be alive. She knew that thinking like this would not help her mood.

It was Agatha and Tim's day and she was happy for them and tried to stay that way. She was also relieved that John and Amy brought the twins with them. She liked to have everybody there. Lots of the villagers and those patients who were well enough from the hospital flooded into the church and some folk even had to stand outside but since it was such a fine day the atmosphere was jolly. Everybody loved a wedding.

After the ceremony began Catrin found herself turning around in the hope that Mr Melrose would come, even just at the back so that he could see his only daughter being married but it was a vain hope. He didn't appear.

The church was not far from the Station Hotel so they all walked up the street and across the road. Mrs McNorton and Mrs Clements had decked the big back garden with huge tables all laden with food so that no matter how many people turned up they would all be made welcome and given food and drink and there was from the beginning a queue to wish the newly-weds a long and happy life together.

She heard Will telling Anne how pretty she looked and the girl gave him a long hard look.

'Girls don't want to be told how pretty they look,' Anne said, 'that's very Victorian and old fashioned. I don't care about things like that. I'm going to be a doctor.'

Will looked hard at her and then smiled.

'I'm so glad. You are much too intelligent to be stuck with somebody else's babies. You must go to school for that.'

'I intend to,' Anne said. This was news to Catrin and she found it hard to digest until Anne came over and kissed her on the cheek. Then she went away and left them to themselves.

At that moment there was something of a disturbance and a cry from Agatha as she saw her father come in through the back gate. He was wearing a beautiful grey suit and a brilliantly white shirt and she ran right across the lawns to him and flung herself into his arms.

'Oh, Daddy, Daddy, I knew you would come,' she cried like the little girl she had been so eager to forget. He was almost in tears. She took him across to see Tim and watched him shake Tim's hand and wish him well. Catrin was proud of Mr Melrose for his show of courage. Perhaps he was thinking that there would most probably be children and that he might have a hand in bringing them up and maybe amongst them there would be someone who was born to be a chemist or even a doctor. Tim smiled all over his face and shook his new father-in-law's hand so enthusiastically that Catrin winced.

'We could go back and sit in the Hilda House garden,' Catrin suggested to Will as the fuss began to die down.

'And have somebody collar you to do something useful? Definitely not,' he said.

He went into the hotel and found two glasses of champagne and gave one to her and then he said,

'I hope you don't mind but I'm thinking of moving.'

'I knew you wouldn't like being pushed out of Jack's

house,' she said. 'Where would you go?' Her heart beat hard. 'Not back to Sunderland?'

'I wouldn't care if I never saw the place again. There is a house vacant in Prince Row.'

Catrin looked at him.

'It's an up-and-a-down, Will.'

'Yes, I know. That's part of its appeal. You don't mind me leaving Jack's house?'

'Certainly not. You have enough to do without being involved and I have thought that you needed a bit of peace and quiet to yourself which you never get.'

'That's exactly it. You don't think you should do something similar?'

Catrin stared straight into his eyes.

'Live in a tiny house?'

'You don't have a house. All the places you spend time in are as a doctor. I've rarely seen you relax.'

'I'd be on my own.'

'Not necessarily. The house in Prince Row is the end one and the garden is full of flowers and Mr Burton who left a couple of weeks since to go and work at Elvet Colliery has done a lot of work on the house even though it does belong to Jack. He's going to a furnished house as assistant manager and has left everything in very good condition. It doesn't need anything doing to it. You must be so tired of looking after huge places and other people. There is a lovely wooden bench in the garden. If you like we could go and sit there now. It's peaceful.'

'Will—'

'I know. You think you're not fit for me and I'm sure that I'm not fit for you but I'm certainly not fit for anybody else so you will have to put up with the fact that I'm a poor man who has no home.'

Catrin couldn't think of a single word to say. All she felt was joy. They finished the champagne, left the celebrations and went up the hill to where Prince Row lay not far beyond the edge of the town and the Hilda House. The sun was shining in the back garden. Soon it would be evening and the sun would begin to lower itself in the sky but just at present it was warm out there in the sunshine and just for once there was not a breath of wind from the fell. Everything was still and the little grey farmhouses on the fell had glinting windows in the sun and the doors stood open to embrace the evening and the coming night. There was the sound of children playing a ring game, singing a song. Catrin's heart lifted like a bird.

Acknowledgements

I would like to thank my agent Judith Murdoch, my editors Emma Capron, Celine Kelly and Gaby Puleston-Vaudrey and everybody who works at Quercus, they are the best.

The Lost Girl
from
Far Away

Will she find a new family to call her own?

Newly arrived in England, Isabella finds herself all alone
after the tragic death of her mother. Desperate for help,
she stumbles into the nearby town.

Sarah doesn't know what to do with the poor little girl she's
found, so brings her back to the Hilda House where they
can stay together. But when she discovers the girl's tragic
connection to Wolsingham, Sarah knows she'll do whatever
it takes to keep Isabella safe from the town's troubling past.

As the lives of the townspeople become increasingly
entwined, will they find a way to come together? Or will
they fall apart under the past that haunts them all?

Available now in paperback and eBook

QUERCUS

An Orphan's Wish

Will she be able to keep her family together?

After their parents die unexpectedly, Connie, Dom,
Leo and Pearl are forced to journey to Wolsingham,
England, in search of the only family they have left.

Hopeful of a warm welcome, the orphans
are heartbroken to be turned away by their
grandparents, Joshua and Flo Butler, and sent back
out into the cold and unfamiliar countryside.

But when Flo falls gravely ill, the Butlers have no choice
but to ask for help from the grandchildren they abandoned.
With the support of their new community, can the orphans
repair what little family they have left . . . ?

Available now in paperback and eBook

QUERCUS

A Daughter's Wish

Can she overcome the secrets of her father's past?

When Thomas Grant – one of the most eligible young
men in London – proposes to Annabel Seaton,
she can't say she's surprised, but she is delighted.
He's been her best friend since she was a child, and
she can't imagine life without him. What shocks her,
however, is the reaction of her mother and father.

As they permit the engagement, she decides to put it out
of her mind. But before she can be married, tragedy strikes,
and only then does Annabel learn of the shocking secret
that her parents have kept from her.

Determined to learn more, she travels to Durham
on a personal search that will change everything . . .

Available now in paperback and eBook

QUERCUS